Also by Jennifer L. Schiff

A Perilous Proposal

A Sanibel Island Mystery

Jennifer Lonoff Schiff

Shovel
&Pail
Press

A PERILOUS PROPOSAL: A SANIBEL ISLAND MYSTERY
by Jennifer Lonoff Schiff

Book Seven in the Sanibel Island Mystery series

http://www.SanibelIslandMysteries.com

© 2021 by Jennifer Lonoff Schiff

Cover design by Kristin Bryant

Formatting by Polgarus Studio

ISBN: 978-0-578-80289-3

Library of Congress Control Number: 2020924725

"It is a truth universally acknowledged, that a single man in possession of a good fortune, must be in want of a wife."
— Jane Austen, Pride and Prejudice

"Marriage is a fine institution, but I'm not ready for an institution."
— Mae West

PROLOGUE

After a year full of breakups, deaths, and home-improvement woes, things were starting to look up for Guin. She had finally moved into her new home, which was a quick ten-minute walk from her favorite beach. Her relationship with Bill O'Loughlin, a detective with the Sanibel Police Department, was heating up. (Though she refused to think of him as her boyfriend, not wanting to jinx things.) And she hadn't stumbled across a dead body in months.

Now if only Ginny, her boss at the *Sanibel-Captiva Sun-Times*, would stop asking her to review books. Guin had nothing against books. In fact, she liked nothing better than to curl up with one at bedtime and read herself to sleep. But reviewing books? That was a whole other matter.

But since the paper's regular book reviewer had moved, Ginny had called upon Guin to help out. As the paper's general assignment reporter, covering everything from restaurant and store openings to human interest stories and murder, Guin felt she had more than enough on her plate, especially with the season kicking off. But there was no saying no to Ginny. So she had agreed to review Wren Finchley's latest novel, a thriller titled *Shot Through the Heart*.

Guin wouldn't just be reviewing the book, though. She would also be interviewing the bestselling author. As part of his upcoming book tour, Finchley would be giving a talk at the Captiva Yacht Club, to benefit the "Ding" Darling

Wildlife Society, and he had specifically requested Guin be the one to interview him.

Finchley, like his main character, was a man of mystery. No one knew what he looked like, and there was little known about him. Indeed, this book tour would be the first time anyone actually saw Finchley in the flesh. And Captiva would be his first stop.

As Guin stood outside Finchley's suite at the San Ybel Resort & Spa on Sanibel, she checked her bag one last time. Recorder? Check. Notepad and pen? Check. Pepper spray? Check. (She hadn't liked that Finchley had insisted the interview take place in his hotel room, but it was either that or no interview.)

As an added precaution, Guin had texted Ginny, telling her that if she didn't hear from her in a couple of hours to call the police. She also texted her best friend Shelly, a huge Finchley fan, to let her know she was going in.

When she was done, Guin put away her phone, checked to make sure her pepper spray was in easy reach, took a deep breath, and knocked.

"Yes?" came a male voice.

"It's Guinivere Jones, from the *Sanibel-Captiva Sun-Times*," said Guin. "I'm here to interview Mr. Finchley."

"Come in," replied the voice. "The door's open."

CHAPTER 1

Guin walked into the room and immediately stopped upon seeing the smiling man standing a few feet away from her.

"Birdy?!" she said. "Why didn't you tell me you were on Sanibel? Are you here to see Wren Finchley?" She glanced around the room. "You want to let him know I'm here?"

Birdy didn't move.

"Mr. Finchley?" Guin called.

There was no reply.

"Where is he?"

"You're looking at him," said Birdy.

Guin stared.

"*You're* Wren Finchley?"

Though really, she shouldn't have been that surprised. The plot of Finchley's first book, *Death in the Jungle*, which she had read in preparation for the interview, had sounded so familiar. No doubt because Birdy had told her the story when she had first met him.*

"I don't understand."

"I will explain everything to you shortly," Birdy replied. "But first I thought we might catch up. Can I get you something to drink?"

"Just some water," Guin replied.

She watched as he made his way to the minibar.

---

* See Book 4, *Bye Bye Birdy*

Guin had first met Bertram "Birdy" McMurtry, a world-famous ornithologist and nature photographer, while covering one of his sold-out nature talks and tours on Sanibel. Although she hadn't initially liked him, finding him a bit full of himself, the two had since become friends. (Escaping death together tends to do that.) However, Guin hadn't heard from Birdy in months. No doubt he had been too busy writing thrillers.

Birdy handed Guin a bottle of water and led her to a sitting area.

"Please, have a seat," he said, gesturing at the couch.

"First, tell me why all the secrecy."

Birdy smiled.

"Still as feisty as ever. No wonder you broke things off with poor Ris. I always thought he wasn't man enough for you."

Guin frowned. She still felt guilty about breaking up with Harrison "Ris" Hartwick, a professor of marine biology who had once been voted one of Southwest Florida's sexiest men and also happened to be a good friend of Birdy's. Ris had asked her to run off to Australia with him after he had lost his job at Florida Gulf Coast University (after being falsely accused of inappropriate behavior). But Guin had turned him down, and he had moved to Australia without her.

"You're stalling," said Guin.

Birdy gave her an appraising look.

"You're looking well. You have a bloom to you, a certain rosiness of the cheek, and your hair is as wild and glorious as ever."

Guin felt self-conscious and absently touched her hair.

Birdy continued to smile at her.

"Come, have a seat," he said, sitting down on the couch and patting the space next to him.

Guin sat down several feet away.

"So, tell me," said Birdy. "Are you seeing anyone?"

Guin thought about telling him about the detective but shook her head instead.

"I've been too busy with work and the house."

"That's right, you bought a place on Sanibel."

Guin nodded.

"I did. There's still work to be done, but it's getting there."

"I'm sure it's utterly charming, just like you."

Guin did her best not to roll her eyes.

"And what about you?" she said. "You planning on ever settling down?"

"Actually, that's why I'm here." He was looking right at Guin, and Guin suddenly felt uncomfortable. "Do you mind if I fix myself a drink?"

"No," she said. "Go right ahead."

Birdy went over to the minibar and poured himself a Scotch. Then he returned to the couch.

"Now, where were we?"

Guin looked at him. Was that nervousness she sensed?

"I asked if you ever thought about settling down."

Birdy leaned forward.

"Has anyone ever told you that you have the most beautiful blue eyes?"

Now Guin knew something was up.

"What's going on, Birdy? What do you want? Is this about the book?"

"Can't a man tell a woman she's beautiful? Or is that a crime now?"

Guin gave him a look, and Birdy leaned back and sighed.

"Very well," he said.

He took another sip of his Scotch, then placed it on the side table and got down on one knee, taking Guin's left hand.

"Guinivere Jones, will you do me the great honor of marrying me?"

"Excuse me?" said Guin, staring at him. "Are you

drunk?" She looked over at the nearly empty glass of Scotch. "How many of those things have you downed?"

"I assure you," Birdy replied, still kneeling. "I am not the least bit inebriated."

Guin wasn't convinced.

"So, what do you say?"

"I say you're crazy."

"I give you my word, I am entirely sane."

Guin wasn't so sure about that either.

"What's going on, Birdy? The truth."

Birdy sighed and got up.

"I take it that's a no then."

"That would be correct."

"Would you at least think about it?"

"There's nothing to think about. Now tell me, what's going on?"

"I need your help."

"What kind of help?"

"It's a bit complicated."

"Try me."

"I may have let slip that you and I were engaged."

"So, let it slip that we got unengaged."

"I can't do that."

"Why not?"

"As I said, it's a bit complicated."

"Uncomplicate it."

"Very well. I shall try. I suppose you could say I underestimated my charm."

Guin rolled her eyes.

"So this is about yet another woman."

Birdy had a habit of attracting and dating semi-psychotic women who were interested in a long-term commitment, but Birdy wasn't the long-term commitment type. And the relationships often didn't end well.

"Not just any other woman. Natasha Ivanova."

"Natasha Ivanova?"

"She's a… fellow ornithologist, from Moscow. Very respected over there. And very beautiful. We met at a symposium in St. Petersburg. One thing led to another and, well… As you know, it gets rather chilly in St. Petersburg in winter and…"

"Spare me the intimate details," said Guin.

"The thing of it is, Natasha became rather attached to me and was quite upset when I told her I was otherwise engaged."

"I see," said Guin. "And by otherwise engaged you mean engaged to me."

Birdy nodded.

"But why me?"

Birdy smiled.

"Well, you did pose as my fiancée, and rather convincingly too."

Guin scowled.

"So, what's the problem? How is she to know you lied to her? She's there and you're here."

"Actually…" Guin had a bad feeling again. "Natasha got herself a position as a visiting lecturer at the University of Central Florida and is insisting on meeting you."

"She wants to meet me? Why?"

"I would think it rather obvious."

"So she's here, now?"

"No. She doesn't arrive until January."

"Oh, well then, she'll probably have gotten over you by then."

Birdy shook his head.

"You don't know Natasha."

Guin sighed.

"I guess I can pretend to be your fiancée for a few hours. Just let me know when she wants to get together. Now, shall we discuss Wren Finchley's latest book?"

But she could tell by Birdy's expression something was wrong.

"I'm afraid it's not that simple."

"Why not?"

"She wants to come to the wedding."

"Wedding? What wedding?"

"Our wedding."

"But there is no wedding. And even if there was, why would we want to have one of your exes attend?"

"Please, Guin, do this one little thing for me. I'm begging you."

He got back down on one knee and clasped her hand.

"Get up, Birdy. I said it before, and I'll say it again: I am not marrying you."

"Then my life is over."

"Aren't you being a bit melodramatic?"

Birdy shook his head.

"You don't know Boris."

"Boris? I thought we were talking about Natasha."

"Boris is Natasha's... Let's just say he wasn't happy about Natasha and my relationship and will no doubt be keeping an eye on her."

"I see," said Guin, though she didn't really. "And if you don't marry me, what? Boris is going to come after you, like the character in your novel?"

In his (or Wren Finchley's) latest novel, the hero, an ornithologist who was really a spy, gets involved with a beautiful Russian spy, and her handler/lover goes after him, nearly killing him.

Birdy nodded.

"This is crazy."

"I know it sounds crazy, but I swear to you on my parents' grave, I am telling you the truth. These people mean business."

Guin looked at Birdy. She had never seen him look so serious. What if he was telling her the truth? What if, just like his protagonist in *Shot Through the Heart*, Russian spies were after him?

"Look, it wouldn't need to be forever. Just until Natasha and Boris left. Though, after the honeymoon, you might change your mind," he said, smiling at Guin.

Guin, however, wasn't paying attention. Her wheels were turning. Her mother had been nagging her more than usual the last few months, complaining about her lack of grandchildren and asking Guin why she couldn't settle down. Maybe marrying Birdy wouldn't be such a bad thing. Though she had no intention of actually marrying him.

"We could always *pretend* to get married. Stage a fake wedding."

"A fake wedding?"

"You know, make it look like we got married, but we wouldn't be legally wed."

"It would have to be believable if we're going to fool Natasha and Boris."

And my mother, Guin thought.

"I'm sure we could make it look believable. So when do Natasha and Boris head back to Mother Russia? We should plan it for right before they leave."

"Actually," said Birdy, rubbing the back of his head.

"Yes?" said Guin.

"I told them we were getting married on Valentine's Day."

"You told them we were getting married on Valentine's Day? Are you insane?"

"It just popped out."

Guin was staring at him.

"That's barely three months away! I can't plan a wedding, even a fake one, in that little time. And every place will be booked. What were you thinking?!"

"It's already taken care of."

"It is?"

Birdy nodded.

"The wedding is to be held right here, at the San Ybel."

"It is?" said Guin again. "When? How?"

Birdy smiled.

"I took the liberty of reserving the date some months ago."

Guin stared at him.

"Awfully presumptuous of you."

"I just believe in being prepared."

"What about food and flowers and music? Did you take care of all of that too?"

"No. I thought I'd leave that to you and Hermione to sort out."

"Hermione?" said Guin. The name sounded vaguely familiar.

"She's the resort's wedding planner."

"What about Bettina? Is she on board with this?"

Bettina was Birdy's agent/publicist, who was not exactly fond of Guin.

"She understands."

Guin wasn't so sure about that.

"What about an officiant?"

"Already taken care of."

Guin raised an eyebrow.

"Who did you get?"

"KC Kellerman."

"As in Weddings by KC?"

Birdy nodded.

Guin didn't know KC personally, but she had seen her ads in the paper.

"And she's willing to go along with this little charade?"

"Absolutely. KC and I go way back."

Birdy smiled as he said it. And Guin wondered how well acquainted the two of them were.

Guin thought of something else.

"What about invitations? We'll have to get going on that right away."

"Communicate with Bettina. She's a whiz at that sort of thing."

Great. The last thing Guin wanted to do was communicate with Bettina.

"Fine," Guin sighed. "It shouldn't be that difficult as I assume it will be a small wedding."

Birdy avoided her gaze.

"It will be a small wedding, right?"

"Define *small.*"

Guin was getting a bad feeling again.

"Forty people?"

Birdy shook his head.

"Fifty?"

"I was thinking we could keep it to around two hundred."

"Two hundred?" said Guin, exploding. "No. Absolutely not. No way."

"I'm a celebrity, Guinivere. My fans will expect a lavish affair."

"Let me make myself crystal clear, Bertram McMurtry: If you want me to marry you, the wedding will be a small intimate affair."

"How small are we talking about?"

"Fifty people tops. And that's thirty more than I want."

Birdy shook his head.

"Absolutely not. That would barely cover my sponsors."

Guin was ready to smack him.

"I don't give a damn about your sponsors. If you want me to marry you, it's a small wedding or nothing."

"Fine," Birdy sighed. "A hundred people."

Guin shook her head.

"Sixty, and that's my final offer."

They stared at one another. Finally, Birdy blinked.

"Very well. Sixty it is. Though that does not include press and photographers."

"Press? We are not having the tabloids cover our fake wedding."

"It will look odd if no one's there to report on it."

Guin pursed her lips.

"Two media outlets, max, and I get to approve them. Ditto the wedding photographer."

"You drive a hard bargain."

"So it's a deal?"

"Deal," said Birdy. "Just one more little thing."

"What?" said Guin.

"You can't tell anyone the wedding is just for show."

"No one? Not even… Shelly?"

She had been about to say, "the detective," but stopped herself.

"Especially not Shelly."

"But…"

"I'm serious, Guinivere. We need people to believe we're really getting married. Otherwise…"

"But what am I supposed to tell people? It's not as though we've been dating."

"Tell them that from the moment I first saw you, I knew you were the one, but that it took a near-death experience for me to realize I couldn't waste another day. So I flew to Sanibel, to tell you in person how I felt and begged you to marry me."

Birdy was looking at her strangely, and Guin felt her heart flutter just the tiniest bit. She hadn't really noticed before, but he had the most beautiful long eyelashes that framed his hazel eyes. And the rest of his face (and body) wasn't so bad either.

"Yes, well," said Guin, pulling herself together. "Fine for you, but what about me? It's not as though I've been going around telling people I've missed you or that we've been secretly dating."

"I'm sure you'll think of something. I know: tell them we've been secretly corresponding. That I wooed you with my words and you were unable to resist."

Guin looked dubious.

"I'll think of something. Now, if we can move on from wedding planning, I have a proposal for you."

Birdy grinned.

"Oh? Do tell."

"How about we discuss your new book?"

CHAPTER 2

Guin reached into her bag and pulled out her microcassette recorder and her list of questions.

"Okay if I record the interview?" she asked Birdy.

"Be my guest."

Guin pressed the record button.

"So why the pseudonym?"

"I wanted the novels to stand on their own. I didn't want people pre-judging them or buying them because they were written by Birdy McMurtry, world-famous ornithologist and award-winning nature photographer." Guin did her best not to roll her eyes. "Like J. K. Rowling."

"J. K. Rowling?"

"She adopted the pen name Robert Galbraith for her Cormoran Strike novels, so people wouldn't compare them to the Harry Potter books."

"Right," said Guin. "And why espionage fiction? It seems a far cry from bird watching."

Birdy smiled.

"Bird watching can be quite treacherous. You'd be surprised at the lengths people will go to spy on their prey."

Guin raised her eyebrows, then moved onto the next question.

"Some of the situations you write about seem almost real. Are any parts of your novels based on things that actually happened to you or people you know?"

Again Birdy smiled.

"Maybe."

Guin pressed him but he was evasive. So she moved on. Finally, over an hour after her first question, Guin announced she was done. As she put her things back in her bag, her stomach rumbled. She glanced at her watch. It was after noon.

"Hungry?" said Birdy.

"I'm fine," Guin replied. Though she was a bit hungry, having had only coffee for breakfast that morning.

"Let me buy you lunch."

Guin slung her bag over her shoulder.

"Thanks, but I need to work."

"What about dinner then?"

"I can't tonight."

"How about tomorrow? I'm leaving Sanibel right after the book talk, and we still have a lot to discuss."

Guin hesitated.

"Fine. Tomorrow."

"Excellent," said Birdy. "I'll have dinner served here in the suite. There's an enchanting view of the Gulf from the lanai."

"I'd prefer someplace public."

"Afraid to be alone with me?" said Birdy, grinning.

"Not at all. It's just…"

She struggled to come up with an excuse.

"Don't worry that pretty head of yours. We shall dine wherever you like. Where would you like to go?"

"How about Bleu Rendez-Vous?"

"An excellent choice," said Birdy. "It's been ages since I've seen Yvette and Gabriel." They were the owners of Bleu Rendez-Vous. "I shall make us a reservation this afternoon. Will seven do?"

"Seven is fine," said Guin.

Birdy walked her to the door.

"Oh, I nearly forgot! Stay right there."

Guin paused by the door as Birdy went into the bedroom. He emerged a minute later.

"Everything okay?"

"Perfectly fine," said Birdy. "I just wanted to give you this."

He reached into his pocket and produced a small velvet box.

Guin stared at it.

"Take it," said Birdy, holding out the box to her.

Guin looked up at him.

"Go on," he said.

Guin reluctantly took the box.

"Now open it."

Guin slowly lifted the lid. Inside was what looked to be an antique diamond engagement ring.

"It belonged to my mother," said Birdy.

"It's beautiful," said Guin. "But I can't accept this."

She closed the lid and tried to give the box back to Birdy.

"Please," said Birdy, pushing the box back toward her. "I think my mother would have wanted you to have it."

He took the ring out of the box and slid it onto Guin's ring finger.

"It fits perfectly."

Guin held up her hand. The ring was truly beautiful. She had never seen anything like it.

"I…"

"Please," he repeated. "We are engaged, after all."

Guin again glanced at the ring.

"All right. For appearance's sake. But once this little charade is over, I'm giving it back."

"What if you change your mind?"

"About you or the ring?"

"Both," said Birdy.

"I won't," said Guin. "Now, I really should get going. I'll see you at the book talk."

Guin stopped at Jerry's and got herself a sandwich. Then she drove to the *Sanibel-Captiva Sun-Times* offices, which were located on Periwinkle Way.

"Is Ginny around," she asked the young woman seated at the front desk.

"I think she's on the phone," said the young woman. "And you are?"

"Guin Jones," said Guin. "I write for the paper."

"Oh!" said the young woman. "I knew the name sounded familiar. I'm Francie. I'm interning here through May."

"Nice to meet you, Francie. So where are you in school?"

"I'm at FGCU. I'm a Journalism major."

Guin was tempted to tell Francie to change majors, journalism being a hard profession with little pay. But she just smiled.

"I'll see if Ms. Prescott is available."

She picked up the phone and entered Ginny's extension.

"Hi, Ms. Prescott? Guin Jones is here to see you."

Francie nodded, then hung up.

"She says to go back."

"Thanks," said Guin.

"So, what's up, Buttercup?" said Ginny, as Guin knocked and entered.

"Just thought I'd stop by."

Guin went to remove a pile of magazines and newspapers from one of the chairs.

"Hold that up a sec," Ginny commanded.

Guin held up a magazine.

"No, not that," said Ginny. "Your left hand."

Guin turned and held up her left hand. She had forgotten about Birdy's ring.

"Come closer."

Guin obeyed, going over to Ginny's desk. Ginny immediately grabbed Guin's hand.

"Don't tell me O'Loughlin proposed to you."

"Actually," said Guin. "It was Birdy."

"Birdy?" said Ginny. "Birdy McMurtry asked you to marry him? I didn't know you two were even dating." She looked thoughtful. "When did he propose? Is he here on the island?"

"Funny story," said Guin, leaning against Ginny's desk. "It seems he and Wren Finchley are one and the same."

"Well, I never," said Ginny, shaking her head. "So this was all a ruse so Birdy could pop the question?"

"Something like that," said Guin.

"And you said yes."

Guin nodded.

"And here I thought you and O'Loughlin were finally... Well, congratulations. So, when's the big day?"

"February fourteenth."

"Valentine's Day?"

Guin nodded.

"It was Birdy's idea."

"Huh. Never took him for a romantic. And where are you two lovebirds getting hitched?"

"Here on Sanibel at the San Ybel."

Ginny whistled.

"Nice."

"What about the honeymoon?"

"We haven't discussed it."

Guin could feel herself blushing.

"Well, congratulations to you both."

"You and Joel will come, won't you, to the wedding?"

"Wild horses couldn't keep me away. And I'll make sure Joel comes too."

Joel was Ginny's common-law husband, who didn't like parties or crowds. But for Guin, he'd probably make an exception.

"Now, how are those articles coming?"

"Good."

"Excellent," said Ginny. "And I've got another assignment for you. I need you to cover the new exhibit opening up over at the Watson MacRae Gallery right after Thanksgiving."

"Can't you get someone else? You know I'm uncomfortable reviewing art."

Ginny waved a hand.

"You'll be fine. And besides, Glen will be there with you."

Glen was a freelance photographer who worked regularly for the paper. He was originally from Fort Myers but had been living in New York City, working in finance. Then his wife divorced him, and his father became ill, and he moved back to Fort Myers, turning his former hobby into a business. He and Guin had become close over the last year, and he had been helping her with the house. (In addition to being a talented photographer, he was also a talented carpenter/handyman.)

"Okay," said Guin, resignedly. "When exactly is the opening?"

"The Wednesday after Thanksgiving."

Guin entered it into her calendar. She would be going to New York to spend Thanksgiving with her family, but she'd be back before the gallery opening.

"Anything else?"

"I have a few other story ideas, but I'll email them to you."

Ginny's phone started ringing, and she immediately picked up.

"Virginia Prescott."

She listened and nodded her head, then asked whoever it was to hold on a sec.

"I need to take this," she told Guin.

Guin gave her the okay sign, then turned and left.

CHAPTER 3

Guin arrived at Bleu Rendez-Vous promptly at seven the next evening and greeted Yvette, the owner. Birdy had yet to arrive. Yvette escorted Guin to a table near the back and asked if she'd like something to drink. Guin asked for a glass of rosé, then glanced around. Nearly every table was occupied.

A server brought over her wine, and Guin sipped it as she scrolled through her social media feeds. A couple of minutes later, she heard loud whispering at the two tables next to her. She looked up and saw that Birdy had arrived. He was chatting amiably with Yvette. Several of the patrons were whispering and pointing. No doubt fans of his.

Finally, Birdy excused himself and headed to their table.

"Sorry about that," he said, taking a seat.

"No worries," said Guin. "Would you like a drink?"

He signaled to the server, a young woman in her twenties, who was standing off to the side.

"Yes?" said the young woman.

"Do you have any single-malt Scotch?" he inquired.

"I'm not sure," said the young woman. "I'll check."

She hurried off, and Guin saw her speaking to Yvette, who shook her head. A few seconds later, she returned.

"I'm sorry, we don't."

"Oh, well," said Birdy. "I'll have a gin and tonic."

He smiled at the young woman, who smiled back, then hurried off to get his drink.

"You're looking lovely this evening," Birdy said to Guin. He glanced down at the table, where Guin's hand was resting. "And I see you're wearing the ring."

Guin nodded.

"Though it doesn't feel right."

"I'm sure one of the jewelers on the island can adjust it."

"That's not what I meant."

The two silently regarded each other.

"I meant I feel funny wearing your mother's ring."

"I told you, she'd want you to have it."

Guin glanced at the ring, turning her hand from side to side.

"Do you know anything about it? It looks a bit Art Deco."

"You have a good eye. It is Art Deco. She spied the ring in an antique jewelry shop, and my father surprised her with it."

"It's lovely," said Guin. "But you know I can't keep it," she added in a low voice.

Birdy was about to say something when the server came over with his drink.

"Here you go!" she said, placing the gin and tonic in front of him. "Can I get you two anything else?"

"Some menus?" said Guin, smiling up at her.

"Of course!" said the young woman. "I'll be right back."

"So, I was thinking," said Birdy, after the server had placed two menus on the table. "We should put an announcement in the paper."

"An announcement?"

"Regarding our engagement."

"Right," said Guin, taking another sip of her wine.

"After all, we want to make sure Boris and Natasha see it."

"Right, Boris and Natasha."

"And your mother will probably want to put something in the *Times*."

"Right, the *Times*."

Guin took another sip. The thought of having her engagement announced in the *New York Times* made her feel a bit ill.

"Are you okay?" asked Birdy.

"Yes, fine," said Guin, squeezing the stem of her wine glass.

"Then it's all settled. I'll have Bettina take care of it."

Guin frowned.

"Something wrong?"

"Just make sure she lets me see the announcement before she submits it."

"Of course," said Birdy.

"So, tell me more about Boris and Natasha," said Guin, after their entrees had been cleared away.

"What do you want to know?"

"You said Natasha was an ornithologist."

Birdy nodded.

"She's an associate professor at Moscow State University in the Faculty of Biology, though she lectures around the world."

"And what about Boris?"

"He's… your typical apparatchik."

"Apparatchik?"

"Loyal bureaucrat."

"Ah, so is he also at Moscow State University?"

"You could say that," said Birdy.

Guin tilted her head.

"He's a…" Birdy paused. "Let's just say he's an administrator."

"And does he have a last name?"

"It's Sokolov. Now, can we please stop talking about Boris and Natasha?"

"Okay," she said, taking a sip of her red wine. (Birdy had ordered a bottle to go with dinner.) "So when will you be back on Sanibel?"

"Not until after the new year."

"Not until January? Are we talking beginning of the month or later?"

Guin didn't know why, but she suddenly felt a bit panicky.

"I'm not sure. I have to check the schedule. Bettina has me flying all over the place for this book tour." He looked at Guin and smiled. "What's the matter? Can't bear to be without me?"

"Hardly. I'm just worried about planning a wedding in less than three months when the groom won't even be here."

"You don't need me. I told you, Hermione and Bettina will take care of everything."

That's what I'm afraid of, Guin said to herself.

She took another sip of her wine. (She was on her second glass. Third, if you counted the rosé.)

"It's just... It is my wedding, and..."

"You can do as much or as little as you like. Bettina and Hermione are only there to help."

"Thanks," said Guin. Though she didn't believe it.

The server came over.

"Could I interest you in some dessert and coffee?" she asked them.

"What do you have?" asked Birdy.

"We have a homemade crème brûlée, a delicious chocolate mousse, and a rustic apple tart."

"Guinivere?"

"They all sound good," she replied. (Guin had a notorious sweet tooth.) "You pick."

"We'll have the chocolate mousse and the apple tart."

"And can I get you both some coffee?"

"I'll have a decaf cappuccino," said Guin.

"And I'll have a double espresso," said Birdy.

"Thank you for dinner," said Guin, as they left the restaurant.

"My pleasure," said Birdy.

It was dark outside, and Guin slipped on the steps and stumbled.

"Are you okay?" said Birdy, rushing to her side.

"I'm fine," she replied, somewhat mortified.

She took a step and winced. It was her ankle.

"Let me drive you home."

"That's really not necessary, Birdy."

"You're limping, and you did have quite a bit to drink. I insist."

Guin made a face.

"I didn't have that much, and I'm perfectly fine."

She took another step and collapsed as a searing pain shot up her left leg from her ankle.

"That does it," said Birdy. "I'm driving you home."

"Really, I'm fine," Guin insisted. Though her ankle hurt, and her head was starting to pound from all the wine she had. (Guin was a bit of a lightweight when it came to alcohol.)

"Don't be a martyr. Let me drive you."

Guin saw he was determined to have his way.

"Fine," she said with a sigh.

"Shall I carry you?"

"No!" It was bad enough he was driving her home.

He ignored her and scooped her into his arms, carrying her to his SUV. She hid her head for fear someone might recognize her, only raising it as he placed her on the passenger seat.

"Where to, my lady?"

Guin gave him her address and ten minutes later he pulled into her driveway.

"Nice place," he said.

"How can you tell in the dark?"

"You could always invite me in," he said.

Although she could barely see his face in the dark, Guin knew he was grinning.

"Another time."

She opened the door and started to get out, but as soon as she put her left foot down, she felt another shock of pain.

"Here, let me help you," said Birdy, materializing next to her.

"I can make it," said Guin, pushing him away. Though she winced as she did so.

"Stop being so stubborn. I can tell you're in pain. Let me help you."

Guin gave in and allowed Birdy to help her. When they got to the door, she fumbled for her keys.

"Here, let me," he said, taking her purse.

He quickly found the keys and opened the door.

"Thank you for driving me home," Guin said.

"You sure you don't need help, say getting undressed and ready for bed?"

"I'll be fine," said Guin, feeling her cheeks grow warm. "Just go. I'll see you tomorrow at the book talk."

"Very well," said Birdy. He reached over and gave Guin a kiss on the cheek. "Good night, Guinivere."

"Good night, Birdy."

She closed the door, then leaned against it, closing her eyes. As she stood there, she felt something furry brush against her legs.

"Hi, girl," she said, opening her eyes and seeing her black cat. "Did you miss me?"

Fauna looked up at her.

"I just need to get some ice for my ankle. Then we can have a cuddle."

CHAPTER 4

The next morning, Guin's ankle still hurt, but it was definitely better. The ice had clearly helped. She dislodged Fauna, who had been curled up next to her on the bed, and went to the bathroom to swallow two ibuprofen. Could she make it to the beach? She hated the thought of not getting in her beach walk. After gingerly walking around her room, she decided to chance it. Though she wrapped her ankle with the ACE bandage she kept in her first-aid kit.

She turned on her phone and texted Shelly, her best friend on the island, asking her if she wanted to go for a beach walk. Like Guin, Shelly was an avid shell collector and made jewelry from the shells she collected, which she sold on Etsy and at local art fairs. Shelly immediately texted back. Of course she did! As Guin didn't have her car, she asked Shelly if they could meet by her beach. And Shelly replied, "No problem!"

After testing out her ankle a bit more, Guin decided to bike to the beach, which was less than a half-mile away. Shelly arrived a minute later and immediately noticed the bandage wrapped around Guin's left ankle.

"You okay?" she asked.

"I'm fine. I just tripped and sprained it leaving Bleu Rendez-Vous."

"Who were you having dinner with at Bleu Rendez-

Vous? Were you dining with the detective?"

"No, I was with Birdy."

Shelly stared.

"You were having dinner with Birdy? I didn't even know he was on Sanibel."

"Yes, well," said Guin, feeling uncomfortable.

"So, how is Mr. McMurtry? Is he giving a lecture? I hadn't heard anything. And why were you having dinner with him?"

May as well get it over with, thought Guin.

"He, uh... You see... We're kind of getting married."

"WHAT?!" said Shelly, her eyes looking like they were about to pop out of her head. "You're marrying Birdy McMurtry?!"

Guin nodded.

"Oh my God!" said Shelly. "When did he ask you to marry him?"

"The other day."

"And you didn't tell me?!"

"It was kind of a surprise."

"I'll say!" said Shelly. "Steve is not going to believe it! We were sure you and Bill were, you know."

"I know," said Guin, a bit wistfully. It hurt just thinking about the detective.

"You don't sound excited."

"It's my ankle," Guin lied. "It kept me awake."

"You poor thing. So, you and Birdy, huh?" Shelly shook her head. "I mean, I know he was crazy about you."

"You did?"

Shelly nodded.

"You'd have to be blind not to see how he looked at you. But a proposal... He didn't seem like the type to settle down."

"I know. I thought so too."

"So when's the big day?"

"February fourteenth."

Shelly grabbed Guin's arm.

"You're getting married on Valentine's Day?"

Guin nodded.

"Where, in New York?"

"No, here, on Sanibel, at the San Ybel."

"But that's less than three months away!"

"I know, but Birdy's arranged everything. Well, almost everything."

"Do you need help? I'd be happy to help you. Oh, a wedding!"

"What about your jewelry business?"

It was Shelly's busy season, after all.

"How many times does a woman get to help her best friend plan a wedding? I can do both. So, who are you planning on asking to be your maid of honor?"

Guin hadn't thought about it. She had lost touch with most of her friends up north after moving to Sanibel. And while she had a couple of cousins she could ask, they both lived far away and probably were busy that weekend.

"Would you be?"

Shelly clasped her hands to her heart.

"I'd be honored. Are you sure, though?"

Guin nodded.

"I'm sure."

"This is going to be so much fun!" said Shelly. "When do we start?"

"I don't know. I need to meet with the wedding planner over at the San Ybel."

"You want me to come with you?"

"I think I should meet with her first."

"Well, let me know how it goes."

"I will. First, though, I need to cover the Wren Finchley book talk."

Shelly grabbed Guin's arm again.

"You're going to the book talk, the one at the Captiva Yacht Club?"

Guin nodded.

"Why?"

"It's totally sold out. And you know I love Wren Finchley. Though Steve's the one who really loves him."

"You want to come with me?"

"Do I?" said Shelly. "Can you get me in?"

"I'm sure," said Guin. "The talk is at four, and I need to get there ahead of time. You want to pick me up at three?"

"It's a date! Oh, I'm so excited! You know no one's ever seen Finchley. I mean, some people no doubt have. But there's no photo on the back of his books, and there's next to nothing about him online."

"I know," said Guin.

Shelly was staring at her.

"What?"

"I can tell by the look on your face you know something. Spill."

There was no keeping anything from Shelly. Though certain things she would have to.

"I guess you'll find out anyway."

"Find out what?"

"Wren Finchley is really Birdy."

Shelly stopped.

"What do you mean?"

"I mean Wren Finchley is Birdy's pen name, his pseudonym."

"You're kidding me? Birdy is really Wren Finchley?"

"Technically, it's the other way around. But yes."

"Oh my God! You're marrying Wren Finchley?!"

"Shhh!" said Guin, her eyes darting around the beach. Fortunately, there was no one near them. "No, I'm marrying Birdy."

"Toe-may-toe, toe-mah-toe," said Shelly. "Now you *have* to get me into that talk!"

"Just do me a favor and don't tell anyone—not even Steve—about Wren being Birdy. At least until after the book talk."

Shelly pouted.

"I mean it, Shelly. And don't say anything about the wedding."

"Why not?"

Guin didn't have a good answer. She just didn't want word getting around the island until she'd had a chance to speak with the detective.

"Just promise me."

Shelly sighed.

"Okay, I promise."

"Good. Now catch me up on what's going on in your world."

And Shelly did.

After filling their shelling bags with lightning whelks, little horse conchs, colorful scallops, glossy lettered olives, common nutmegs, and banded tulip shells, Guin and Shelly headed back to the parking area.

"Could you do me a favor and give me a lift over to Bleu Rendez-Vous?" asked Guin.

"Why?"

"Birdy insisted on driving me home. The Mini's still there."

"Did you invite him in for a nightcap, to celebrate your betrothal?" asked Shelly, grinning a bit too broadly.

"No."

Shelly pouted.

"So, can you give me a lift, or do I need to call Island Taxi?"

"I'll drive you. Hop in."

Shelly dropped Guin off at the restaurant, and Guin drove the Mini home. Thank goodness it was her left ankle and not her right.

She parked the Mini in the garage and hobbled inside. She probably shouldn't have gone for such a long beach walk. But she was glad she did. She undressed, took two more ibuprofen, then got in the shower. The hot water felt good. When she was done and had gotten dressed, she grabbed an ice pack from the freezer and wrapped it around her ankle. Then she propped her left foot up on a chair as she sat at her computer.

Although she had no shortage of work to do for the paper, she was feeling distracted. She opened her browser and typed *Natasha Ivanova Moscow State University*. There wasn't a lot, but Guin was able to find a photograph. She stared. Natasha was a statuesque blonde, with clearly defined features. A knockout, as her late father might have said. She continued to stare at the image on the screen. Natasha reminded Guin a bit of Maria Sharapova. Were all Russian woman so good looking? (She knew it wasn't the case, but at the moment it felt that way.)

Next, she ran a search for *Boris Sokolov*. While there were many men with that name, she didn't think any of them were the right one. *Odd*, she thought. She thought about taking a deeper dive, but she did have work to do. So she abandoned her search and pulled up her piece on how and where to celebrate Hanukkah and Christmas on the islands.

CHAPTER 5

It was a good thing Guin had set a calendar reminder for the book talk. Otherwise she wouldn't have been ready when Shelly came to get her. As it was, Shelly was early.

"I'm coming! I'm coming!" Guin shouted. Though she realized Shelly probably couldn't hear her.

She had debated what to wear, finally deciding on a pretty blue maxi dress. Then she had put on a little makeup and combed her hair, leaving it down. Finally, she got out her heart pendant and fastened it around her neck. Then she slid the diamond engagement ring Birdy had given her onto her ring finger.

Shelly honked her horn again, and Guin grabbed her bag and headed to the door, Fauna trotting after her.

"I'll be back soon," Guin informed the forlorn-looking feline. (She really ought to get her a playmate. She had seemed so lonely since Flora had died.)

She knelt and stroked the black cat.

Again came the sound of Shelly's horn.

"All right already!" shouted Guin.

She hurried to the door.

"Sorry," she said as she got in the car.

"If we don't get good seats, I'm blaming you," said Shelly, annoyed.

"The talk doesn't start until four," Guin replied.

"But Finchley is famous. People will have been lining up since dawn."

Guin highly doubted that.

"Birdy probably saved us seats."

"He better have," said Shelly. Then she hit the gas.

They arrived at the Captiva Yacht Club twenty minutes later to find the small parking lot full. So they parked at the resort next door.

"You sure he saved us seats?" whispered Shelly, looking at the line of people slowly filing in.

"Positive," said Guin, though she wasn't.

Finally, it was their turn.

There were two women checking people in and handing out nametags. Guin gave the first one her name and introduced Shelly as her guest. They were each handed a nametag, then made their way inside. The place was packed, which surprised Guin. Clearly, Birdy—Wren—was more popular than she had realized. And the crowd was evenly divided between men and women, attesting to Birdy's—Wren's—crossover appeal.

Guin glanced around and recognized a few familiar faces.

"I hope he saved us seats," said Shelly nervously.

They made their way to where the talk was to be held, and Guin was relieved to see a seat with her name on it and one next to it labeled "Shelly."

"See," said Guin.

"I'm sorry I doubted you," said Shelly. Though Guin had doubted herself. "Oh, look, food!" she said, taking Guin's arm and dragging her to a table filled with tea sandwiches and cookies. There were also urns filled with iced tea and lemonade. Shelly took a plate and piled it with sandwiches and cookies. ("I skipped lunch," she informed Guin.) Then they returned to their seats.

At four on the dot, a woman stepped up to the podium. According to her nametag, her name was Nan.

"Greetings," said Nan. "Thank you all for coming. We are quite fortunate to have with us today bestselling author Wren Finchley. His latest book, *Shot Through the Heart*, came out earlier this month and shot to the top of the *New York Times* bestseller list."

She smiled and continued.

"As you may know, Captiva is the first stop on Mr. Finchley's book tour, and all proceeds from the event will go to support the 'Ding' Darling Wildlife Society."

She paused, looked down at her notes, then back up at the audience.

"Many people have wondered, who is Wren Finchley? Indeed, the man is as big a mystery as his books. Even I didn't know who he was until just a few minutes ago. But now his secret is about to be revealed, and I know you will be delighted. So without further ado, I give you... Wren Finchley!"

Guin glanced around and saw several people leaning forward and whispering. Would they be surprised to learn who he really was? A minute went by. Then two. Guin wondered if something had happened to Birdy. And her mind flashed back to his last time on Sanibel, when he had been poisoned and then shot. Surely, no one here sought to harm him.

Finally, Birdy emerged, and the whispers grew louder.

"Isn't that Bertram McMurtry?" Guin heard several people murmur.

Birdy stood at the podium and smiled at the assembled crowd.

"Greetings, everyone, and thank you, Nan, for inviting me to speak at the Captiva Yacht Club. Many of you already know me as Birdy McMurtry, world-renowned nature photographer and ornithologist. But I am also Wren Finchley, bestselling author."

"I love you, Birdy!" called a woman. Guin heard another

woman telling her to shush and hid a smile.

"Thank you," said Birdy, smiling at the audience. "I love you, too."

There was some chuckling.

"So, many of you are probably wondering, why the pen name and all the secrecy?"

Several people in the crowd nodded. He then proceeded to tell them. When he was done, he spoke at length about his new book, then took questions.

"So, are your novels based on things that happened to you?" asked one lady. "Brett Marlow's exploits seem so real."

Brett Marlow was Birdy's protagonist, an ornithologist who secretly worked for the CIA.

Birdy smiled at the woman.

"Some of the stories I relate in my books are based on actual events, fictionalized, of course."

"So, are you really a spy?" a man called out.

Again, Birdy smiled.

"If I were, I'd have to kill you," he replied. Which elicited laughter from the audience.

There were several more questions, which Birdy answered. Then Shelly's hand shot up.

"Yes?" said Birdy, looking at her.

"I heard a rumor that you recently got engaged," said Shelly. "Is that true?"

"What are you doing?" Guin hissed. "I told you not to say anything."

Birdy grinned.

"As a matter of fact, it is."

There was chatter in the audience.

"Who's the lucky lady?" shouted a man off to Guin's right.

Birdy zeroed in on Guin.

"Guinivere, would you please join me?"

Guin was mortified and stayed in her seat, shaking her head.

"Go on!" Shelly nudged her.

Guin glared at her.

"For the record, you are no longer my friend."

Shelly ignored the comment and nudged Guin a second time. Guin could see everyone looking at her. She sighed and stood up, then made her way to the podium. A flash went off, startling her. She finally made it to the stage (it wasn't that far, but it had seemed a mile away), and Birdy reached out and took her hand, gently squeezing it.

"Ladies and gentlemen," he said. "I'd like to introduce you to my fiancée, Ms. Guinivere Jones, a very talented writer in her own right."

Guin spied several people taking pictures and prayed word of the engagement didn't leak out before she had a chance to speak with the detective.

"When are you two getting married?" someone called out.

"Where's the wedding?" shouted another.

"I'm afraid the answers to both those questions are a secret," Birdy replied.

Guin felt herself relax slightly.

Several hands shot up.

"I'm afraid that's it for questions," Birdy announced. "However, I will be signing books after I take a short break. Please, help yourself to food. And if you haven't bought a copy of my book already, you can do so at the table over there," he said, pointing.

He then escorted Guin to a small room at the back of the building.

"Well, I think that went rather well, don't you?" said Birdy.

Guin was scowling.

"Oh, come on, Guinivere. You'll get wrinkles if you continue to do that."

Guin continued to scowl.

"Are you going to tell me what's bothering you?"

"I thought we were going to wait to announce the engagement."

"Don't look at me. Your friend Shelly was the one who brought it up."

Guin squinted.

"Did you put her up to it?"

"*Moi?* Why would I do such a thing? I assure you, Guinivere, Shelly came up with the question all on her own."

Guin wasn't so sure about that, but she let the matter lie.

"Now put a smile on that pretty face of yours," said Birdy. "We have a public to greet."

Guin forced herself to smile and allowed Birdy to take her hand. He led her over to the table where he was to sign books. There was a long line.

"I should get going," said Guin.

"Can't you stay?" said Birdy, still holding her hand.

"No. I need to type up your talk and send the piece to Ginny right away."

"Very well," said Birdy.

Guin started to pull away but Birdy pulled her back, causing Guin to nearly collide with him. Then he gently placed a hand under her chin and kissed her.

Guin could swear she heard a woman sigh and felt her cheeks burning. She wanted to slap him, but people were watching. Finally, he released her. She glared at him, then turned and went in search of Shelly.

"Let's go," Guin hissed, grabbing Shelly's arm. She had been on the line, waiting for Birdy to sign her book.

"What about my book?" whined Shelly.

"He can sign it later. We're leaving."

Shelly was pouting, but she followed her friend out the door.

"What's the hurry?"

"I have work to do."

"Can't it wait? It's not every day you get engaged."

"Nothing's more important to Ginny than a deadline."

Shelly shook her head. She didn't understand what was up with her friend.

CHAPTER 6

As soon as she got into Shelly's car, Guin sent the detective a message.

"URGENT: Need to speak with you ASAP."

It was only a matter of time now before everyone on Sanibel and Captiva knew about the engagement. And she had to speak with the detective before that happened.

"You want to get a drink?" Shelly asked her as she started the car. "You look like you could use one. That is if you won't miss your deadline."

Guin knew that Shelly knew it had been an excuse. She glanced at the clock on the dashboard. It was after five.

"Okay. Maybe just a quick one nearby."

"How about the Green Flash?"

Guin gave her a thumbs-up.

They made their way to the restaurant and got a table for two outside, overlooking Pine Island Sound. There were a handful of boats docked and several brown pelicans. A server came over and took their order.

"So why the hurry to get out of there?" asked Shelly. "The real reason."

"I…"

Guin was saved from having to explain by her phone. She looked down and saw that Detective O'Loughlin was calling her back.

"I need to get this," she said, getting up and moving away.

"So, what's so urgent?" asked the detective. "Please tell me you didn't find another dead body."

"No, no dead bodies."

"Well, that's a relief. So, what's up? We still on for dinner tomorrow?"

"About that," said Guin.

The detective waited, but Guin couldn't bring herself to tell him about the engagement over the phone.

"Do you need me to bring anything?"

"That's what was so urgent?"

"I'm on my way to Bailey's."

She felt guilty about lying, but...

The detective sighed, and Guin thought she heard him mumble "women."

"Just bring yourself—and maybe something for dessert."

"Okay," she replied. "What time should I get there?"

"Six is good."

"Okay, see you tomorrow."

She ended the call and saw their drinks had been delivered.

"Everything okay?" asked Shelly.

"Fine," said Guin, taking a seat. She took a sip of her drink and prayed no one spilled the beans to the detective before dinner the next night.

That evening Guin tossed and turned in bed, unable to sleep. She worried that the detective would learn about her engagement before she could explain. Finally, around five-thirty, she gave up. She went over to the window to see if it was raining, but it was too dark to see anything. Though she didn't hear raindrops. She went to the bathroom, then sat on the edge of her bed. She thought about going shelling. Plenty of people shelled in the dark. Though Guin didn't like to.

Fauna nudged her, and Guin went to give her some food. While she was in the kitchen, she made herself some coffee and read the paper online. Finally, around six-thirty, she went to get dressed. Then she headed to the beach.

It was still dark out when Guin arrived, though the sun would soon be rising. She had turned on the flashlight app on her phone, so she wouldn't trip over anything. (Her ankle was much better, though it was still a tad sore.) And she saw a few other flashlight beams in the distance. No doubt fellow shell seekers.

Guin had found many beautiful shells during her time on Sanibel. However, she had yet to find a junonia, considered the prize specimen among shell enthusiasts. Maybe today would be the day. Though she doubted it.

She walked along the wrack line, where the water lapped against the sand, her head down. As she made her way west, the sky began to go from dark blue to light, and the clouds turned cotton candy pink. Guin stopped to look out at the Gulf. She closed her eyes and slowly inhaled, listening to the sound of the sea and the birds. Then she slowly let out her breath.

"Beautiful morning," said a familiar voice.

Guin opened her eyes to see her friend Lenny, a retired middle school science teacher, standing a few feet away. Like Guin, Lenny was originally from New York City, though he had moved to Sanibel long before Guin had and now, as a Shell Ambassador, roamed the beaches in search of people who needed help identifying shells.

"It is," Guin agreed.

"You find anything good?"

"I got a pretty gaudy nautica. You?"

Lenny held up an orange lion's paw.

"Wow!" said Guin. "Where'd you find that?"

"Over there," said Lenny, pointing to a shell pile.

Guin wasn't fond of shell piles. Too much work.

They walked in silence a little way, both scanning for shells.

"So, you heading north for Thanksgiving?" Lenny asked her.

Guin nodded.

"I am. I'm leaving Sunday. You?"

"I'm meeting up with some of my Kiwanis buddies over at Timbers."

"That sounds nice."

"They do a good job."

They continued to walk.

"So I heard a crazy rumor at bridge last night."

Guin stopped.

"Oh?"

"Yeah, Annie said that you and that nature photographer, Birdy McMurtry, were getting hitched."

Guin swallowed. Lenny was looking at her.

"Is it true?"

Guin desperately wanted to tell Lenny the truth, but she couldn't.

"It is," she said.

"Huh. And here I thought you and the detective… Guess I'm out of the loop."

Guin felt miserable.

"So when did he pop the question?"

"Just the other day. It was a surprise. I was planning on telling you. Word just kind of got out. My mother doesn't even know."

Guin quickly made a mental note to speak to her mother.

"So when's the big day?"

"February fourteenth. But you can't tell anyone. It's not public yet."

"You're getting married on Valentine's Day?"

Guin nodded.

"Here on the island?"

Guin nodded again.

"I'll send you an invitation."

"Thanks," said Lenny. "Though you don't have to."

"Don't be ridiculous!" said Guin. "I want you there."

Lenny smiled, then they continued to walk. When they reached the spit of beach that jutted out into the Gulf, just past Beach Access #7, Guin stopped.

"I should head back."

"You go on," said Lenny. "I'm going to walk a bit more. Gotta get in my steps."

Guin noticed Lenny was wearing one of those fitness watches.

"Is that new?"

Lenny nodded.

"Won it in a raffle and thought I'd check it out. It's kind of addictive."

Guin smiled.

"Well, have a good Thanksgiving if I don't see you."

"You too, kiddo."

As soon as Guin got home, she made herself a pot of extra strong coffee. As she was drinking it, her phone started vibrating. Birdy had sent her a text.

"Give KC a call."

Guin stared at the message. She wondered why KC wanted to speak with her. She continued to sip her coffee. When she was done, she looked up KC's number.

"May as well get this over with."

She entered the number into her phone, but the call went into voicemail. Guin was relieved. She left a message, then went to her office. (One of the nice things about the house was that she finally had a dedicated office space. It was small, but it had a view of the backyard and water.)

She was hard at work on her holiday article when her phone started vibrating again. She picked it up and saw "Weddings by KC" on the caller ID.

"Hello?" said Guin.

"Is this Guin Jones?" said a cheery female voice.

"Speaking. Is this KC?"

"That's me!"

"Thanks for calling me back," said Guin. "Birdy said you wanted to speak with me?"

"That's right," said KC. "I like to get to know all my brides and grooms before I marry them."

"I see," said Guin.

"Do you have some time this afternoon by any chance?"

Guin had work to do but no actual appointments.

"What time were you thinking?"

"Say three o'clock over at the Bailey Tract? Figured we could walk and talk. Less pressure."

"I'll see you then," said Guin.

Guin decided to bike to the Bailey Tract as it was a beautiful day, and her ankle wasn't hurting her. She arrived right at three but didn't see KC. A minute later, a white SUV with "Weddings by KC" printed on the side pulled into the lot. A woman a few inches taller than Guin, with wavy almost white-blonde hair and twinkly blue eyes, got out and smiled at Guin. Guin waved.

"You must be Guin," said KC.

"And you must be KC."

"That I am," said KC, smiling again. "So, shall we go for a walk?"

Guin nodded, and they headed off.

"So you're the one who finally snared Birdy."

"I wouldn't say 'snared,'" said Guin. "That makes it

sound like I trapped him when it was entirely his idea."

"Well, in any case, congratulations. You got yourself a winner."

Guin wasn't so sure about that.

"So, how do you know Birdy?"

"Oh, Birdy and I go way back."

Guin wanted to ask KC if she and Birdy had dated, but she didn't want to be rude.

"I used to volunteer at Ding Darling."

"Ah," said Guin.

"Birdy kind of took me under his wing. Made a proper birdwatcher out of me."

"Do you still volunteer?"

"No time," said KC. "The wedding business has really taken off. Seems like everyone wants to get married on Sanibel or Captiva nowadays."

They continued to walk.

"Birdy told me all about you."

"He did?" said Guin. "What did he say?"

"That he knew you were the one."

Guin stared at her.

"When was that?"

"When he got out of the hospital. He said you were his angel."

"He said that?"

KC nodded.

"He did."

"What else did he say?"

"He said you were different from the other women he had dated. That you really seemed to care about him, not his celebrity. And that you were smart and beautiful," she added with a smile.

Guin had been about to say they had never dated but stopped herself. Had Birdy really said all of that to KC?

"Is something wrong?" asked KC.

Guin shook her head.

"No. I just didn't realize Birdy talked about me."

KC smiled. She seemed to smile a lot. But the smiles seemed genuine.

"A lot of people think Birdy's full of himself, that he doesn't care about other people. But that couldn't be farther from the truth. When my daughter got sick and needed medical care—this was when I was just starting my business and had barely a dollar to my name—Birdy paid for everything, no questions asked. And he's helped a lot of other folks too."

Guin stopped and looked at KC. She had had no idea.

"And most women, they just see some famous guy, not the man. But I can tell you're different."

"You can?"

KC nodded.

"I did some research on you."

"You did?"

"Yup. Read a bunch of your articles. And I know you're divorced."

They continued to walk.

"I also know you were seeing Ris Hartwick."

Guin swallowed. KC had clearly done her research. Did she also know about her and the detective and that the wedding was just for show? She wanted to ask but dared not.

KC stopped and looked at her.

"So my question to you is: Will you, Guinivere Jones, take Birdy for better and for worse, for richer and for poorer, in sickness and in health?"

Guin felt a trickle of sweat roll down her back and swallowed. At least KC hadn't said, "until death do you part." Still, Guin hated lying. It always made her perspire. She just hoped KC didn't notice.

She nodded, and KC smiled.

They continued to walk and made small talk until they

were back at the start of the trail.

"So, do you have any questions you wanted to ask me?" said KC.

"I'm good," said Guin, not wanting to talk about the wedding.

"Well, if you think of anything, just send me a text or give me a call. I'm pretty busy on weekends, but I'll always get back to you."

"Thanks."

Guin walked with KC to her SUV.

"Bye," she said. "It was nice to meet you."

"It was nice meeting you too. Birdy's a lucky man."

KC got in, and Guin watched as she pulled away. What had she gotten herself into?

CHAPTER 7

Guin stopped at Jean-Luc's Bakery to get dessert for herself and the detective. When she got home, she called Birdy to let him know she had met with KC. He didn't pick up, so she left a message. Then she stared out her office window. She was watching a great egret stalk an invisible prey when her phone started vibrating.

"Birdy?" she said, not looking at the caller ID.

"No, it's Glen. Did I catch you at a bad time?"

"Oh, sorry, Glen. I thought you were someone else. What's up?"

"I just wanted to make sure it was still okay for me and the guys to work on the house while you're away next week."

Guin had almost forgotten.

"Oh yeah. That would be great. Just promise me you'll take Thanksgiving off."

"Don't worry about us," he replied. "You just have a good time up north."

Guin wasn't so sure about that.

"Speaking of Thanksgiving, do you have plans?"

"Just having a quiet dinner with the folks."

Glen's parents lived in an assisted living facility in Fort Myers, not far from Sanibel.

"You're a good son. I'm sure they appreciate having you around. You cooking or going out?"

"Mom's insisting on cooking, even though I told her I

would treat if they wanted to go out. I'm to be the sous-chef."

"I thought you didn't like cooking."

"I never said I didn't like it, just that I wasn't very good at it. But I've been practicing."

"You have?"

"I have. Ramen noodles and grilled cheese get old fast. Also, I hear that women like men who know how to cook."

Guin smiled.

"It's true. But you have lots of other fine qualities to recommend you."

"Such as?"

"You can fix practically anything, and you're a great photographer."

"Thank you. So can I cook you a meal when you get back from New York?"

"I'd like that."

"Anything I should stay away from?"

"I'm not a fan of cream sauce or liver."

"Good to know."

"So, can I ask you a favor?"

"Shoot."

"Would you mind feeding Fauna while you're here and giving her fresh water? I can probably get one of the neighbors to do it or hire a pet sitter. It's just…"

"No problem. You want me to clean the litter box too?"

"If you don't mind. I hate to even ask, but…"

"Don't worry about it. Happy to help."

"Thanks. I owe you. So, any plans for the weekend?"

"I'm photographing a wedding."

"Anyone I know?"

"I doubt it. They're from out of town. They're getting married over at the San Ybel."

"Nice."

At the mention of the San Ybel, Guin thought about her

own wedding. They would need to hire a photographer, even though the wedding was just for show. Could she ask Glen? Though that might be a bit awkward. She had a feeling that he might be interested in her as more than a friend. (They had shared a kiss when both were feeling lonely and had had a few drinks.) But in many ways, Glen would be the perfect choice.

"So I'll see you at the gallery opening?"

"Hmm?" said Guin.

"I said, I'll see you at the gallery opening, the one after Thanksgiving."

"Oh, right. See you there!"

"Then maybe we can grab a bite to eat and catch up."

Guin nodded.

"Sounds good."

"Great. So, I'll see you when you get back. And don't worry about the house or Fauna. They're in good hands."

"I know," said Guin. "Have a good Thanksgiving."

"You, too," said Glen.

Guin was pacing. She needed to head to the detective's for dinner, but how was she supposed to tell him she was engaged to another man?

She went into her walk-in closet and changed into one of her nicer sundresses, even though they would be dining in, then put on a little makeup. Then she went into the kitchen and gave Fauna some dry food and fresh water. She glanced up at the clock. She was running late. She grabbed her bag and her keys and headed to the door. Then she remembered, the pastries! She quickly ran back to the kitchen and grabbed the box.

Of course, there was traffic getting to the Causeway, making her even later.

Finally, she arrived at the detective's apartment block.

She parked the Mini and hurried up the stairs. Then she took a deep breath and rang the doorbell.

"It's open!" called the detective.

Guin turned the knob and entered.

"I'm in the kitchen!" he called.

Guin followed the smell of roasted garlic and found the detective hovering over a crowded stovetop with an apron on. She smiled at the sight.

"Smells good!" she said.

"Dinner will be ready in a few. You want some wine? There's a bottle of white in the fridge."

"Here," she said, holding out the box of pastries. "These are for you."

He glanced at the box.

"Put it in the fridge."

Guin did so and retrieved the bottle of white wine while she was there.

A few minutes later, the detective announced that dinner—a mixed salad, garlic bread, and spaghetti with a white clam sauce (made with fresh clams)—was ready. Guin helped him bring everything to the table.

"You look nice," he said, giving her a once over.

"Thank you," she replied.

They sat and helped themselves.

Neither said anything for several minutes, the detective being a man of few words.

"This is really good," said Guin, taking another bite of the pasta. "If this detective thing doesn't work out, you could open a restaurant."

The detective grunted, but she could tell he was pleased by the comment.

"So, how's work? You find out who's been breaking into those cars?"

Someone, or several someones, had been burglarizing cars around the island, mostly at night.

The detective scowled.

"It was a bunch of kids. Probably bored. We keep telling people to lock their cars, but they don't."

"Well, I'm glad you finally caught them. Maybe now it'll stop."

They continued to eat, Guin trying to figure out how to tell the detective—Bill—about her and Birdy.

"You working on anything interesting?" he asked her.

"Just the annual holiday roundup. Trying to fit everything in. It seems like each year there's more to do on Sanibel and Captiva."

The detective nodded and twirled some pasta on his fork.

"So what are you doing for Thanksgiving? You going up to Massachusetts to see Joey?"

Joey was the detective's son.

The detective shook his head.

"Not until Christmas. That's when the baby's due."

"Baby? I didn't know Joey and his wife were expecting."

The detective nodded.

"Due Christmas day."

"Oh, wow."

Guin moved a clam around with her fork. She knew she was stalling.

"What about you?"

"I thought I told you. I'm going to New York."

"That's right," said the detective.

He took a bite of his garlic bread.

"You looking forward to it?"

"I'll be happy to spend some time with my brother. My mother, not so much."

"You two don't get along?"

"She's just…" Guin searched for the right word. "A bit difficult."

"What woman isn't?" said the detective.

Guin scowled.

"Excuse me?"

"You know what I mean."

Guin wasn't sure that she did and didn't like the implication. She put down her fork, and the detective glanced over at her plate.

"You done?"

"Yes."

He reached over and took it, placing it on top of his.

"You need some help?" Guin asked him.

"You can grab the salad bowl."

She picked it up and followed him into the kitchen. Then she watched as he washed the dishes.

"I heard an interesting rumor," he said, looking down at the sink.

"Oh?"

"One of my officers was at this book talk with his wife." Guin froze. "It was given by this author they like, Wren Finchley. You ever hear of him?"

Guin held her breath.

"The guy's not bad."

"You read *Shot Through the Heart*?"

The detective nodded. "And his first one. Anyway, Carlos, he's the officer, says to me that during the Q and A some woman asks if the author is engaged."

Guin dug her nails into her palms.

"And you'll never guess who he said he was engaged to."

He turned and looked at Guin.

"Is there something you'd like to tell me, Ms. Jones?"

He looked down at Guin's left hand, but she had purposely not worn the ring.

Guin swallowed.

"I can explain."

The detective continued to look at her, and Guin could feel perspiration trickling down her back.

"So the paper lost its regular book reviewer a few months ago. And Ginny asked several of us to help out. And one of the books she asked me to review was by Wren Finchley, who I had never heard of."

She paused and looked at the detective, who had stopped washing the dishes.

"Finchley was apparently starting this big book tour, and his first stop was Captiva. And he specifically asked for me to interview him and cover the talk."

"What's that got to do with you being engaged to him?"

"I'm getting to that."

"So I go to Finchley's hotel room. Only it's not Finchley there, it's Birdy."

The detective was giving her a look.

"You know, Birdy McMurtry, the wildlife photographer."

"I know who Birdy McMurtry is," said the detective.

Guin could feel sweat dripping down her back.

"So, funny thing. It turns out Finchley and Birdy are one and the same."

"Which one asked you to marry him?"

"Birdy. But we're not really getting married," she hastily added, then winced. She wasn't supposed to say anything. But she couldn't stand lying to the detective.

"Then why does everyone on Sanibel and Captiva think you're engaged to the guy?"

"The whole thing is just for show. See, Birdy got into a bit of a pickle with these Russians. And in order to get them to leave him alone, he told them he was getting married."

The detective looked skeptical.

"I know it sounds crazy, but it's the truth."

Guin could tell the detective wasn't buying it.

"Why you?"

"I had already posed as his fiancée, back when he was last here. So I guess he figured I could do it again."

"So you're not really getting married?"

"Well, there's going to be a wedding, but we won't actually be married."

"I don't follow."

"It's a pretend wedding, just to convince Boris and Natasha that Birdy's really tying the knot."

"Boris and Natasha, like the cartoon?"

Guin knew how it sounded. She had watched *The Adventures of Rocky and Bullwinkle and Friends* when she was a kid.

"Natasha's an ornithologist, like Birdy," she explained. "Though I think she may be a spy. And Boris is an administrator at the university she works at. Though I think he may be a spy too."

The detective raised his eyebrows.

"And you believe his cock-and-bull story?"

"I realize how it must sound. But it's the truth. Birdy wouldn't lie to me."

The detective shook his head.

"I thought you were smarter than that."

"What's that supposed to mean?"

"It means you shouldn't go believing some story just because some famous, good-looking guy expects you to believe it."

"You're not serious? You don't actually think I'm going along with this just because Birdy's a good-looking celebrity and I want my fifteen minutes of fame? Do you really think I'm that shallow?"

"I wouldn't blame you if you did."

Now Guin was angry.

"I'm going," she said, marching into the other room to retrieve her bag.

"Guin!" he called. "Stop." But she ignored him. "What about dessert?"

She stopped as she got to the door.

"Keep it," she said.

She left the apartment, slamming the door behind her, then stomped down the stairs to her car.

CHAPTER 8

"Argh!" Guin yelled as she sat in the Mini. "Men!"

Here she was, telling the detective the truth, and he didn't believe her. Fine. She didn't really want to be with someone who thought her shallow and inconstant. It wasn't as though the detective had asked her to marry him. In fact, he had made it very clear he had no interest in or love for that institution, having been married for many years to a woman who didn't love him.

She scowled. This was not how she saw the evening ending. Though what had she really expected? (A part of her had hoped that she and the detective would laugh about it. That he would understand she was just helping out a friend, and the two of them could still secretly see each other. Talk about naïve.)

She sighed and put the car in gear. Maybe it was better this way. But then why did her heart feel like it was breaking?

It was Sunday morning, and Guin was waiting to board her plane. She hadn't heard from Birdy, which she thought odd, and wondered if something had happened to him. (She also hadn't heard from the detective, but she was trying not to think about him.)

She sent Birdy a text, asking if he was okay and letting

him know she was about to board her plane to New York. Then she got in line.

It always felt strange to be back in New York, though she had grown up there. But the city always seemed different each time she visited.

She had wanted to stay with her brother Lance and his husband Owen, but she knew her mother would have never forgiven her if she didn't stay with her. So she had compromised, staying at her mother and stepfather's most of the time and with Lance and Owen just a couple of nights.

Guin adored her older brother. And the two of them had grown closer over the years, even though they now lived far apart.

Lance owned a Brooklyn-based boutique advertising agency, and Owen ran a gallery in Chelsea. Although Guin hadn't seen much of them since she had moved, she talked to her brother at least once a week. But she had yet to tell him about the wedding. She hated lying to him. However, she knew if their charade was to work, she had to convince her family. She only hoped Lance would forgive her when the truth was revealed.

She arrived at her mother and stepfather's apartment to find them out. Though they had left her a note saying they would be back later and that Lance and Owen would be joining them for dinner. Guin shook her head, then made her way to her old room, which had been turned into a guest room. She had just opened her suitcase when she felt her phone vibrating. It was an unfamiliar number, but she answered anyway.

"Guin! I'm so sorry to have been incommunicado, I—"
Guin cut him off.

"Are you okay? Where are you? I've been worried."
Birdy chuckled.

"So you do care."

Guin scowled.

"I'm fine," said Birdy. "I've just been busy. And I misplaced my phone. Had to get a new one. Make sure you enter this number into your contacts, so you know it's me."

"Where are you?"

"New York."

"New York, New York?"

"New York, New York, a helluva town," sang Birdy. "The Bronx is up, but the Battery's down. The people ride in a hole in the ground. New York, New York—"

Guin cut him off.

"You didn't tell me you were headed to New York."

"I sent you my schedule." Which Guin hadn't looked at. "In any case, I'm here, and I'd love to take you and your family out for dinner."

"It's Thanksgiving."

"Only on Thursday."

"I'm staying with my mother and stepfather."

"They need to eat, don't they?"

"I don't know what they have planned."

"Ask them. I'm sure they would love to meet your fiancé."

Guin sighed. He was probably right. As soon as Guin broke the news, everyone would be asking her about Birdy.

"Fine, I'll ask them if they are free this week."

"Wonderful. Let me know what night, and I'll make us a reservation."

"Did you get my message about KC?"

"I did. I knew you'd like her."

"She's great, but I didn't get the sense she knew the wedding was just for show."

"Sorry? What was that? I have to go, Guinivere. Bettina's calling me. Text or call me later about dinner. Gotta run!"

Before she could reply, the line went dead.

That night at dinner, Guin broke the news to her family. Everyone was excited. Except for Guin.

"So, do ornithologists make any money?" asked her mother.

"Birdy's an award-winning nature photographer and has hosted nature documentaries," Guin's brother informed her.

His mother ignored him.

"Yes, but can he support you?"

"I don't need to be supported, Mom. I work, remember? And I still have some of the money I got from selling the house." (The one she had lived in with her ex, Art, until he left her for their hairdresser.) Though she had used most of what remained fixing up her new place on Sanibel.

"Be that as it may, it's important for a husband to take care of his wife."

"Isn't that a bit old-fashioned?" said Lance.

Their mother sniffed.

"There is nothing wrong with a man taking care of a woman."

"Or another man?" asked Lance.

Their mother frowned.

"Birdy's also a bestselling author," said Guin, trying to run interference.

"Oh?" said her stepfather.

Guin nodded.

"He writes espionage novels under his pen name, Wren Finchley."

"You're marrying Wren Finchley?" said Philip, perking up. "I just read his latest novel. The man's a master!"

Guin smiled. She had forgotten that her stepfather loved thrillers.

"I'm just marrying Birdy, but I guess I'm marrying Wren, too."

"Well," said her stepfather. "This calls for a toast." He

raised his wine glass and everyone else followed suit. "To Guin and Birdy!"

"To Guin and Birdy," everyone except Guin mouthed. Then they drank.

"So when is the wedding?" asked Lance.

"February fourteenth."

"You're getting married on Valentine's Day?"

"It was Birdy's idea."

"And where will the blessed event take place?"

"Please tell me you told him you have to be married in New York," said their mother.

Guin shook her head.

"We're getting married on Sanibel at the San Ybel."

Her mother looked as though she smelled something unpleasant.

"Birdy already reserved rooms for everyone."

"I am not staying at the San Ybel," announced her mother.

"Why not? It's a perfectly nice hotel," said Guin. "They even have a spa."

"Please, Guinivere. If I am to go to Florida, I will be staying at the Ritz-Carlton in Naples, like we usually do."

"Your choice. What about you, Lance?"

Lance opened his mouth to speak, but their mother cut him off.

"Lance and Owen will be staying with us."

Guin looked at her brother, but he just shrugged.

"So, do you need any help?" asked her mother.

"I'm good," said Guin. The last thing she wanted was to have her mother supervising her wedding. She had practically taken over the first one, and that hadn't ended well. "But thanks for offering."

Her mother sniffed.

"What about the dress?"

"What about it?"

"You will need something appropriate, even if the wedding is on Sanibel."

Guin stopped herself from rolling her eyes.

"I'm sure I'll find something."

Her mother was looking at her.

"Not on your own. I will fly down to Naples after Thanksgiving and help you find something suitable. I'm sure Harriet knows of someplace decent to get a dress."

Harriet was a friend of her mother's who lived in Naples. (Technically, she was a friend of Guin's step-aunt, Lavinia, who still lived in Bath, in England, where her stepfather hailed from. But Guin's mother now considered Harriet her good friend and would visit her whenever she visited Guin.)

"Fine, Mom, but it's really not necessary."

"Nonsense!" said her mother. "I'm coming and that's that."

Guin looked over at her brother, who was smiling.

"So, um, I was speaking with Birdy, and it turns out he's here in New York and invited us all out to dinner this week. That is if you're available."

"He's here, in New York?" said her mother. "Why didn't you say so?"

"I just did. If you're too busy, I can tell him another time."

"Don't be ridiculous, Guinivere. We will make the time. Philip, do we have plans for Tuesday?"

"I don't think so, dear. Though you're the keeper of the social calendar."

"I'll check it when we get home."

They finished their meal and left the restaurant. Lance went over to give Guin a kiss goodnight.

"Congrats again, Sis. And here I thought you were all in on that detective."

"Yes, well," said Guin, feeling uncomfortable.

He gave her a hug, then headed off with Owen.

CHAPTER 9

"You ready?" asked Lance.

"As ready as I'll ever be," Guin replied.

She was staying with Lance and Owen for a couple of days, and they were off to meet Birdy and their parents in Manhattan.

"You nervous?" he asked her.

Guin nodded.

"I told Birdy to be prepared. He laughed."

Lance smiled.

"I'm sure he can handle himself."

"Yes, but he's never been interrogated by Carol Martin before."

"Mom won't interrogate him."

Guin gave him a look.

"Come on, the car's here."

They arrived at the restaurant a short time later. They didn't see their parents.

"We're with the McMurtry party," said Guin.

"Oh, yes," said the maître d', looking down at his book. "You are the first to arrive. Would you like to have a drink at the bar?"

Guin nodded. She could definitely use a drink. She was tempted to order a margarita, no salt, but she wanted to make sure to keep her wits about her, so she ordered a white wine spritzer. Lance and Owen each ordered vodka tonics.

A few minutes later, Guin heard her mother's voice.

"There you are!" she said, coming over and giving Lance a kiss on the cheek. "It took forever to find a cab. I thought we'd never make it."

Her mother glanced around.

"Where's your fiancé?"

"I'm sure he'll be here any minute."

As if on cue, Birdy entered the restaurant, looking dapper. He made a beeline for Guin, giving her a kiss on the lips. Guin did her best not to flinch.

"Darling, I'm sorry I'm late. I had a devil of a time getting a cab."

"See! We weren't the only ones!" said her mother. "Honestly, it's getting harder and harder to find one nowadays."

Birdy turned to face her and smiled.

"You must be Guinivere's mother. Though you two could be sisters."

This time Guin did roll her eyes, and her mother was pursing her lips.

"Flattery, young man, will get you nowhere."

Birdy wasn't the least bit fazed.

"Shall we get a table?" he said, still smiling.

Guin had to admit, dinner had gone surprisingly well. Birdy had seemingly charmed everyone, even her mother. She had insisted he call her Carol, while she referred to him as Bertram. But he seemed fine with that.

Instead of just talking about himself, as he usually did, Birdy had asked Guin's mother and stepfather about their travels and life in New York. Then he had asked Lance about his agency and Owen about his gallery, seeming to show genuine interest.

It was only after they had talked about everyone else that the conversation turned to Birdy. And he was more than happy to answer their questions and tell them about his exploits. Her parents seemed fascinated. And even Lance seemed to hang on his every word.

All the while, Birdy had made sure to look fondly at Guin and hold her hand, giving everyone the impression they were happily engaged. But it had been hard for Guin to keep up the charade. Yes, Birdy was good-looking. And yes, he was being charming. But she wasn't in love with him. Still, she continued to smile and nod throughout dinner.

When they were done with dessert and coffee, Birdy asked for the check, snatching it over Philip's protests.

Then, as they stood outside, Guin's mother turned to her and in a loud whisper told her that she better not blow it this time, which caused Guin to wince and Birdy to smile. They said goodnight, and Guin watched as Philip hailed a cab and her parents left. That left her and Birdy alone with Lance and Owen.

"It was nice meeting you, Birdy," said Owen, extending a hand.

"Same," said Birdy. "If I have some time, I plan on checking out that gallery of yours."

"That would be great." He reached into his pocket and handed Birdy a card. "Make sure you ask for me."

"I will," said Birdy. "Thank you." Then he turned to Guin. "Care to join me for a nightcap? My suite has a fabulous view of Central Park."

"Thanks," she replied, letting out a fake yawn. "But I'm pretty tired."

"Oh well," he said. "Another time." He then gently planted a kiss on her forward. "Goodnight, dear Guinivere. I shall text you anon."

A car pulled up.

"That's us," said Lance. "You coming, Guin?"

Guin nodded, and they all got in.

"I like him," said Lance, on the drive back to Brooklyn. "He's not what I expected."

"What were you expecting?" asked Guin.

"I don't know. But he's clearly crazy about you."

"He is?"

"Is that so hard to believe? He did ask you to marry him, after all."

"He definitely looked like a man in love to me," said Owen.

Guin wanted to tell them Birdy was just a good actor, but she held her tongue.

"You know, we wouldn't have objected if you had gone back with him to his hotel," said Lance.

"I know," said Guin. "But I have so little time with you."

Lance smiled.

"So who will be giving you away?"

"I hadn't thought about that."

"Well, I know you'll probably want Philip to do the honors, but I'd be happy to step in."

Guin touched his shoulder. Ever since their father died, many years ago now, Lance had looked after Guin, often acting more like a father than a brother.

"Thanks, Lance. I'll let you know."

They arrived back at Lance and Owen's place and got out.

"You want to watch a movie or something?" Lance asked her.

Guin let out a yawn. A real one this time.

"I'm going to pass. But you go ahead. I'll see you in the morning."

The rest of the week was mercifully uneventful. Though Guin's mother kept asking her about the wedding. Finally, it was time to head back to the airport. Guin's mother was still asleep when she left, but Philip was up to say goodbye. She gave him a hug and a kiss, then wheeled her bag to the elevator.

CHAPTER 10

While she had enjoyed spending time with her brother and Owen, Guin was happy to be back on Sanibel. Though her mother would be flying to Naples in a week to help her pick out a wedding dress. Not something Guin was looking forward to, but she couldn't say no.

Guin was also pleased to see all the work that had been done on her house in her absence. The place looked finished, though Glen had originally said it might take him until Christmas. She sent him a quick text, thanking him and asking how much she owed him. Then she went to unpack.

When she went back to check her phone, she found a reply from Glen, saying the house was indeed done and he would send her the bill shortly. He then asked if she was still up for grabbing a bite after the gallery opening. She told him she was, and he replied with a smiley face.

Guin thought about asking him about photographing the wedding but decided to wait until she saw him in person.

There was also a message from Birdy, letting her know that Bettina would be calling her Monday to go over the wedding.

Ugh. Just what she wanted. Not. Though, for a second she thought about telling Bettina to do whatever she wanted. However, knowing Bettina, and how she felt about Guin, Guin decided that would not be a good idea.

Guin sighed and made a note to call Hermione at the San

Ybel first thing Monday, to see where things stood. Then she checked the rest of her messages. Still nothing from the detective. She had written to him several times, though she wound up deleting what she had written before sending it.

As she sat in the window seat, absent-mindedly stroking Fauna, her phone began to vibrate. It was Shelly.

"Hey," said Guin.

"Hey yourself," said Shelly. "You back?"

"I am."

"You want to go shelling tomorrow?"

"What about the farmers market?"

Guin made it a practice to go to the Sanibel Farmers Market every Sunday when it was on.

"We could always go there after shelling."

"Sounds like a plan," said Guin. "What time do you want to meet up?"

"How about I meet you at Beach Access Three at seven?"

"Sounds good. Can we take your car to the market? I'll bring a couple of bags and throw them in your trunk."

"No problem," said Shelly.

"So, how was New York?" asked Shelly, as they combed the beach looking for shells.

"Good," said Guin, her eyes focused downward.

"Was your mom excited about the wedding?"

Guin nodded.

"You should have heard her grill Birdy."

"How did he handle it?"

"Like a pro. You'd think he was used to being interrogated."

"Your mom scares me," said Shelly.

"She does have that effect on people. But she's mostly harmless. Oh, and she's flying down next week to help me pick out a dress."

Shelly stopped.

"Can I come?"

Guin looked at her.

"You really want to? I thought you said my mother scared you."

"True. But how often does a woman get to help her best friend pick out a wedding dress?"

"Just remember, you asked."

Shelly grinned.

"Come on! It'll be fun!"

Guin gave her a look.

"So, where are we going?"

"I don't know. My mother was going to ask her friend Harriet in Naples."

"There's always Nordstrom and Saks at the Waterside Shops."

"True," said Guin.

After ninety minutes of searching for shells, Shelly announced she was hungry.

"Let's go to the farmers market. I want to get one of those waffles on a stick."

"Sounds good," said Guin, smiling.

Monday morning, Guin called over to the San Ybel and asked to speak with Hermione.

"This is Hermione," said a woman with a British accent. "How may I help you?"

Guin was sure she recognized the voice.

"Hi, Hermione. This is Guinivere Jones. My fiancé, Bertram McMurtry, told me to reach out to you."

"Oh, Ms. Jones! How nice to hear from you again. I was most excited when Mr. McMurtry told me of your upcoming nuptials."

Hear from her again? Suddenly, Guin remembered. She

had worked with Hermione back when Art, her ex, had been accused of killing one of his colleagues during a corporate retreat being held at the San Ybel. Back then, Hermione had been in charge of room service.

"So, did you get promoted?"

"I did. Though frankly, managing room service was easier," she said conspiratorially.

"I bet. I can't imagine having to deal with prospective brides all the time."

"It's not too bad. So, shall I arrange an appointment for us to go over things? I don't like to rush brides, but we are on a bit of a tight schedule."

"Uh," said Guin swallowing.

"I have a cancellation tomorrow afternoon at three. Would that work? Otherwise, we could meet at nine on Thursday."

May as well get this over with, thought Guin.

"Let's do tomorrow at three."

"Very good. I'll put you on my calendar. In the meantime, I'll email you some information. Would you mind giving me your email, in case I don't have it?"

"Sure," said Guin. "No problem."

Guin had looked over the information Hermione had sent her and had felt overwhelmed. All the brides in the photos looked so happy to be getting married. And there was so much to decide. How had she done it the first time? She shook her head.

Now here she was, standing in the lobby of the San Ybel, waiting for Hermione. A minute later Hermione appeared, wearing a form-fitting dress, her light brown hair in a neat ponytail. She went up to Guin and smiled.

"Ms. Jones, so good to see you again."

"Please, call me Guin."

They shook hands.

"I thought we could start by showing you the different wedding locations," said Hermione.

"Lead on."

"Shall we go outside first?"

"Sure, why not?"

Hermione led Guin outside, down a path to the beach. Then she turned right, coming to a stop by the adults-only pool area.

"This is where we hold our outdoor weddings," she said, gesturing toward the beach. It has a fabulous view of the Gulf, and we close off the pool area, so you have complete privacy."

"What about the people walking on the beach?"

Hermione smiled.

"We have a white picket fence we use to close off the area and stage employees around the perimeter to keep prying eyes away."

"You can do that?" said Guin.

Hermione nodded.

"What about the sand? Or does everyone go barefoot?"

Hermione smiled again.

"It's up to the couple. If you like, we have special platforms that can be placed on top of the sand. Or you can go *au naturel*."

Guin glanced around.

"Okay."

"We can also hold the wedding in our indoor-outdoor conference area. If you'd care to follow me?"

They made their way back along the path to the other side of the hotel.

"As you can see, we can configure the room several ways, depending on the number of people. You could hold the ceremony outside, on the patio portion, and then open things up for dining and dancing."

Guin's practical side liked the idea of that, though she had always dreamed of having a beach wedding. Then she reminded herself: This wasn't a real wedding. Still.

"So if we decided to go with a beach ceremony, where would the reception be held?"

"We could do it in the pool area if it's nice out. There's also a small private dining room we could use, though it may not fit everyone. Ms. Betteridge indicated you would be having over a hundred guests."

Guin frowned.

"Ms. Betteridge is off. It's more like sixty."

Hermione smiled.

"In that case, you might be able to fit everyone in the private dining room. You can discuss everything with Mr. McMurtry and get back to me. In the meantime, shall we go back to my office and discuss the food and flowers?"

Guin nodded and followed Hermione.

Hermione offered Guin a seat, then handed Guin several sample menus, along with brochures for florists, wedding musicians, and photographers. Guin could feel her heart hammering and had the urge to run, but she remained seated.

"I know it can be a bit overwhelming," said Hermione sympathetically.

"It is a bit. Though I was married before."

"As I said, you don't have to decide everything right this minute. But it would be good to finalize everything by early January if not sooner."

Guin nodded.

"So have you thought at all about whether you would prefer sit-down service or a buffet?"

"Definitely a buffet. I was thinking we could do cocktail food or tapas. You know, have a table where people could help themselves and maybe some servers passing around hors d'oeuvres."

"I think that's a lovely idea. Though Ms. Betteridge seemed to think you would be doing a sit-down meal."

"Did she now?"

Guin really needed to have a chat with Bettina, much as she didn't want to.

"But of course, the final decision is up to you and Mr. McMurtry." Hermione paused. "Have you thought about the cake?"

"The cake?"

No, Guin definitely hadn't thought about it.

"We offer several different options, or you can provide your own."

"What did Ms. Betteridge say?"

Hermione smiled.

"We didn't actually discuss the cake." There was another pause. "And you'll need to decide on flowers and the music. Ms. Betteridge made some suggestions."

"Of course she did," said Guin.

Again, Hermione smiled.

"Look over the brochures and just let me know what you decide."

"By January."

"Yes," said Hermione.

"Anything else?" asked Guin.

"Just the photographer. Though Ms. Betteridge said she had one."

Guin raised her eyebrows. This was news to her.

She got up and extended her hand.

"Thank you, Hermione. I'll be in touch soon."

Hermione rose and shook Guin's outstretched hand.

"And if you have any questions, don't hesitate to call, text, or email me. We want all of our brides to be completely satisfied."

Guin forced herself to smile. Then she turned and left.

Her head and her heart were pounding as she headed to

the Mini. It was all too much. Then she felt her phone vibrating. She pulled it out and glanced at the caller ID. It was Bettina. Of course. She thought about letting the call go to voicemail.

"Hi, Bettina. What's up?"

She had been relieved when Bettina hadn't rung her the day before. But she had been foolish to think Bettina wouldn't ever call.

"You know what's up. I'm calling to discuss this sham of a wedding."

Well, at least Guin didn't have to pretend with Bettina.

"I'm just leaving the San Ybel now."

"Did you meet with Hermione?"

"I did."

"And?"

"And she gave me a lot to think about."

"Please tell me you didn't make any decisions."

Guin was tempted to tell her everything was set, but she didn't.

"Not yet."

"Thank God for that."

"It is my wedding, Bettina."

"Correction, it's Birdy's wedding. You are merely a prop."

Ouch.

"And I can't have you embarrassing him."

Guin rolled her eyes.

"I have no intention of embarrassing Birdy."

"Maybe not intentionally, but you have no idea what an event like this entails."

"I'm pretty sure it entails two people getting married. And, in case you've forgotten, this isn't my first wedding."

"I haven't forgotten. And that's why everything has to be perfect. We need people to forget that fact. It's about Birdy, remember? So it needs to be spectacular."

"Spectacular? Is that what Birdy wants, a spectacular wedding? Because last we spoke, he said it was up to me."

Guin could hear Bettina sighing.

"Be that as it may, my job is to make sure this wedding goes off without a hitch and that Birdy's guests are suitably impressed."

"Speaking of Birdy's guests, why did you tell Hermione we'd be having over a hundred people? Birdy promised me we could limit the guest list to sixty."

"That's ridiculous."

"Ridiculous to you, but Birdy promised."

Another sigh.

"Fine. Whatever. Let me know who you plan on inviting, and I'll send them an invitation."

"I'd rather mail the invitations myself. Are there even invitations to send?"

"Of course. I had my assistant order them."

Guin frowned. She had neglected to discuss the invitations with Birdy, and now Bettina had gone and ordered them.

"Could you send me one, so I could at least see what they look like?"

Bettina sighed again.

"Very well."

"Thank you. And please, Bettina, don't make any more decisions without running them by me first."

There was a beeping on the line.

"I need to get this," said Bettina.

Before Guin could say another word, Bettina had ended their call.

CHAPTER 11

Guin met Glen at the gallery a little before five.

"You ready?" he asked her.

"As ready as I'll ever be."

Guin hadn't heard of the artist before she had been assigned the story, contemporary art not being her thing. But she didn't want to sound ignorant or unhip. So she had visited the woman's website and read reviews of her previous shows. Most of the reviews had been glowing. The artist specialized in mixed media, and her works commanded five and even six figures. This was her first show on Sanibel.

Glen was more knowledgeable about contemporary art and knew the artist, albeit not personally. As soon as he spied her, he went up to her and told her how much he enjoyed her work, which elicited a smile. Then he introduced Guin.

Guin found something nice to say about the woman's work, then asked if she could ask her a few questions. When they were done, Guin went in search of the gallery owner, to ask her some questions about the exhibit. By six, Guin felt she had what she needed, having spoken to the artist, the gallery owner, and several people attending the opening.

"Shall we get a bite to eat?" asked Glen, putting his camera away.

"Sure," said Guin. "Want to go over to Traders 2?"

The restaurant was just across the way.

"Lead on."

They were seated at a table near the window and ordered.

"You're so good with people," said Guin, taking a sip of her white wine spritzer.

"You have to be when you're a photographer," said Glen, taking a sip of his beer.

"I wish I was better."

"You did fine in there. You're good at getting people to talk about themselves."

"I try. It's just contemporary art isn't really my thing. Though I found her work interesting."

They continued to make small talk as they ate.

When they were nearly done, Glen handed Guin an envelope.

"Is this your bill?"

He nodded.

"I'll get a check to you this weekend."

"No hurry."

"So, speaking of work…"

"You have another home improvement project you want me to tackle?"

Guin smiled.

"No, it's a photography job."

"You need a new headshot?"

"No, I need a wedding photographer."

"Who's getting married?"

"Me," said Guin.

"You? So the rumor's true?"

So, he had heard.

"You're really marrying McMurtry?"

Guin nodded. She saw the pained look on Glen's face and wanted to tell him the truth. But she didn't.

"When's the wedding?"

"Valentine's Day."

"You serious?"

"Birdy picked the date."

"Well, I'd like to help you, but I'm booked."

"Any way you could…?"

Glen shook his head.

"I don't cancel bookings. Sorry."

He looked around and signaled for the check. Was it Guin's imagination or was Glen upset?

"You okay?"

"I'm fine. I just need to go. I've got a lot of work to do."

The waiter came over with the check and Glen handed him his credit card before Guin could get hers out.

"How much do I owe you?"

"Nothing. It's on me."

She started to protest but Glen stopped her.

"Consider it my wedding present."

The waiter returned, and Glen quickly signed the credit card receipt.

"I'll send the photos to Ginny."

He got up and started to walk away.

"Wait!" called Guin, but it was too late. Glen had already left.

Guin stared. What had just happened?

Before Guin knew it, it was January. December had been a blur, what with planning the wedding, picking out her wedding dress (a whole other story), Christmas, and fending off reporters calling her about her upcoming nuptials. She hadn't been prepared for that. Though she should have been. Birdy was a celebrity, especially now that people knew he was also Wren Finchley. And people loved celebrity gossip.

She had begged Birdy to do something, or have Bettina do something, but the reporters still kept calling and emailing her. Hopefully, things would die down after the wedding. Already she was regretting agreeing to it, especially as it had driven a wedge between her and the detective.

She hadn't seen or heard from him since their dinner, and she missed him. She had even written to him, asking if they could meet or at least talk, but he hadn't replied. When she told Shelly she thought the detective was ghosting her, Shelly had said, "What did you expect?"

And the detective wasn't the only one who was keeping his distance. Since the gallery opening, she hadn't seen or heard from Glen either. And it seemed he was doing less work for the paper. Her other colleague at the paper, Craig Jeffers, who was like an uncle to her, also didn't seem overjoyed about the wedding. Though he had told Guin that if she was happy, he was happy for her.

Craig was an award-winning crime reporter who had moved to Sanibel from Chicago with his wife Betty a few years before Guin moved there. He had covered several murders with Guin, teaching her everything he knew, and the two had become close.

Aside from Craig, Glen, and the detective, however, Guin's friends seemed thrilled for her. Especially Shelly. She basked in all the attention as Guin's best friend and matron of honor and was happy to speak to reporters.

Now, finally, Birdy would be returning to the island, hopefully taking some of the pressure off of Guin.

"You look amazing," said Birdy.

He had just arrived to pick Guin up and was standing in her entryway.

"Thank you," Guin replied. "Though I feel a bit overdressed."

She had had her hair done and had bought a new dress for the occasion, their official engagement party, being held by Pierre and Paulette Marchand, friends of Birdy's who lived on Captiva.

"You look perfect. And everyone will be dressed up. After all, Pierre isn't known as *le vicomte de vêtements* for nothing."

"The viscount of clothing?"

"Because of his stores. He's one of the leading retailers in Quebec."

"Right," said Guin. She knew that, having researched him. But she had temporarily forgotten. "And remind me how you know them?"

"Pierre is an amateur birder. We met on one of my first tours, and he became a regular."

"And they have a place on Captiva?"

Birdy nodded.

"They bought it last year. It's quite spectacular. Views of the water on both sides."

"Any idea how many people will be there?"

Birdy looked thoughtful.

"They said they were keeping it small, so probably no more than a hundred."

"A hundred? You call that small?"

Birdy smiled at her.

"For Pierre and Paulette, that's an intimate gathering."

Guin shook her head.

Birdy placed his hands on Guin's arms.

"You'll be fine."

Guin wasn't so sure.

"I think I'm getting a headache."

"It's just nerves. Though you have nothing to be nervous about. Now, turn around."

Guin eyed him suspiciously.

"Do as I say."

Guin slowly turned, until her back was facing him.

Birdy began to massage her neck and shoulders. At first, she tensed. Then she began to relax. It felt rather good.

"There now," he said a couple of minutes later. "Feel a bit better?"

Guin hated to admit it, but she did.

"Now let's go. I don't want to be too late."

"Fine," she said with a sigh.

He held the front door open for her, then closed it behind him.

"Wow," said Guin, as they drove down the Marchands' driveway. Like many of the houses on Captiva, it was hidden behind a wall of shrubbery. So you had no idea what the actual house looked like unless you were standing in front of it.

Birdy got out of the SUV and handed the keys to the waiting valet.

Guin had let herself out and was taking in the grounds. The property had clearly been professionally landscaped, probably by R.S. Walsh, and had a mixture of native and tropical plants and trees. It was like being in a curated jungle.

"It must cost a fortune to maintain this place," said Guin, gently laying a hand on a colorful hibiscus bush.

"Probably. But they can afford it," said Birdy. "Come, let's go inside."

Guin accompanied him up the stairs. As they approached the front door, they could hear music.

The door was ajar, so they let themselves in. Immediately Guin's eye was drawn to the large plate-glass windows, which no doubt provided a spectacular view of the Gulf in the daytime. She glanced around. The main room was enormous, with high ceilings and marble floors. And there were people everywhere.

Guin had been in a handful of large houses on Captiva and Sanibel, but this was definitely one of the most elegant.

"I guess the clothing business is doing all right."

"Indeed," said a female voice.

Guin turned to see a woman with bright red hair,

probably around her mother's age, smiling at her. Guin felt her cheeks turning pink.

"I'm Paulette Marchand," said the woman, extending a hand. "And you must be Guinivere. Birdy's told us so much about you."

"He has?" said Guin, trying not to stare. Paulette was dressed in a multicolored kind of caftan that seemed to coordinate with her hair.

Paulette nodded, then turned to Birdy.

"Though he didn't tell us he was planning on proposing, naughty boy. You know, Angelique was quite upset by the news."

"Is she here?" asked Birdy, glancing around.

Paulette nodded.

"And the children?"

"They're with their father."

Guin glanced from Paulette to Birdy. Who the heck was Angelique?

As if reading her mind, Birdy turned to her.

"Angelique is Paulette and Pierre's daughter."

"They were quite the item, back in the day," said Paulette, turning to look at Guin.

"What happened?" said Guin, looking from Paulette to Birdy.

"He went off on one of his little adventures, and Angelique met Jacob," which she pronounced the French way.

"Jacob?" said Guin, imitating Paulette's pronunciation.

"Angelique's husband. Soon to be ex-husband. Frankly, we didn't think Birdy would ever settle down. But…" She smiled at Guin, then looked over at Birdy. "He has once again surprised us."

Birdy put an arm around Guin.

"Yes, well, I think Guin and I were both taken by surprise."

You can say that again, Guin thought.

"So, Guinivere, you must tell me truthfully. What did you think of our Birdy when you first met him?"

Guin looked up at Birdy and grinned.

"I thought he was rather full of himself."

Paulette laughed.

"She's got your number, hasn't she Birdy?"

"And my heart, too," said Birdy, taking Guin's hand and placing it on his heart.

Paulette smiled and shook her head.

"The great Birdy has finally been snared in love's net."

Guin continued to smile, though the metaphor pained her.

"Well, you two enjoy yourselves," said Paulette. "And help yourselves to food and something to drink. I'll see if I can find Pierre."

"Shall we?" said Birdy.

Guin nodded. She could use a drink. She also wanted to ask him about Angelique.

They headed over to the bar and Guin got herself a glass of white wine.

"Birdy, old man!" said an older gentleman, slapping Birdy on the back. "How are you? Is this the lucky lady?"

Birdy smiled.

"Guin, allow me to introduce you to Bartholomew Adams, one of Captiva's top real estate agents, and an old friend."

"Pleased to meet you," said Guin, wondering how many "old friends" Birdy had.

"So with the two of you getting married, you'll probably want your own place here on the island," said Bartholomew, grinning at Guin and Birdy. "And I have the perfect house! It's—"

Guin cut him off.

"Thank you, but that won't be necessary. I just bought a place on Sanibel."

"Not on Captiva?"

"I prefer Sanibel. It's a bit mellower."

"Yes, well," said Bartholomew. "And how many bedrooms and baths?"

"Two bedrooms, two baths, and an office. I'm a writer."

"A writer, eh?"

"Guin writes for the *Sanibel-Captiva Sun-Times*," Birdy explained.

"Very good, very good," said Bartholomew. "Give Ginny my best."

Guin smiled.

Bartholomew reached into his pocket and pulled out a card, handing it to Guin.

"Well, when you're ready to upgrade, give me a call."

She politely thanked him, then asked Birdy if they could get some food.

They were helping themselves when Guin heard a familiar voice.

"Guinivere, is that you?"

Guin cringed. The voice belonged to Susan Hastings, better known as Suzy Seashell to her shell-obsessed fans. Suzy ran a blog called Shellapalooza and considered Guin the competition.

"I couldn't believe it when I heard the news!" Suzy said, placing a hand over her heart.

"Hi, Suzy," said Guin, clasping her drink a little tighter and plastering a smile on her face.

But Suzy wasn't looking at her. She was looking at Birdy.

"I don't know if you remember me," she said, smiling at Birdy. "I've been on two of your bird-watching tours. And my husband, Karl, is a huge fan of your Brett Marlow books. He was at your recent book signing. I would have gone, but I was too busy to attend. Had to close on yet another million-dollar listing."

She continued to smile, and Birdy smiled back at her.

Guin wanted to throw up.

"But Guin, I simply don't understand," said Suzy, turning back to her. "I had thought you and Dr. Hartwick…"

"Ris and I broke up nearly a year ago, Suzy." *As you no doubt know*, she wanted to add. "And, well, Birdy made me an offer I couldn't refuse."

She squeezed Birdy's arm and smiled up at him. She should have pursued a career in acting.

"Yes, well," said Suzy, clearly flustered. She turned back to Birdy. "So does this mean you'll be settling down here on the islands?"

Birdy glanced at Guin.

"We haven't decided yet. My only desire is to make Guin happy."

He gently stroked Guin's face.

"Yes, well," said Suzy, clearly flustered. "If you two will excuse me? I should go find Karl."

She walked swiftly away, and Guin breathed a silent sigh of relief.

"I thought she'd never leave."

They proceeded to fill their plates with food, taking them to one of the standing tables placed around the room. As they ate and drank, they were congratulated by several people.

Guin smiled and chatted politely with each of them, but she was exhausted by the effort.

"Can I get you something else to drink?" asked one of the servers, noticing Guin's nearly empty wine glass.

"A white wine would be great," said Guin. (This would be her third drink, but she wasn't counting.)

The server, a young woman in her twenties, returned a couple of minutes later.

"Thanks," said Guin, immediately taking a sip of the white wine.

The room had continued to fill, and Guin felt herself

growing warm as Birdy chatted with yet another "old friend."

"Birdy," she said, interrupting his conversation a few minutes later. "I need to get some air."

He looked down at her. Guin's face was quite flushed.

"Are you okay?" he said, concerned. "Should I come with you?"

"No, you stay here. I'll be fine."

Guin made her way to the deck, which was separated from the main room by large glass sliders. The sliders had been left partially open, so guests could easily go back and forth. There were a handful of people outside, talking quietly. Guin went over to the railing and took a deep breath, closing her eyes. She still felt hot and was suddenly overcome with a wave of nausea. Before she could stop herself, she heaved over the railing. The chatter around her immediately stopped. Guin felt mortified and rubbed her hand over her mouth.

"Are you okay, dear?" asked a woman.

Guin shook her head. She could feel herself about to throw up again.

"Get Birdy," she croaked. Then she heaved over the railing a second time.

The woman, appalled, hurried inside. A minute later, Birdy appeared.

Guin was still leaning over the railing, gripping it tightly. She felt slightly better, having now thrown up whatever she had eaten, but she still felt weak and dizzy.

"Are you okay?" asked Birdy, gently touching her arm.

Guin shook her head, and Birdy felt her forehead.

"I'm getting you out of here now."

"I'm sure I'll be fine in a minute," she replied. Though she highly doubted that.

"Oh, there you are, Birdy!" came a female voice. "I've been looking all over for you!"

Guin raised her head to see an attractive (bleached) blonde, probably around her age, coming towards them.

"Not now, Angelique," said Birdy.

Angelique was about to say something when she noticed Guin.

"Are you okay?" she asked Guin. "You don't look well."

"My fiancée will be fine," said Birdy, taking Guin in his arms. "I just need to get her home. Now."

"Too much to drink?" said Angelique, still looking at Guin. "I know parties like this can be a bit overwhelming." She turned to Birdy. "Why don't you come back after you drop her off? Then we can catch up."

Guin knew that look. Angelique definitely had more than talk on her mind.

"Another time, Angel."

"Always the knight in shining armor," sighed Angelique. "Very well, take care of your *fiancée*. I'll give you a ring tomorrow."

Birdy nodded, then led Guin out.

"Can you make it downstairs?" he asked her.

Guin nodded weakly and took a couple of steps. Then she collapsed.

CHAPTER 12

Guin came to in the SUV. She had felt another wave of nausea and had ordered Birdy to stop the car. But nothing came up.

As soon as she got home, she rushed to the bathroom and knelt over the toilet. Birdy followed her.

"Are you going to be okay?"

"I don't know."

He knelt and felt her forehead. She was like ice, and her face was drained of color.

"I should take you to the hospital."

Guin shook her head.

"It's probably just food poisoning."

"Maybe," said Birdy, not convinced. "I still think we should get you checked out."

Guin shook her head again.

"If I'm not better tomorrow, I'll go to urgent care."

Guin made to get up, but her legs were shaking, so Birdy helped her.

"Thanks. You can go back to the party now."

"I'm not going anywhere."

"We're alone now, Birdy. You don't have to play the part of concerned fiancé. Go, have your little chat with Angelique."

"Angelique can wait. I'm not going anywhere until I know you're okay."

Guin was too weak to argue with him.

"Here," he said, taking her arm. "Let me help you get into bed. What you need is a good night's rest."

"I need to brush my teeth," she said, shaking him off. "I have an awful taste in my mouth."

Birdy stepped out of the bathroom and told her he'd be just outside if she needed him.

Guin shut the door and began to brush her teeth. As she did she went over the events of the evening and what she had eaten and drank. True, she had had two and a half glasses of wine. But that would hardly make her sick. Could she have had a bad oyster? Though Birdy had eaten more than she had.

She stared at herself in the mirror, then rinsed out her mouth.

She went into the bedroom and found Birdy there.

"I thought you might need some help getting undressed."

"Thanks, but I can manage."

He didn't move.

"Do you mind?"

"We are about to be married."

"Not legally."

"It's not like I've never seen a woman's body before."

"Well, you're not going to see this woman's body. Now let me get changed."

"Call if you need me."

Guin waited for Birdy to leave the bedroom, then quickly got undressed and pulled on her nightshirt. A second later, there was a knock on the door.

"Yes?" she said.

Birdy entered.

"I brought you a glass of water."

Fauna rushed in and jumped on the bed. Birdy put the glass on the nightstand.

"You can go now," she told him, climbing into bed. "I'll be fine."

"I'm not leaving until I'm sure you're okay."

Guin scowled.

"I'll be fine," she repeated. "I have Fauna to keep me company."

"Unless Fauna knows how to dial 911, I'm staying."

"Suit yourself," said Guin, rolling over.

Birdy pulled up a chair.

"I have a guest room," she informed him.

"What if you take ill in the middle of the night?"

Guin pulled the sheet up over her head, ignoring him.

"Good night, Birdy."

"Good night, Guinivere."

He continued to watch her until he was sure she had fallen asleep. Then he quietly removed his shoes and his clothes (except for his underwear) and climbed into the bed. Guin didn't move. He watched her for another minute, then closed his eyes and drifted off to sleep.

The sun came streaming into the room, waking Guin up. She had a horrible headache and felt weak. She had had the craziest dream, that she and Birdy had gotten married and were on their honeymoon and had slept together. Then she heard the snoring and nearly screamed.

There he was, next to her. And, oh my God, was he naked? She started to lift the sheet then stopped.

She silently made her way to the bathroom. Then she tiptoed back into the bedroom. Birdy was sitting up, his chest bare, except for a bit of chest hair. Guin tried not to stare.

"You okay?"

She nodded.

"I'm fine. Just a bit woozy."

Birdy went to get up.

"Stop!"

Guin closed her eyes as Birdy got out of the bed.

"You can open your eyes."

Guin slowly opened her eyes. Birdy had his pants on and was buttoning his shirt.

"You should get back into bed. You still look quite pale."

"That's just my natural skin tone. I need coffee."

"I don't think that's a good idea. I'll get you a glass of water."

Guin started to protest but Birdy shot her a look.

"Be right back."

Guin sat on the edge of her bed.

"Here," he said, handing her a glass of water.

Guin took several sips and immediately felt nauseated again.

"You don't look so good."

Guin ran into the bathroom, but only dry heaved.

"We should take you to see a doctor."

"I'm fine," Guin insisted. "I just drank the water too quickly."

Birdy looked skeptical.

"Get back into bed."

"But... Fine," said Guin, not in the mood to fight. "Just bring me my laptop."

He stayed put.

"What now?"

"I'm worried about you."

"I appreciate your concern, but it's probably just food poisoning."

Birdy didn't look convinced.

"Why don't you call the Marchands and see if anyone else got sick?"

"Fine," he said, after several seconds. "Just promise me you'll let me take you to see a doctor if you're not better this afternoon."

"I promise," said Guin.

Guin must have fallen asleep. When she opened her eyes, there was no sign of Birdy, and she had no idea what time it was. She glanced at her alarm clock. It said it was nearly noon. She stared at it, not believing it was that late.

"You're awake."

Birdy was back.

"I didn't realize I had fallen asleep."

"How are you feeling?"

"Better."

Birdy didn't move.

"Really."

She got out of bed and stood up.

"See, fine."

Birdy looked skeptical.

Fauna came in, meowed, jumped up on the bed, and pawed Guin.

"I need to feed her."

"I gave her some food and fresh water earlier."

"Thank you. So, did you speak to the Marchands?"

"I did."

"And?"

"No one else reported falling ill."

"Doesn't mean anything. I need a shower."

"Need some help?"

"No, thanks. I can manage."

"Call me if you want me to scrub your back."

"Don't you have someplace to be?"

"Nope. My place is here with you."

Guin made a face.

"Lucky me. Well, don't feel you have to wait around. I may be a while."

She made her way to the bathroom, locking the door behind her.

CHAPTER 13

Guin stood under the shower, her eyes closed, letting the hot water cascade over her. It felt wonderful, and she allowed her mind to drift. It was only when she felt her fingers start to prune that she turned the water off.

She dried herself, then wrapped the towel around her torso and peeked into the bedroom. There was no sign of Birdy. She quickly got dressed, then went into the living area. Birdy was on his phone, pacing.

"I need to go," he told whoever it was. Then he put his phone in his back pocket. He looked over at Guin. "You're looking better."

"Thanks. I feel better. You can go now. I'll be fine."

"What if you have a relapse?"

"I'll be fine, Birdy. Besides, I can't work with you around."

He grinned.

"Afraid you won't be able to control yourself?"

Guin snorted.

"Hardly. I just need quiet when I'm writing. And don't you have things you need to do?"

Birdy looked thoughtful.

"Okay, I'll go. But I'll be back later."

"You really don't have to."

Birdy held up a hand.

"I know I don't have to. I'm just concerned about you.

How about I bring you some chicken soup?"

"Fine," said Guin, knowing it was no use arguing with him. Besides, she liked chicken soup. Her father always used to bring her some when she was little and was sick.

"All right then. I'll see you later."

"What time?"

"Going somewhere?"

"No, I just want to be prepared."

Birdy smiled.

"Say six?"

"Okay."

He went over to Guin and gave her a kiss on the forehead.

"Good. Your forehead feels normal."

"Thank you, Dr. McMurtry."

He smiled again.

"I'll see you around six."

"Can't wait."

As soon as Birdy left, Guin got to work. She had a lot of articles to write before the wedding, and there was no time to waste. At six o'clock the doorbell rang.

"Coming!" called Guin.

She peered through the sidelight and saw it was Birdy. He was carrying a bag. She opened the door to let him in.

"What's in the bag?" she asked him.

"Chicken soup."

He went into the kitchen and retrieved two bowls. Then he divvied up the soup.

"Looks good," said Guin.

She was starving.

She had made herself some dry toast earlier, which she had managed to keep down. But she hadn't eaten anything since, for fear of regurgitating it.

Guin got out two spoons.

"Do you want something to drink?"

"I brought a bottle of San Pellegrino for us to share," he said, removing the bottle from the bag.

Guin retrieved two glasses, then sat down at the counter. She picked up the spoon and dipped it in the soup.

"This is good," she said, savoring the broth. She took another spoonful then paused, waiting to see if the nausea returned. But her stomach merely grumbled. Clearly it wanted food. Guin was tempted to pick up the bowl and slurp down the contents, she was so hungry. But she controlled herself.

Birdy glanced over at her, not saying a word.

"So what's the deal with you and Angelique?" Guin asked him when she was nearly done with her soup.

"Jealous?"

"Hardly. Just wondering what was up with the two of you. Her mother said you two used to date."

"A long time ago," said Birdy. "I met Angelique through Pierre."

Guin waited for him to go on.

"I was visiting him in Montreal. Angelique had just returned from Paris."

"When was this?"

"Long before I met you."

Guin made a face.

"And before she met her husband?"

Birdy nodded.

"And you two were an item?"

"I don't know if I'd go that far. Angelique had recently had her heart broken, and I..."

"Go on," said Guin.

"I was young and horny."

Guin smiled, despite herself.

"So, what happened?"

Birdy sighed.

"We had a few laughs, hung out. But I had a big assignment in Africa. Angelique wanted to come with me, but I told her no."

"How come?"

"The places I was to visit were no place for someone like Angelique, used to the creature comforts."

"I take it she didn't agree."

"She begged me to take her along. But I refused."

"Were you in love with her?"

Birdy shook his head.

"Angelique was a pleasant diversion, nothing more."

"Did she know that?"

Birdy sighed.

"I told her that first night that I wasn't interested in anything long-term, that my occupation required considerable travel, and I wasn't ready to settle down and play house with anyone."

"But she didn't believe you."

"No."

"So what happened?"

"She met Jacob a week after I left."

"Her husband."

Birdy nodded.

"It was not a good marriage by all accounts."

"So why did she marry him?"

"He was rich and part of her social set. It was a good match on paper."

"I see," said Guin.

"And they have children?"

"Two girls."

"And they're getting divorced?"

He nodded.

"Pierre told me the other day."

"Did she know you were here on Sanibel?"

"I don't know. Maybe. Why?"

"Isn't it obvious?"

Birdy's face was blank.

"She no doubt had hopes for a reunion."

"If she knew I was on Sanibel, she must also have known that I was engaged to be married."

"Maybe she didn't believe you were really engaged. Or maybe she thought that if you saw her, you'd forget all about me."

"Has anyone ever told you that you have an active imagination?"

"You want the short list or the long one?"

"I made it very clear to Angelique long ago that we were over."

"Maybe she has a short memory."

"Trust me, nothing is going on between me and Angelique Marchand."

Guin shrugged, then lifted her bowl and slurped the last of her soup.

"I take it you liked the soup."

Guin put the bowl down.

"It was very good. Thank you."

"And you feel okay?"

"If you mean, do I feel like I'm going to throw up? I'm good."

"Well, there's more soup if you want it," said Birdy.

"I'll save it for tomorrow."

"Speaking of tomorrow…"

"I know what you're going to say, but I'm still going to your talk over at Ding Darling."

"Just promise me that if you have a relapse you'll stay home and rest."

"I'm not an invalid, Birdy. Besides, Ginny's counting on me."

Birdy eyed her.

"Very well."

Guin had insisted on meeting Birdy at Ding Darling. (He had offered to pick her up, but she politely declined.) But when she arrived, the parking lot was full. Clearly, she should have arrived earlier.

She made her way up the stairs and entered the Education Center. The room was full of Birdy's adoring fans, most of whom were over sixty. She glanced around but didn't spy him. Though she spotted Glen. Was he there to photograph the event? Ginny hadn't said anything. She saw him raise his camera and take a few photos. Then she made her way to the lecture room. All the seats looked to be taken, so she positioned herself off to the side.

A bell sounded and the remaining people filed in. Then Birdy was introduced by the head of the Ding Darling Wildlife Society.

He gave a slide show presentation, peppering his talk with humorous anecdotes. When he was done, the audience gave him a standing ovation. Birdy smiled and thanked them, then took questions.

Finally, it was over. There was a reception afterward, but Guin didn't plan on hanging around. She had gotten what she needed. She looked around for Glen but didn't see him.

Birdy saw her and went over.

"Did you enjoy my presentation?"

"Yes, it was very good."

He smiled.

She was still looking around when she saw a woman who looked like Angelique. Their eyes met, then the woman hurried away, exiting the Education Center.

"Hello? Anybody home?"

"Sorry," said Guin, looking back at Birdy. "Did you say something?"

"I asked if you were free for dinner later."

Before Guin could reply, they were interrupted by a jovial-looking woman with short hair and blue-rimmed glasses, probably in her early seventies.

"Is this your fiancée?" she asked Birdy.

"It is," said Birdy smiling.

"You two make a lovely couple," said the woman.

Then Guin spied Glen heading out the door.

"I need to go," she told Birdy and the woman.

"Are you okay?" Birdy asked.

"I'm fine. I just need to go."

She hurried to the door and practically ran down the stairs.

"Glen!"

He ignored her, quickening his pace.

"Glen, please, wait!"

She ran into the parking lot, trying to catch him. However, she was so intent on catching him, she didn't hear the car.

"Guin!" Glen shouted, seeing it.

Guin turned to see a large car barreling toward her. It was the kind that many older people and one of the local taxi companies drove. Terrified, she flung herself between two parked cars, crashing into one of them and landing with a thud on the asphalt.

"Are you okay?"

It was Glen.

She shook her head.

"Can you move?" he asked her.

Guin looked down. Her entire right side hurt. She started to get up, but as soon as she put pressure on her right leg, she was lanced with pain.

"Let me help you," said Glen, gently helping her up.

Guin winced. Her right leg and her right arm and shoulder were killing her. And was that blood?

"What were you doing, running into the lot like that?" he said, leading her over to a bench.

"Chasing after you! Didn't you hear me?"

Glen ran a hand through his hair.

"I'm sorry."

"You should be."

Glen looked ashamed. But Guin didn't care. She was angry at him for blowing her off. But first things first.

"Did you see who was driving that vehicle? Did you get a look at the license plate?"

Glen shook his head.

"No. I was too busy worrying about you."

Guin sighed.

"It was probably some elderly man who hit the gas instead of the brake pedal."

Glen frowned. That's not what it had looked like to him.

"Anyway, thank you for the warning," Guin continued. "If you hadn't called out…" She shivered.

"You should get your arm looked at. Your leg, too."

Guin looked down. Her arm and leg did look pretty bad. Felt bad, too. But she hoped they were just bruised not broken. As for the blood…

"I should go to the bathroom, get these scrapes cleaned up."

She made to get up, but pain again shot through her right leg.

"Let me help you. Lean on me."

Glen gingerly led her up the ramp to the women's restroom.

"I think I can make it from here," she said.

"I'll be right here if you need me," he said, standing outside the door. "Actually, I'll see if they have a first-aid kit. Be right back."

Guin gritted her teeth as she went inside. The pain in her leg was pretty bad, but she didn't think she had broken it. Probably just a bad bruise.

There were no towels in the bathroom, so she made do with toilet paper, wetting it and applying soap, then wiping away the blood.

"You okay in there?" Glen called. "They're looking for a first-aid kit."

"I'm fine!" Guin called back. "You can go now."

But Glen stayed put.

A few minutes later, Guin emerged.

"I told you you could go."

"I wanted to make sure you were okay."

Guin was hobbling, and Glen could tell she was in pain.

"Can I give you a ride home?"

Guin was about to reply when Birdy came running toward them.

"Are you okay? Someone said you were injured, some kind of accident in the parking lot."

"I'm fine, both of you. Just a little banged up."

Birdy looked at Glen.

"What happened?"

"A car nearly ran her over."

"How did that happen?"

Neither Glen nor Guin said anything.

"Really, Birdy, I'm fine. Just a little shaken up. Glen said he'd give me a lift back to my place."

"Thank you, but I'll see that Guin gets home," said Birdy, a bit testily.

"Don't you need to speak with your fans? I wouldn't want to deprive them of your presence."

The two men glared at each other.

"Glen's right, Birdy. Go back inside. I'll be fine."

"Don't be ridiculous. The talk is over. I'm driving you home and that's that."

Guin looked up at Glen.

"I'll be fine, Glen. Thanks for the offer."

Glen frowned, then turned to go. She watched him leave, wishing he was the one taking her home. They needed to talk. But she didn't want to get into an argument with Birdy.

"I'll be right back," said Birdy.

He returned a few minutes later, then helped Guin to his SUV. Guin could tell from his expression he was angry. They drove to the exit and Birdy turned on his right turn signal.

"Hey, where are we going? My place is the other way."

"I told you, I'm taking you home."

"I thought you meant my home."

Birdy shook his head.

"We're going back to my place, where I can keep an eye on you."

Guin started to protest, but she was suddenly overcome with exhaustion.

CHAPTER 14

"We're here," said Birdy.

Guin hadn't realized she had nodded off. She opened her eyes and saw they were parked in front of a pretty white cottage.

"Welcome to Casa Birdy."

"Where are we?"

She glanced around but didn't see any other houses.

Birdy smiled.

"Come."

Guin opened her door.

"Wait. Let me help you," said Birdy.

"I'm not an invalid," Guin snapped. Though as soon as she put her right foot on the step, she winced with pain.

Birdy quickly went around to the passenger side, scooped her into his arms, and carried her up the short flight of stairs to the house.

"You can put me down now."

"Don't you want me to carry you over the threshold?"

Guin made a face.

Birdy quickly entered the code into the lock, then opened the door. He paused, Guin still nestled in his arms, so she could take in the view. The house was just a few yards from Dinkins Bayou. And you could see the water from the living area.

"Shall we go out onto the deck? Maybe we'll see a pod of dolphins."

Before Guin could reply, he carried her to the deck, then gently set her down on a chair.

Guin looked out at the Bayou, then turned to him.

"So, are you renting, or do you own this place?"

"Just renting. But if you like it, I could make an offer."

Guin looked out at the water again and watched a boat cruise by. Then something caught her eye.

"Is that a boat dock... and a boat?"

Birdy smiled and nodded.

"It is. The owner left it."

"Awfully trusting of him."

"I paid him for it."

"Do you even know how to operate a boat?"

"Please, Guinivere. What do you take me for? I learned how to drive a boat before I could drive a car."

Guin knew very little about Birdy's childhood. She would have to ask him about it.

"Can I get you something to drink?"

"A glass of water would be great."

"Flat or sparkling?"

"Sparkling, if you have it."

"Coming right up!"

He returned a minute later with a glass of sparkling water, complete with a small wedge of lime.

Guin took the glass and thanked him. She took a sip, then noticed him looking at her.

"What?"

"Let me see your leg."

"It's fine, Birdy. I just bruised it."

He went over to where she was seated and knelt next to her. Then he gently lifted her sundress, pulling it up to her thigh.

"What do you think you're doing?"

"Examining your leg."

Guin watched as Birdy proceeded to touch it in various spots, gauging Guin's reaction.

"I think it's just badly bruised. Like I said."

"I'll be the judge of that."

Next, he examined her arm, gently moving it.

"Ouch," said Guin.

He finished his examination and stood up.

"Well, the good news is, I don't think you broke anything."

"What are you, an orthopedist?"

Birdy smiled.

"Just an ornithologist. Though I did study human biology and anatomy in school. The places I go, it comes in handy. You sit there. I'm going to get some arnica."

"Arnica?"

"It's good for pain and bruising. Never leave home without it."

He went down the hall and returned with a jar of ointment. He knelt again and gently applied the cream to Guin's leg, rubbing it in in slow circles. Guin closed her eyes. It felt good. She opened her eyes to see Birdy smiling at her.

"Shall I put some on your arm too?"

Guin nodded, and he gently rubbed some onto her arm.

"Better?"

Again, Guin nodded. Then she yawned.

"Tired?"

"Not really."

She yawned again.

"Go ahead and close your eyes."

"I should type up my notes."

"You can borrow my laptop."

"Thank you. That would be great."

"I'll set you up as a user. Be right back."

He disappeared, then returned a short time later with a laptop.

"Do you want to work out here or shall I set you up at the table?"

Guin was tempted to stay outside, but it was starting to get dark.

"I should probably sit at the table."

Birdy helped her inside, then set up the laptop.

"Type away, and let me know if you need anything."

"Thanks," said Guin.

She had been busy typing away when Birdy asked her what she wanted for dinner.

"Dinner?"

She looked down at the clock on the laptop. How had it gotten to be so late?

Birdy smiled.

"I can whip us up something, or I can order food from the Sunset Grill. It's just down the road."

"Let's do that, if it's all right with you."

"I'm the one who suggested it," said Birdy. "Just tell me what you'd like."

Guin pulled up the menu on the laptop and gave Birdy her order.

A half-hour later, he went to get it, leaving Guin alone in the house. She gingerly got up to take a look around. Her right leg still hurt, but the arnica was definitely working.

The place had a small but modern open kitchen, and there was a powder room right when you walked in. She peered down the hallway where Birdy had gone to get the arnica. She suspected the master bedroom was that way. She hobbled to the other side of the living area. There was a short hallway leading to what she assumed was another bedroom. She made her way down the hallway and peeked in. It was a guest room, which Birdy was using as an office space. Attached to it was a bathroom.

Guin heard a car and hobbled back to the living area.

Birdy walked in a minute later.

"Dinner is served!"

After dinner, Birdy insisted on doing the cleanup. He also insisted that Guin sleep in his room. Guin had protested, saying there was no way she was sleeping with him. Birdy explained that he would sleep down the hall in his office, but Guin didn't trust him and made him swear he wouldn't sneak into her bed in the middle of the night. He swore he would behave, then gave her a t-shirt to sleep in and a new toothbrush.

After he had gone, Guin looked for her phone and realized she had left it in her bag, which was in the other room. She hobbled to the living area to retrieve it. The message light was blinking. There were emails, texts, and voicemails. She debated whether to wait until morning to look at them but worried there might be something urgent.

She began with voicemail. They were messages from Glen and Ginny, both asking if she was okay. She texted Glen that she was fine, no broken bones, and thanked him for his concern. She had started to text Ginny when she decided it would be better to call her.

Ginny immediately picked up.

"I was getting worried there. What's this about you nearly getting run over?"

"It was probably some old man in a Caddy forgetting which pedal was the break," said Guin.

"That's not what I heard."

"Oh?"

"One witness said it was a woman, and that she wasn't that old."

This was news to Guin.

"Where'd you hear that?"

"I've got my sources. But you say you're okay?"

"Yes, I'm at Birdy's."

"Oho!" said Ginny. "And is he taking good care of you?"

"He is. And before you ask, I'll have the piece on Birdy's talk to you tomorrow."

"I wasn't going to ask, but good to know."

"What about the piece on the Sanibel-Captiva Rotary Club Arts and Crafts Festival?"

"Almost done," said Guin.

"Good, good. Oh, and you'll be happy to know, I just hired an arts reporter."

"You did? Does that mean I don't have to cover any more gallery openings?"

Ginny chuckled.

"It does."

"So, anyone I know?"

"I don't know. You know Angelique Marchand?"

Guin froze.

"You hired Angelique Marchand?"

"I did. You know her?"

"We've met. But I thought she was just here temporarily."

"Well, according to her, she's here for the season."

"And does she know anything about art or music or journalism?"

"Apparently she's very involved in the art scene up in Montreal, and her parents are big supporters of BIG ARTS. She's also written for several magazines."

Guin scowled. She had a bad feeling about Angelique working for the paper.

There was a knock on her door.

"You okay?"

It was Birdy.

"I'm fine!" Guin called. "Just talking to Ginny!" She turned back to her phone. "Sorry about that."

"Nothing to be sorry about. Thanks for checking in. I was getting worried."

"I'll have those articles to you tomorrow."

"I know you will," said Ginny. "Now take care of yourself."

"I will," said Guin.

She ended the call and thought she heard something. She hobbled to the door and opened it. Birdy was standing just outside.

"Were you eavesdropping?"

"No, I just needed a few things."

Guin gestured for him to come in.

"So did you know your friend Angelique is now working for the paper?"

Birdy shook his head.

"What's she doing for them?"

"She's the new arts reporter."

Birdy lifted his eyebrows.

"You look surprised."

"I suppose I shouldn't be. Angelique was always a patron of the arts. Though working for a small local paper seems a bit beneath her."

"Hey, I work for that small local paper!"

"You're different."

"I just hope there isn't a problem."

"A problem?"

"Angelique didn't seem to like me very much."

"She doesn't even know you."

"And I got the sense she didn't want to."

"Should I speak with her?"

"And say what?" Guin shook her head. "I'll deal." Then she remembered. "So what is it you need?"

"My toothbrush."

Guin watched as he went into the bathroom.

"Got it." He looked over at Guin, who was wearing the t-shirt he had given her. "You look quite fetching in that. You sure you don't want some company?"

"Positive," said Guin, folding her arms over her chest.

Birdy sighed dramatically.

"Then I shall sleep alone, unloved."

Guin rolled her eyes.

"Goodnight, Birdy," she said, then ushered him out of the bedroom.

CHAPTER 15

The next morning, Guin insisted Birdy drive her home right after breakfast. He helped her inside, despite her protests, gave her a jar of arnica to help with her bruises, and said he would check on her later.

Fauna was waiting for Guin, giving her a dirty look.

"What?" said Guin.

The cat meowed.

"I did not abandon you," Guin informed the huffy feline. "I had an accident, and Birdy insisted I spend the night at his place."

Fauna looked indignant, meowed again, then trotted to her food bowl, which was empty.

Guin opened a can of cat food and refilled Fauna's water bowl. Then she went to get changed. Her leg and her arm still hurt, but the combination of pain relievers and arnica had made the pain bearable, just.

Dressed in a pair of loose-fitting capris and a t-shirt, she hobbled to her office and opened her laptop. She had emailed herself her write-up of Birdy's talk and proceeded to shape it into an article. Before she knew it, it was lunchtime. She gingerly made her way to the kitchen and opened the refrigerator. She frowned. Then she remembered the chicken soup. She poured some into a bowl and heated it in the microwave. When she was done, she washed the bowl, then headed back to her office.

By Friday, Guin was feeling better and able to drive. (Both Birdy and Shelly had stopped by to check on her, bringing her food.)

There was an exhibit opening at BIG ARTS that evening, which Angelique would be officially covering. But Ginny had asked if Guin would tag along, show Angelique the ropes. That was if she was feeling up to it. She was, if only to see Angelique in action.

Birdy insisted on accompanying Guin and drove her to the gallery. He dropped her off in front, then went to park the SUV. As soon as she entered the gallery, Guin spied Angelique. Glen was beside her, which surprised Guin. She didn't know he would be there. He and Angelique were laughing about something, which irked Guin. Then she saw Angelique place a hand on Glen's arm.

"Shall we?"

Guin jerked. She hadn't seen or heard Birdy come in. She had been too busy watching Angelique and Glen.

He offered Guin his arm, and they made their way around the room, pausing in front of the various paintings and sculptures. Then Birdy excused himself, and Guin was alone.

"I'm glad to see you up and about."

Guin turned to see Glen.

"And I see you brought your fiancé."

Guin saw where Glen was looking. Birdy was talking to Angelique on the other side of the room. Angelique had placed a hand on Birdy's face. It was an intimate gesture.

"I take it they know each other."

Guin nodded.

"They used to date."

"Used to?"

Guin looked up at him, then back at Birdy and

Angelique. Angelique had removed her hand, and was that a look of annoyance Guin saw on Birdy's face?

"She's a very attractive woman," said Glen, also looking at the couple.

"If you like that type," said Guin.

Glen smiled.

"I understand she's getting a divorce."

Guin turned back to Glen.

"She told you that?"

He nodded.

They watched Birdy and Angelique for another minute.

"Well, I should finish up," said Glen. "Still need to get a few more photos. Glad to see you're okay."

"Thanks," Guin replied.

She watched Glen make his way around the room, then went over to Birdy and Angelique.

"I hope I'm not interrupting anything."

Angelique turned.

"We're done," said Birdy, before Angelique could say anything.

Guin turned to face her.

"Congratulations by the way."

Angelique looked confused.

"On your job with the paper."

"Oh, that."

She didn't seem particularly excited about it.

"If you need any help…"

"I'm sure I can handle it. Not like covering art openings is a lot of work. I could do it in my sleep."

Guin wondered how that would work.

"Well, if you ever have any questions about anything, feel free to ask," said Guin.

"How sweet," said Angelique. "But I'm sure I'll be fine." Guin saw her looking at Glen. Then she turned and looked at Birdy. "I must be off. But think about what I said."

Guin then watched as Angelique made her way over to

Glen, placing a hand on his arm.

"I think I've seen enough," said Guin. "Let's go."

"Shall I pull the SUV around?" asked Birdy.

"I think I can make it to the lot."

They made their way to Birdy's SUV. Then Birdy helped her get in.

"Shall we get something to eat?"

"I'm not hungry."

"Well, I am," said Birdy. "Let's go over to Doc Ford's. You can have an appetizer."

Guin sighed.

"Fine, but just a quick bite."

When they had finished, Birdy drove Guin home. She yawned in the car, even though it was only eight o'clock. It was probably the margarita. She knew she shouldn't have had it, but the run-in with Angelique had put her in a bad mood. Now she could barely keep her eyes open.

Birdy had wanted to come in, but Guin insisted he not. She just wanted to go to sleep, though she forced herself to stay awake.

She flopped down on the couch in her living room and turned on the television. After flipping channels, she settled on *Diners, Drive-Ins and Dives*. She stared at the TV, watching as the host, Guy Fieri, made jokes with the owner of some barbecue place in Texas. She went to grab her phone and realized she had left it in her bag. She retrieved it and saw she had a text from her brother, asking if she was okay as he hadn't heard from her. She pressed the phone app and called him.

"You're alive."

"Sorry. I've been meaning to call you."

"Yeah, yeah, yeah."

"I've just been a bit distracted."

"Wedding stuff?"

"Not exactly. I was nearly run over by a car."

"What? Are you okay?"

"I'm fine. Mostly. Just a bit banged up."

"How did you get run over by a car? I thought you weren't supposed to drive over thirty-five down there."

"I was in a parking lot and wasn't looking. And I didn't actually get run over. I jumped out of the way before it hit me."

"Still. I'm glad you're okay. You go to the hospital?"

"No, Birdy took care of me. Gave me some arnica."

"That stuff's awesome. So, you excited about the wedding?"

"I guess."

"You don't sound excited."

"I'm just tired. Long day."

"I hear you. And speaking of the wedding, I tried to convince Mom to stay on Sanibel, but she's insisting we all stay at the Ritz."

"Whatever. I don't really care. I just hope I'll get to see you."

"Of course. I'll make sure of it. So is Shelly throwing you a bachelorette party?"

Guin stared at the television, which she had muted. She hadn't talked to Shelly about a bachelorette party, and frankly she didn't want one. But she could see Shelly arranging something and surprising her. Suddenly she had a vision of Officer Pettit, the hot young officer Shelly had a crush on, doing a striptease in front of a group of their friends. She shook her head to clear the image.

"Hello? Anybody there?"

"Sorry," said Guin. "No bachelorette party. At least as far as I know. So, how are you? How's business?"

Lance smiled.

"Business is good. Booming, actually. After I get back from Sanibel, I have to go to Paris, then San Francisco."

"Poor baby."

"Speaking of Paris, if you and Birdy want to borrow the corporate apartment for your honeymoon…"

"Thanks, I'd love to, but Birdy's in charge, and he's not saying where we're going. I just hope we're not trekking through some jungle."

She yawned.

"Am I keeping you up?"

"No, I just had a margarita with dinner."

"You're such a lightweight. Well, I'm glad you're okay. Just make sure you call Mom this weekend. I think she's pissed she hasn't heard from you."

Guin rolled her eyes.

"Fine, if she asks you, tell her I'll call her Sunday."

"Okay. Goodnight, Sis."

"Goodnight, Bro."

CHAPTER 16

"Are you sure you want to wear that?" asked Birdy.

"What's wrong with what I'm wearing?" asked Guin. She had on a sundress and heeled sandals.

They were heading to the University of Central Florida in Orlando, some four hours away. Birdy had been invited to speak to a group of graduate and undergraduate students there. And afterward there would be a cocktail reception, then dinner with Natasha.

Guin had nearly forgotten about her. Then Birdy had told her about the invitation and insisted that she accompany him. Guin had reluctantly agreed, not thrilled at the idea of driving to Orlando or having dinner with Birdy's possibly psycho ex. Now Birdy was unhappy with her choice of attire.

"You know this is an important evening."

"I've been to your lectures, Birdy. They're not typically formal affairs."

"This one is different."

"Why, because your psycho ex-girlfriend is hosting it?"

"Technically, the university is hosting it. And I would think you would want to make a good impression."

Guin looked at him. He seemed a bit on edge.

"Fine. I'll wear something else. You want to go to my bedroom with me?"

Birdy grinned.

"I thought you'd never ask."

She led him to her closet and gestured.

"Have at it."

Birdy stepped inside and began going through her clothes, shaking his head. Guin wished Shelly were there. She always knew the right thing to wear.

"I need to take you clothes shopping," Birdy announced.

"What's wrong with my clothes?"

"Nothing, if you plan on sitting in front of a computer all day or playing mahjongg at the senior center."

Guin scowled, and Birdy's expression softened.

"Guin, you are a beautiful, desirable woman, but your wardrobe is woefully out of date and dowdy."

"*Dowdy?*"

Birdy turned back to the closet and pulled out one of the dresses Guin had bought with Shelly and her mother in Naples. It was lowcut with a kind of paisley design and hugged her body, but it wasn't constricting like the dress she had worn to the engagement party.

"Wear this," he said.

"Fine," said Guin, taking the dress.

"And do you have a better bra?"

"What do you mean by *better?*"

"You know, something with a bit more oomph?"

"You mean a pushup bra?"

"Exactly!" said Birdy smiling.

Guin opened her mouth to say something, then shut it.

"Fine," she said, going over to her underwear drawer and pulling out a pushup bra.

Birdy was peeking over her shoulder.

"We'll go lingerie shopping, too."

Guin quickly shut her underwear drawer, her jaw clenched.

"Will you excuse me? I need to change."

"Hmm?" said Birdy.

"I said I need to change."

"Go right ahead."

"Alone."

"You are aware that we are about to become husband and wife."

"In name only. Now out!"

Birdy held up his hands and left.

Guin changed, then looked at herself in the mirror. She had to admit, she looked good. The paisley dress was definitely more flattering than the shapeless sundress she had on before. And the pushup bra had her showing some cleavage.

She found Birdy and slowly turned around.

"Happy now?"

He took her in, his eyes slowly appraising her.

"Guinivere, you are a vision."

"I assume that means I'm acceptable."

"More than acceptable. Natasha will be green with envy."

Guin doubted that. She had seen photos of Natasha, who looked like a Russian supermodel.

"Let's go."

Guin had never been to UCF before. The campus was enormous, or felt that way, but Birdy was easily able to find the lecture hall. They parked and headed inside.

"Ptashka!"

Guin turned to see a stunning blonde Amazon heading towards them. She made a beeline for Birdy and kissed him, on the mouth, or, more accurately, in the mouth. Guin didn't know whether she was shocked or amused.

Birdy pushed the Amazon away from him, his face red.

"What the hell do you think you're doing, Tasha? We're in your place of work! And my fiancée is standing right there!"

But Natasha was grinning.

"You are not happy to see me, Ptashka?"

Birdy certainly didn't look happy.

"Where's the lecture?"

"That's it? No asking how I've been? You didn't miss me just a little bit?" she said, holding up two fingers pressed together.

"I'm here to give a lecture, Natasha, not go over old times."

Natasha pouted, then she turned and looked at Guin. Guin could tell by her expression she was not impressed.

"Really, Ptashka? You chose *that* over me?"

She shook her head.

Looking at Natasha, who must have stood at least six feet in her stilettos and had a body that would not look out of place in a *Sports Illustrated* Swimsuit issue, Guin thought the same thing. She also wondered why Natasha kept referring to Birdy as *Ptashka*. She would have to ask him later.

Birdy put his arm around Guin.

"If you're going to be rude to my fiancée, I will turn around and leave."

Natasha tutted.

"So sensitive. No need to be in a huff."

She looked again at Guin and shook her head.

"So you're the one who captured my Ptashka's heart."

"Guin Jones," said Guin, extending a hand.

Natasha looked down at it, then turned back to Birdy.

"This way."

The lecture hall was packed. Birdy spoke for nearly an hour, then took questions. When he was done, a line formed. At least a dozen students wanted Birdy to sign books, and Birdy was more than happy to oblige. Then it was off to the cocktail reception.

Guin sipped a glass of white wine while Birdy chatted

with students and professors. Everyone, it seemed, wanted to talk to him, and Guin was getting bored. Was this what it would be like being married to him? Going to hear him speak, then standing unnoticed in the background while his fans mobbed him?

Of course, they wouldn't really be married. But she'd probably have to go to a few lectures with him, at least until Natasha left the country.

Finally, Birdy excused himself and went to find Guin.

"Sorry about that. Are you ready to eat?"

Guin nodded. She was starving, having only had a few hors d'oeuvres.

"Let me just find Natasha."

She watched as he went in search of her. A few minutes later, he was back.

"She'll meet us by the exit. Come on."

They stood by the door, waiting for Natasha. Guin was starting to wonder if Natasha had gotten lost or changed her mind when she appeared.

"We take my car," she announced, her Russian accent more pronounced.

Guin looked over at Birdy, hoping he could read her mind.

"We'll follow you," Birdy replied.

Guin secretly smiled as Natasha glared at her.

They followed Natasha to a sleek red convertible. Birdy asked her for the name of the restaurant, then they made their way to his SUV.

"She wants you," said Guin, as they drove to the restaurant.

"She was just trying to make you jealous."

"Well, she failed."

They were silent for a moment. Then Guin spoke.

"So why does she keep calling you Ptashka?"

Birdy smiled.

"It's *birdie* in Russian."

"Ah."

They were silent again as they continued to follow the red convertible.

They arrived at the restaurant ten minutes later. It was an Italian place, which surprised Guin. Not that finding an Italian restaurant in Orlando was surprising. She had just pictured them going to some dimly lit Russian establishment. Though she had no idea if such a place existed near the university.

They entered the restaurant and were shown to a table. Natasha stopped a few feet away and frowned. There was a man seated at the table, a broad smile on his face. Birdy placed a hand on Guin's arm.

"Boris," said Natasha. "What are you doing here?"

"Are you not happy to see me, Tasha?" He turned to the rest of the group. "Come, sit!" he said, patting the seat next to him. "And Birdy, how good to see you again. This must be your little American friend."

Guin didn't know what to say or do.

Natasha went over to the table.

"What are you doing here?" she hissed.

Boris continued to smile.

"Why, I came to join you and your friends."

Natasha glared at Boris, then turned to Birdy.

"Let's go."

"You must stay!" said Boris. "I ordered a bottle of Champagne. It would be rude to leave. Tell her, Birdy."

Birdy looked at Natasha.

"Fine," she said, pulling out a chair.

Boris patted the seat next to him. Natasha scowled, then did as directed. Next Boris turned to Guin.

"Sit across from me, so I can get a good look at you."

Guin hesitated.

"Don't be shy. I don't bite. Well, sometimes." He gave a belly laugh.

"I'm sorry," Birdy whispered in Guin's ear. "I had no idea he'd be here."

He then took the seat next to Guin, across from Natasha. The two of them exchanged a look.

"So, what brings you to Florida, Boris?" Birdy asked him. Boris smiled.

"This and that. And of course, I couldn't miss your wedding."

Guin squeezed Birdy's hand.

"How did you know we would be here?" asked Natasha.

Boris turned and smiled.

"Really, Tasha, do you need to ask?"

Guin could feel the tension rising. Fortunately, they were saved by the busboy, coming to fill their water glasses.

"Tell the server to bring the Champagne!" commanded Boris.

The busboy nodded and scurried off.

The server appeared with a bottle seconds later. He showed it to Boris, who nodded. Then he carefully opened it and poured some into Boris's glass. Boris took a sip, smacked his lips, and sighed.

"Is there anything better than Champagne?" he said. "Other than vodka, of course."

He signaled for the waiter to pour the rest. The waiter did as instructed, then stepped away.

Boris raised his glass.

"To the happy couple."

No one looked happy.

"Come, come!" he said. "You look like you are at a funeral. This is a festive occasion. Raise your glasses!"

They complied. Then they watched as Boris took a healthy sip of Champagne. He looked around.

"Drink!" he commanded. They drank. "Is good, yes?"

"Yes," said Guin. "Thank you."

Boris leered at her.

"Good, good. Now, tell me, how did you capture our Ptashka's heart?"

CHAPTER 17

"Well, that was uncomfortable," said Guin, as she and Birdy got into the SUV.

"But you handled it beautifully. I think Boris may have a bit of a crush on you."

Guin snorted.

"Great. So, are you okay to drive? You drank a lot in there."

Birdy, Natasha, and Boris had done vodka shots after the Champagne. No doubt some macho Russian thing. Guin had passed, for fear of passing out.

"I'm fine. I'm used to it. Besides, Boris and Natasha drank more than me."

"True," said Guin. "But that doesn't mean it's safe for you to drive."

"What do you suggest? You drank, too."

She had, though not as much as the rest of them.

"We could always find someplace to stay. Leave first thing tomorrow."

As soon as Guin said it, she regretted it.

"Now that you mention it," said Birdy, fake yawning, "I am a bit tired. Shall we search for a hotel?"

Guin didn't like the look on Birdy's face, but she got out her phone and began to search.

"Nothing low rent," said Birdy. "I can't stand those places with cheap polyester bedspreads and noisy air conditioners."

Guin stopped scrolling and looked over at him.

"You want to look for a place?"

"Very well." He pulled out his phone. "Hmm…" he said, staring at the screen. "There's a Four Seasons and a Ritz-Carlton not too far away. Decisions, decisions. Eeny meeny miny moe…"

"Just pick a hotel!" Guin practically shouted. The alcohol and Birdy's proximity had made her a bit on edge.

Birdy looked at her.

"Touchy, aren't we? Well then, the Ritz-Carlton it is. Happy now?"

"Ecstatic."

He dialed the number and held the phone up to his ear.

"Yes, good evening. This is Bertram McMurtry, I'd like to reserve a suite for the evening…"

Fortunately, the hotel wasn't far from the restaurant, and there was no line at the reception desk. It was only when they got upstairs that Guin realized she didn't have any toiletries or a change of clothes.

"No worries," said Birdy. "I'll simply call housekeeping and have them deliver a package of essentials."

"What about something to sleep in?"

Birdy looked at her.

"Do what I do and sleep in the buff."

"I don't think so," said Guin.

"It's much better for you, you know."

"Be that as it may, I am not sleeping in the buff with you."

"Really, Guinivere, don't you trust me?"

"No."

Birdy placed a hand over his heart.

"You wound me."

Clearly, the alcohol brought out Birdy's hammy side.

"Maybe I can find something in one of the shops, assuming they're open."

"Do as you wish," said Birdy, flopping down on one of the oversized couches.

Guin looked around. She had to admit, the suite was very nice.

"I'll be back in a few. Can I get you something?"

"I'm good. I'm used to roughing it."

Guin snorted. As if spending a night in a suite at the Ritz was roughing it.

She went down to the lobby and found a shop that sold clothing. She purchased an extra-large t-shirt that would work as a nightshirt and bought one for Birdy, too. Then she headed back up to their room.

"Here," she said, handing him the t-shirt.

"What's this?"

"Something for you to sleep in."

"I told you, I—"

"Not if you're planning on sleeping with me."

Birdy smiled.

"Is that an invitation?"

"I meant, in the same room. Though I bet the sofa has a pull-out bed."

Birdy frowned.

"We did sleep together on Sanibel."

"I was unconscious. It didn't count. Look, I'll sleep on the couch. You can sleep in the bedroom."

"Did you see the size of the bed? A whole family could sleep on it."

Guin held her ground.

"You're being ridiculous," said Birdy. "Look, I give my word of honor. I'll keep to my side. You can stuff a bunch of pillows between us, a kind of Maginot Line, if you will."

"And you know how that worked out for the French."

Birdy sighed.

"If I promise to wear the t-shirt and keep to my side, then will you sleep with me?"

Guin gave him a look.

"You know what I mean."

Guin was tired from the bickering and all the Champagne she had drunk.

"Fine. But I trust you to keep your word. No funny business. And keep your drawers on."

Birdy gave her the Boy Scout salute.

"I promise."

"Okay, I'm going to get changed and brush my teeth. Then I'm going to bed. Did room service send up a toothbrush and toothpaste?"

"They did. They're in the bathroom."

Guin took her t-shirt and went to change. After she had brushed her teeth and washed her face, she washed her underwear, so it would be fresh the next morning. Then she climbed into bed. She wished she had a book with her and thought about getting her phone. Instead, she closed her eyes and imagined herself at the beach. Soon she was asleep.

That night, she dreamed she had gone to see the detective and told him that she had called off the wedding, that he was the one she wanted. He had then taken her into his arms and kissed her. Next thing Guin knew, they were in bed, the detective's arms wrapped protectively around her.

The dream felt so real. It was as if she could feel the detective's body pressed against her, his…

Suddenly Guin's eyes flew open.

There was a body wrapped around her all right. But it wasn't the detective's. She shoved Birdy away.

"What the hell do you think you're doing?" she said.

"Hmm?" said Birdy, who had been sound asleep. Or so he wanted Guin to believe.

"Just what do you think you were doing?"

"Sleeping?"

Guin eyed him. So much for the Maginot Line.

"This was a bad idea."

"I don't know about that," said Birdy.

She could tell he was smiling, even though it was dark.

"I'm going to sleep on the couch."

"Don't be ridiculous."

Guin got up, taking a pillow with her.

"Come back here!" called Birdy. "I swear I had no idea!"

But Guin didn't believe him. She slammed the door to the bedroom behind her and went in search of a blanket. Then she settled herself on one of the oversized couches and squeezed her eyes shut. She was mortified by how her body had reacted to Birdy. Though her brain thought it was Detective O'Loughlin.

"Argh!" she screamed, covering her head with the pillow.

"Rise and shine, sleepyhead."

"Mmph?" said Guin.

Birdy was squatting next to the couch, gently shaking her.

"Time to get up and hit the road."

Guin buried her head in her pillow.

"Come on," said Birdy.

Guin turned and opened her eyes a crack. He had opened the curtains and sunlight was streaming into the room.

"What time is it?"

"Seven a.m. And I have an appointment on Captiva I can't be late for."

Birdy was already dressed.

"Can I at least take a shower?"

"Yes, but be quick."

Guin roused herself and made her way to the bathroom. She brushed her teeth, then took a shower. She emerged with one towel wrapped around her head and another around her body.

"Don't you look fetching," said Birdy.

Guin scowled, then went to get her dress from the closet. She retrieved it, then went back into the bathroom. A few minutes later, she emerged, dressed, her hair combed but still wet.

"Is there any coffee?"

"We can pick up a cup downstairs or else stop at a Starbucks."

"Okay," said Guin. Then she let Birdy escort her out of the suite.

Guin turned on the radio as they drove away from the hotel, not wanting to talk. They briefly stopped to get coffee, and that loosened Guin's tongue. She turned down the radio and asked Birdy about Boris. Birdy was tight-lipped, saying only that Boris did whatever he wanted and the less said about him the better. Which only made Guin more curious.

Throughout dinner, she had played the role of dutiful fiancée. She had smiled or laughed when Birdy said something witty and allowed him to put his arm around her and hold her hand. That had seemed to please Boris, though it clearly annoyed Natasha, which was fine by Guin. She instinctively didn't like the woman.

She asked Birdy if he thought Natasha would still be coming to the wedding, and he told her nothing had changed. Guin frowned. She had hoped that their performance the night before would have convinced Natasha that Birdy was over her and they wouldn't have to go through with the wedding.

Guin looked over at Birdy, who was frowning. She was going to say something but decided not to. Instead, she turned up the radio and stared out the window.

Guin had never been so happy to be home, despite Fauna practically attacking her at the door and giving her another lecture about leaving her alone without any food. Though Guin had filled her bowl with dry food before she left. In an attempt to make amends, Guin gave the cat a whole can of wet food, which Fauna inhaled.

Fauna fed, Guin went to change. Then she checked her messages. Ginny had sent her new assignments. And there was a text from the detective, asking her to call him. She immediately dialed his number.

"I can't talk right now," he said. "Meet me at Jean-Luc's at one."

"Is everything all right?" asked Guin.

"Just meet me at Jean-Luc's at one."

"Okay, I will, but…"

The detective had hung up.

Guin looked at her phone. Well, that was odd. She looked at the time. It was nearly noon. She was hungry, having had only coffee and a muffin on the ride home. But she could wait until one to eat. But why had the detective called her? Why did he want to meet? Had he come to his senses and realized he couldn't live without her?

Get a hold of yourself, Guin, a little voice scolded her. *It's probably police business.*

But what has that got to do with me? Guin asked the voice.

Meet him and find out, said the voice.

Guin sighed, then opened her laptop and got to work.

CHAPTER 18

Guin arrived at Jean-Luc's Bakery at five to one. She glanced around but didn't see the detective's car. She thought about waiting for him outside but decided to go in and see if Jean-Luc, the owner, was around.

The counter and the handful of tables were all occupied, and there was a short line for food.

Guin went up to the counter but didn't see Jean-Luc.

She waited until it was her turn, then smiled at the young man behind the counter.

"Hi, Jake," she said. "Looks like you're busy."

"Oh, yeah," Jake replied. "This time of year, I don't think I sit until three."

"Hope you have comfortable shoes."

He nodded.

"Can I get you something?"

"I'm waiting for a friend, but I was wondering if Jean-Luc was around."

"He's off today."

"Jean-Luc took a day off—in season?"

Jake smiled.

"I know, right? But he ran into an old friend and…" He shrugged.

"Old friend, eh?"

Guin was curious. Jean-Luc was a good-looking Frenchman, recently divorced, and a self-professed lover of women. But she hadn't heard about him seeing anyone. And he never left his shop, except when he went back to France late summer.

"Does this old friend happen to be female?"

"I don't know. He didn't say. And I haven't seen her— or him," he quickly added.

Guin was about to say something when she heard someone clearing his throat. She turned around.

"Detective! I didn't hear you."

"I didn't want to interrupt your conversation."

"Can I get you something, Detective O'Loughlin?" Jake politely asked him.

"Give me one of those ham and cheese crepes."

"Ms. Jones?" asked Jake.

"I'll have the goat cheese, walnut, honey, and arugula galette—and a sparkling water."

"Coming right up!"

"So, is everything okay?" Guin asked the detective.

"We'll talk outside."

They waited in silence for their order, the detective insisting on paying, as usual, then they took their meal outside. They sat at one of the covered tables, and Guin looked over at the detective. He took a bite of his crepe, not looking at Guin, and Guin took a bite of her galette.

"Mmm..." she said, closing her eyes. When she opened them, she saw the detective looking at her. "You want a bite?"

The detective was frowning.

"You need to call it off."

"Call what off?"

"You know what I mean: the wedding, the engagement, the whole thing. It isn't safe."

"But I gave Birdy my word. Besides, it's a bit late for that. Everything's set. Though once Boris and Natasha go back to Russia..."

The detective cut her off.

"Listen to me, Guin. You need to stop this charade now,

before you get hurt."

Guin stared at him. She had rarely seen him like this.

"I mean it, Guin. You don't know these people."

"By these people do you mean Boris and Natasha?"

The detective nodded.

"McMurtry, too."

"I appreciate your concern, *Bill*." (It still felt odd to call him by his name.) "But I can handle them."

"I don't think you can. Do you have any idea who you're dealing with?"

Guin regarded him.

"If there's something you want to tell me, just spit it out."

"I did some digging."

Guin waited.

"I couldn't find a lot. So I asked a buddy of mine who's got connections if he had any intel."

"Why?"

"Because I didn't buy McMurtry's cock-and-bull story about some Russian broad being so in love with him that she'd hunt him down for leaving her. And that the only way to get her off his case was for you to marry him."

When he put it that way, he had a point.

"So I had my friend check out the Russians. And while he was at it, I had him look into McMurtry, too."

"Who does your friend work for, the CIA?"

The detective didn't reply.

"So, what did your friend find out?"

"They're bad people, Guin."

"Bad as in…?"

"Bad as in not the kind of people you'd want to run into in a dark alley."

"Birdy and Natasha are ornithologists. That's not exactly a dangerous profession, though the early mornings can be killer."

She chuckled, but the detective didn't look amused.

"Did you know that *birdwatcher* is slang for *spy*?"

Guin nearly choked on the bite of galette she had just swallowed.

"It is?"

The detective nodded.

"Come on. You don't really think…"

Though as she started to speak, her mind flashed on Birdy's books, the ones he'd written as Wren Finchley. What if they were true? She shook her head. Birdy assured her they were fictional. Though…

"How much do you really know about the guy?"

Guin opened her mouth then shut it. How much did she really know about Birdy?

"You don't really think he would hurt me, do you?"

The detective looked at her.

"I don't know."

Guin frowned. She didn't want to believe Birdy would knowingly put her in harm's way.

"Is your friend absolutely sure? Maybe he was mistaken."

The detective was looking at her. Guin knew what that look meant.

"Just do me a favor and stay away from them."

Guin looked down at her galette, no longer hungry.

"Anything else?"

"No, just promise me you'll call off the wedding."

"I told you, I can't do that."

Guin didn't know why, but she had suddenly become determined to go through with the wedding.

"Is it worth possibly risking your life?"

"My life?"

"If these people are after Birdy, they may see you as a roadblock and try to get you out of the way."

Guin stared at the detective. Could the food poisoning incident and the parking lot accident have been intentional, a way of scaring her off, or worse?

"I know that look," said the detective. "What's going on in that brain of yours, Nancy Drew?"

Guin made a face. She hated it when the detective called her Nancy Drew.

"Nothing."

The detective didn't look convinced.

"I'll have a talk with Birdy. But I'm not making any promises."

"Just be on your guard."

"I will."

Guin got up to go.

"Aren't you going to finish your crepe?"

"I'm not hungry. You can have it."

"I'm full. Just promise me you'll take care of yourself."

Guin looked at him. She knew that the detective cared about her. But she resented the way he often treated her, as though she were naïve or fragile and might break.

"Thanks for lunch," she said. Then she turned and headed to her car.

She was tempted to call Birdy as soon as she got in the Mini, but she waited until she got home. Fortunately, it was less than ten minutes away.

She was about to enter his number when she changed her mind and called Craig instead.

He immediately picked up.

"Guin?"

"Are you at home?"

"I am. Why?"

"Can I come over?"

"Is everything okay?"

"I'm not sure. I have a delicate matter I want to discuss, and I don't want to do it over the phone."

She was suddenly paranoid her phone could be bugged.

Though she knew that was probably ridiculous.

"Sure, come on by. Betty and I are playing bridge later, but I'll be home for a bit."

"Great. I'll be right over."

"Come in," said Craig, opening the door.

"Thanks for letting me stop by."

"Of course. So, what's up?"

He led Guin over to the sitting area, but she continued to stand.

"I just had lunch with the detective."

Craig waited for her to continue.

"He doesn't want me to marry Birdy."

"Understandable."

"Yes, but not for the reason you're thinking. He's convinced that Boris and Natasha are spies and that Birdy is one too."

"And O'Loughlin believes this because…?"

"He has a friend who works for the CIA, or so he says, and asked him to do some digging."

"Hmm," said Craig. "And you don't believe him?"

"I don't know what to believe."

"Have you talked to Birdy? Asked him about it?"

"Not yet. I was going to call him when I got home, but I wanted to talk to you first."

"I'm flattered, but I'm not sure what I can do."

"You can use your connections to find out if what the detective said is true."

"I'm retired, Guin."

"Come on, Craig. We both know you're the most connected guy on the island—and I'm guessing you still have some connections inside the government."

"Maybe," said Craig. He was trying to suppress a smile. "Tell you what. Give me everything you know about Boris and Natasha, and I'll see what I can find out."

"What about Birdy?"

"I can inquire about him, too. Though are you sure you want me to? What if my sources uncover something unpleasant?"

"All the more reason."

"Okay, then," said Craig, getting up. "Anything else?"

"No, that's it. Just, if you could keep this a secret."

"Of course."

Guin went over and gave Craig a quick kiss on the cheek. "Thanks, Craig. You're the best."

"You want to stay? Betty should be back any minute."

"Thanks, but I should get going. I have work to do."

"Okay, I'll let you know what I find out."

He then walked her to the door.

CHAPTER 19

Guin was finding it hard to work. She kept replaying her conversation with the detective. She didn't want to believe that Birdy would place her in danger, but she was starting to have her doubts.

She was staring into space when her phone started to vibrate, startling her. The caller ID said it was Birdy.

"Birdy?"

"Is everything okay? Your text said it was urgent."

"I'm fine, but we need to talk."

"About?"

"The wedding—and Boris and Natasha."

Birdy sighed.

"Must we?"

"We must."

"Very well. Can we discuss it on the boat?"

"The boat?"

Then Guin remembered.

"I was thinking of taking it out for a spin later."

Guin hesitated.

"You said you wanted to talk."

"Fine. When?"

"I was thinking we could go on a sunset cruise."

Guin had always wanted to go on a sunset cruise.

"So shall we say a little before five at my place?"

"Okay. Do I need to bring anything?"

"Just yourself."

A half-hour later, Guin went into her closet to change. It could get chilly on the water, so she picked out a pair of jeans and grabbed a sweatshirt. She stared at herself in the mirror, then went to grab her phone and called Shelly.

"What's up?"

"Birdy invited me to go on a sunset cruise with him in Pine Island Sound."

"How romantic!"

"That's not why I called."

"It isn't?"

"Well, it is, but…"

"Is everything okay?"

"I don't know. I had lunch with the detective and—"

"You had lunch with O'Loughlin? Did he beg you to call off the wedding?"

"In a manner of speaking."

"I knew it! He's in love with you, Guin, and doesn't want to lose you!"

"I don't think so, Shell."

"So what did he want?"

"He thinks Birdy isn't being truthful."

"About?"

"About… a lot of things."

"What man is? Are you getting cold feet?"

"I don't know."

"Go on your romantic sunset cruise, then call me back."

"But—"

"Go! Have fun. You could use some. And don't worry about Birdy. Every man has secrets. It's what makes them interesting."

Guin wasn't so sure about that. Her ex managed to keep his affair with their hairdresser a secret. That didn't make him interesting. It made him a jerk.

"Fine. I'll go."

"That's my girl. You can tell me all about it tomorrow."

Guin parked in Birdy's driveway then walked up the steps to the front door. She rang the doorbell, but no one answered. She pressed it again, then called his name.

"I'm by the dock!" Birdy called.

Guin went around to the back of the house. Birdy was on the boat, and there was a large cooler next to him on the dock.

"What's in there?" asked Guin, pointing to the cooler.

"Provisions."

"Provisions?"

"For our cruise. In case we get hungry or thirsty. So, you ready?"

"As ready as I'll ever be."

Birdy helped her onto the boat, then grabbed the cooler.

"Nice boat," said Guin, glancing around. She looked over at the steering wheel and all the instruments. "You know how to operate it?"

Birdy scoffed.

"Please, Guinivere."

"That's right: you learned how to drive a boat before you could walk."

"A slight exaggeration."

He smiled and cast off.

It was a beautiful evening. The water was like glass, and there was a soft breeze blowing. Guin closed her eyes, breathing in the salty sea air, then she opened them.

"So who taught you how to pilot a boat?"

"My father."

"Were you close to him?"

Birdy shrugged.

"He wasn't around much. But he had a boat and liked to go fishing when he was home. He would take me with him.

One day I asked if I could steer, and he let me. The rest, as they say, is history."

They made their way into Pine Island Sound, and Guin spied a dolphin.

"Look!" she said, excitedly.

Birdy smiled.

Guin watched the dolphin as it came up for air then dove back down. Then she turned to Birdy.

"There's something I need to ask you."

"Ask away."

Guin took a deep breath.

"This whole story about you needing to marry me because of Boris and Natasha. Is it a lie?"

Birdy turned and looked at her.

"Why would I make up such a ridiculous story?"

"I don't know," said Guin. "But I get the feeling there's something you're not telling me."

"Like what?"

"I spoke with Detective O'Loughlin."

Birdy frowned.

"And?"

"I told him the truth."

"I told you—"

"I couldn't lie to him, Birdy."

Birdy continued to frown.

"He did some digging, into Boris and Natasha."

Birdy didn't say anything.

"He's convinced they're spies, and that you are too."

"I think he's confusing us with the characters in my books."

"I don't think so."

"And did he happen to tell you how he came to this conclusion?"

"Not exactly."

"Please, Guinivere. The man clearly has a thing for you

and would say anything to make you distrust me."

"He's not like that."

"Oh? You were sleeping with him before I arrived on the scene, were you not?"

Guin stared at him.

"Who told you that? Were you spying on me?"

"Has it never occurred to you that the detective might be jealous? Think about it, Guin. Here he is, a small-town detective. And this dashing celebrity swoops in and steals away his lady love. Are you really surprised he would try to discredit me?"

"I... uh..."

Guin didn't know what to say. When Birdy put it that way...

"Trust me, Guinivere. I would never make up such a ridiculous story or knowingly place you in danger."

He said it with such conviction. Guin didn't know who to believe. She just hoped Craig would be able to ferret out the truth.

"Now, it's a beautiful evening, and we're missing the sunset."

Guin looked out at the sky. It looked like an impressionist painting.

"Some wine?" said Birdy, retrieving a bottle from the cooler. "It's a 2016 Flâneur La Belle Promenade chardonnay I picked up. It's made from organically grown grapes and was one of the top wine picks of twenty-eighteen."

"Is it safe to drink on the boat? It's getting a bit dark."

Birdy scoffed, then uncorked the bottle. He sniffed.

"Heavenly. Here," he said, handing Guin the cork. "Breathe in the aroma."

Guin placed the cork under her nose. She had to admit, it did smell good.

Birdy took out two odd-looking round glasses and filled them with wine.

"Here you go," he said, handing one to Guin.

Guin stared at the glass. It felt heavy.

"They're special spill-proof glasses," Birdy explained.

"Ah," she said.

"Shall we toast?" He raised his glass. "Here's to us."

Guin didn't raise her glass.

"What's the matter?"

"How about a different toast?"

"What would you prefer?"

"How about, here's to your new book being a bestseller?"

"It already is."

Guin made a face.

"Then how about we drink to the sunset?"

Birdy smiled.

"To the sunset."

They touched glasses and drank.

The wine was excellent. Guin took another sip, closing her eyes as she did so.

"Methinks the lady likes it," said Birdy, smiling at her.

"It's nice. It tastes a bit fruity. Not sweet though. More dry. I can't explain it."

Birdy smiled again.

"You have a good nose. Would you like some cheese and crackers?"

He reached into the cooler and pulled out a plastic-covered cutting board with several kinds of cheese, a cluster of grapes, and crackers on it.

"You thought of everything."

"I try."

He placed some cheese on a cracker and was handing it to Guin when she noticed a boat coming toward them. At first, she didn't think anything of it. Several boats were cruising through Pine Island Sound or stopped, no doubt there to enjoy the sunset. But this boat wasn't slowing down, and it seemed as though it was on a collision course.

"Birdy," said Guin, a note of worry in her voice. "That boat." But Birdy had seen it, too.

"What does he think he's doing? Here, take this," he said, handing Guin the cutting board. He started the engine. "Hold on tight. Things could get a bit bumpy."

Guin quickly put the cutting board back in the cooler, along with her wine glass.

In a flash, Birdy had the boat in gear and was in motion. But the other boat continued to make a beeline for them.

"What's wrong with him?" Guin asked, staring behind her. She tried to see who was driving the boat, but it was now almost dark, and the boat was still too far away, though it was gaining on them.

As Birdy sped up, people on the other boats started yelling.

"He's gaining on us!" Guin shouted, a note of terror in her voice.

"We'll be fine once we get into the bayou," Birdy told her. But Guin wasn't so sure.

There were several boats in their path, but Birdy skillfully maneuvered around them. Finally, they entered the bayou.

Guin had been too scared to look back.

"We lost him," said Birdy.

Guin turned but didn't see the other boat.

A few minutes later, they were back at Birdy's dock. He helped her off the boat.

"What the hell was that about?" she asked him.

"I don't know," said Birdy, a somber look on his face. "But I'm going to find out."

Birdy insisted Guin stay and help him finish the wine, cheese, and crackers. She was still a bit shaken up, so she agreed, though she didn't have much of an appetite.

"You have no idea why that boat was chasing us?" Guin asked him, taking a sip of her wine.

"No," he replied. But something in his expression made Guin doubt him.

She took a last sip, then got up.

"Well, thanks for the cruise and the wine."

"You're leaving?"

"It's been a long day, and I'm tired."

"You're welcome to sleep here," Birdy said.

"Thanks, but I prefer my own bed."

Birdy sighed dramatically and got up.

"Very well. At least let me walk you to your car."

"Well, goodnight," said Guin when they had reached the Mini.

"You sure you won't change your mind?"

Guin shook her head.

"Then safe home and sweet dreams," said Birdy. "I'll see you soon."

Guin opened the door and got in.

CHAPTER 20

As soon as she got home, her phone buzzed. It was Shelly. So much for waiting for tomorrow.

"So, how was the sunset cruise?"

"It was okay."

"Just okay?"

"It was fine."

"Fine? Really? That's all you have to say? Your dashing fiancée takes you on a romantic sunset cruise, and all you can say is, 'It was okay' or 'Fine'?"

Guin sighed.

"We ran into some trouble."

"What kind of trouble?"

"We got chased by another boat."

"For real?"

Guin nodded.

"It was coming right toward us. Thank goodness Birdy has quick reflexes."

"Wow. Sounds just like a scene from one of his books!"

Guin paused. It did sound like something out of one of Birdy's—or Wren Finchley's—books.

"At least you escaped."

"We did. Just. But it was a bit unnerving."

"I bet. So, any idea who was chasing you?"

Guin had an idea, but she didn't want to say anything to Shelly.

"Do you think it was Natalia and Igor?"

Natalia and Igor were the Russian spies in Birdy's latest book.

"Natalia and Igor are fictional characters, Shelly. They're not real."

"How do you know? They seemed pretty real in the book."

Guin attempted to distract her.

"Hey, you want to meet up and go shelling tomorrow?"

"Uh, hello? Do birds fly?"

Guin smiled.

"Where do you want to start?"

"How about Algiers?"

"Sounds good. Shall we say seven?"

"Seven it is!"

Although it was only seven, the beach was teeming with shell seekers, and Guin and Shelly struggled to find good shells. That's what happened on Sanibel in season. If you weren't on the beach by sunrise, you risked losing out.

"Is it me or does the beach seem more crowded than usual?" asked Guin, glancing around.

"There are definitely more people than there used to be," said Shelly. "But it's January, so…"

"We should plan a trip to the Ten Thousand Islands."

"I'm game. Though there are more people going there, too," said Shelly. "I miss the good old days."

"When was that?"

"Back when we first moved here."

"That wasn't that long ago."

"Ten years is a long time."

"And you really think there were more shells then?"

Shelly nodded.

"I do. Though I know a lot of it has to do with climate and currents and wind. The Shell Club's actually doing a lecture on it next meeting. We should go."

"Can't. I'll be on my honeymoon." Which Guin was dreading.

"Duh! How could I have forgotten? So, do you know where Birdy's taking you?"

Guin shook her head.

"Not even a clue?"

"No. I just hope he doesn't plan on us trekking through some jungle."

Shelly made a face.

"Yeah, not my idea of a honeymoon either. But you know how Birdy loves a good jungle."

"Speaking of your upcoming nuptials... I was thinking I could throw you a bachelorette party."

"Thanks, but you don't have to."

"But I want to! Please?"

Guin's vision of Officer Pettit doing a striptease in front of the Shell Club returned and she shivered.

"How about a barbecue instead?"

"Okay," said Shelly, a bit sulkily. "Though a bachelorette party would be way more fun."

"I prefer a barbecue. Besides, you know I don't have a lot of female friends on the island. I just need to check with my mom. She's flying in this weekend, and I don't know what her plans are."

"Invite her!"

Guin couldn't picture her mother at one of Shelly and Steve's barbecues, but she said she would.

"Will your brother and Owen also be coming?"

"They're not flying down until Tuesday."

"Their loss. Well, check with Carol and get back to me. It'll probably be Sunday."

"Okay," said Guin.

She looked down at her shelling bag. It was nearly empty.

"I think I'm giving up."

Shelly looked down at her bag, which contained maybe a dozen shells, mostly colorful scallops.

"I'm going to see if I can find a few more things. I could really use some rose petal tellins."

"Good luck."

Guin was about to head back when Shelly stopped her.

"So is everything set for the big day?"

"I think so. Though I should probably check in with Hermione. Thanks for reminding me."

"No problem. If you need any help…"

Guin smiled at her friend.

"You'll be the first person I call. Now, I need to get going. Still have some more articles to write."

"What are you working on?"

"Some Shell Festival stuff, and I'm doing a piece on this new vet CROW [the Clinic for the Rehabilitation of Wildlife] hired."

"Sounds like fun. Well, I won't keep you."

"Thanks. Happy hunting."

Guin turned and made her way off the beach.

Guin spent the rest of the morning working, not leaving her desk (except to go to the bathroom) until a little after one. She could feel her stomach rumbling, so she went to the kitchen to fix herself some lunch. Fauna followed her.

Guin glanced over at the cat bowl. It was empty. So she added some dry food.

"Now what will I have?" she said, opening the refrigerator. "Hmm…" She eyed the deli drawer and took out a package of tortillas and a bag of shredded Mexican cheese. "How about a cheesy quesadilla?"

She took out a skillet and turned on a burner. Then she placed the tortilla in the pan and covered it with cheese. When the cheese had nearly melted, she added some salsa.

Then she folded the tortilla in half and pressed down.

"Not bad," she said, taking a bite of the gooey quesadilla. She took another bite and stared out the bay window into the backyard. A great egret was bobbing its head, clearly on the hunt for something. Guin watched as it slowly made its way across the grass.

She took another bite of her quesadilla and drank some seltzer.

When she was done, she washed her plate and placed it in the drying rack. Then she went to check the mail.

Most of it was junk, but one envelope caught her eye. There was no postage on it, nor return address, and her name and address were written in block letters. She frowned, wondering if she should open it. But her curiosity got the better of her. She carefully sliced the top open. Inside was a neatly folded sheet of paper, bearing the typewritten words CALL OFF THE WEDDING OR ELSE in all caps.

Or else what? Guin wondered. She examined the piece of paper and the envelope, but there were no identifying marks. She thought about throwing them away. Then she thought better of it and grabbed her phone. She speed-dialed the Sanibel Police Department and asked to speak with Detective O'Loughlin. The operator informed her that he was out, so she left a message. Then she sent him a text.

He called her back five minutes later.

"I'm coming over there," he announced. "Don't go anywhere, and don't touch that letter or the envelope."

Guin wanted to point out that she already had and ask him when he would be there, but he had hung up. She looked at her phone, wondering if she should call him back, then sighed and went back to her office, leaving the envelope and the letter on the counter.

Twenty minutes later, the doorbell rang.

"Where's the letter?" asked the detective as soon as Guin had opened the door.

Guin led him over to the kitchen counter. The detective pulled out a pair of gloves and put them on. Then he picked up the letter, examining it. Next, he examined the envelope. When he was done, he took out a plastic evidence bag and placed both the letter and the envelope inside.

"You going to have them checked for fingerprints and DNA?"

The detective nodded.

"What if there isn't anything?"

"The lab should be able to find something."

"So what do you think it means?"

"Clearly, someone wants you to call off the wedding."

Guin made a face.

"Obviously. So you think the sender wanted to scare me?"

The detective looked at her.

"You still planning on going through with this farce?"

"You really think I would cancel the wedding just because of some anonymous letter?"

"Tell me you love him."

"Excuse me?" said Guin.

"Tell me you're in love with the guy."

"I…"

Before she could answer, the detective stepped in front of her. She could feel his breath on her face, and his tawny eyes boring into her.

"Tell me you're in love him."

Guin opened her mouth, but the next thing she knew the detective had closed the distance between them and was kissing her. Guin had no idea how long they had been standing there, kissing, until he stepped away. He was smirking, and anger flared up inside her.

"Get out," she commanded. She was shaking.

"Fine. I'm going. But don't let McMurtry fool you. I don't trust him, and you shouldn't either."

"Goodbye, *Detective*," said Guin. "Let me know what you find out about the note. That is, of course, unless *you* left it for me."

She was looking at him, but his face had become a mask, unreadable.

He turned and headed to the door. Then he was gone, and Guin was left more confused than before.

CHAPTER 21

"Thanks for seeing me, Hermione."

Guin was seated in the wedding coordinator's office at the San Ybel Resort & Spa.

"Of course!" said Hermione.

"So, I know it's too late to change anything, but I'm worried I forgot something."

Hermione smiled.

"Everything's been taken care of. And no problem regarding the special requests."

"Special requests?"

"I'm sorry. I assumed you and Bettina had spoken."

Guin silently fumed. She had barely heard from Bettina and had no idea about any special requests.

"What exactly did Bettina tell you?"

"She just wanted to make sure we could accommodate those guests with special diets. She also made a few changes to the seating chart."

"The seating chart? I thought we had agreed that it would be a buffet and that people could sit where they wanted to."

Now it was Hermione's turn to look a bit flustered.

"I'm sorry. I thought you and Bettina had discussed it. We're still doing a buffet, but Bettina wanted to assign people to tables, to avoid any potential issues."

"Potential issues?" said Guin. She shook her head and made a mental note to have a chat with Bettina. Then another thought occurred to her. "And did Bettina happen to give you a final headcount for the reception?"

Hermione nodded.

"She said there would be eighty people attending."

Guin could feel the steam starting to build up. Any minute now she would erupt. Eighty was twenty more people than she and Birdy had agreed to. And she was not happy about Bettina going behind her back.

"Is there anything else Bettina told you?"

Hermione looked slightly nervous.

"Maybe we should go over everything one more time?"

"Good idea," said Guin.

Guin was fuming when she left Hermione's office. Bettina had gone and changed nearly everything without saying a word to her, telling Hermione that she had approved all the changes. Ha! Guin realized, though, that she only had herself to blame. She hadn't checked in with Hermione or Bettina in weeks, assuming everything was taken care of. And she knew what happened when you assume.

Guin had been too embarrassed to say anything to Hermione. Besides, it was too late to change things back. She would just have to live with it. She thought about calling Birdy, to let him know of Bettina's perfidy, but what could he do?

She had planned on going back home right after her meeting but abruptly changed her mind and headed for the path that led down to the beach. It was warm out, and she wasn't dressed for the beach, but she didn't care. She needed to feel the sand between her toes.

She walked for half an hour, then returned to her car. Before she started the engine, she called Shelly. She picked up after three rings.

"What's up? Is everything okay?"

"Can we meet for a drink later?"

"Sure. When and where?"

Guin thought for a minute.

"Doc Ford's at five-thirty?"

"I'll be there."

"Can you believe that bitch?"

Guin was still angry.

Shelly shook her head.

"She has a lot of nerve."

"I'll say."

"Did you tell Birdy?"

"No. What good would it do?"

"Well, someone needs to put her in her place."

"Ladies."

Guin turned up to see Marty Nesbitt. Marty was an administrator of one of the Facebook shelling groups and a bit of a character. Somewhere in his sixties, with thinning gray hair that he wore in a ponytail, he could be seen on the beach and at the local watering holes sporting one of his many Hawaiian shirts. While well-meaning, he was also quite annoying and devoid of self-awareness.

"What's this I hear about you getting married, Guinivere? If I knew you were hot to tie the knot, I would have proposed," he said, waggling his bushy eyebrows.

"Maybe next time," said Guin, not in the mood to chat with Marty.

"Well, if it doesn't work out, you know where to find me."

"What happened to that woman you were dating?" asked Shelly, who was a member of Marty's Facebook group. "Hilda, wasn't it?"

"You mean Tilda? We broke up a while ago. Decided I should play the field a while longer."

"Uh-huh," said Shelly.

Guin suppressed a smile.

"Mind if I join you ladies?" asked Marty.

"Actually," said Shelly. "This is a private conversation. I'm giving Guin here some pre-marital advice."

Marty looked from one to the other.

"Girl talk," Shelly clarified.

"Oh, got it." He looked around the bar and spied someone else he knew. "Tom!" he said, smiling and waving at a man at the other end of the bar.

Guin and Shelly watched him go.

"Dodged a bullet there," said Shelly, taking another sip of her drink.

"I'll say," said Guin.

"So why did she go and change everything?"

"Because she could. Apparently, nothing I do is good enough for her Birdy."

"She could have at least informed you."

"Yeah, well, that's not Bettina's style."

"Well, you're the one marrying Birdy, not her."

"Tell that to Bettina."

They continued to sip their drinks.

"Can I get you ladies anything else?" asked the bartender.

"Actually," said Guin. "Can I see a menu?"

He handed her and Shelly each a menu, and Guin thanked him.

"Shall we get a bite to eat, or do you need to get home and make dinner for Steve?"

"Steve's perfectly capable of fending for himself, but he's actually out tonight. Some work thing."

Guin smiled.

They placed their order a few minutes later. And by the time they were done eating, Guin was feeling better. She had also decided she would have a little talk with her fiancé about his agent.

As soon as she got home, Guin called Birdy.

"Guinivere! This is a pleasant surprise. Did you miss me?"

"We need to talk about Bettina."

Birdy sighed.

"What did she do now?"

"Just destroyed my wedding."

"And how did she do that?"

"She invited twenty extra people and changed everything."

"I'm sure she had a reason."

"Yes, to make me look and feel like an idiot."

"And what do you propose I do?"

"Talk to her."

Birdy sighed again.

"And what exactly am I to say? She was probably just trying to help."

Guin snorted.

"Yeah, help me to a nervous breakdown."

"Aren't you being a bit melodramatic?"

"She changed the seating, the food, even the flowers!"

"Fine. I'll have a chat with her."

"Thank you."

"You want to come over? I was about to eat. I grilled some fish I caught."

"Thanks, but I just ate."

"You want to come over for dessert?"

Guin heard the suggestive tone in Birdy's voice but ignored it.

"Thanks, but I need to fit into my wedding dress."

"I can help you work off the calories."

Guin rolled her eyes.

"That's kind of you," she said sarcastically, "but I'm not in the mood."

"Too bad."

"But you promise you'll have a word with Bettina?"

"I promise."

"Okay. Thank you."

There was a pause.

"I should go," said Guin.

"If you change your mind…" said Birdy.

"I won't. Good night, Birdy."

He said good night back, then Guin ended the call.

That night Guin had another anxiety dream. She'd been having a lot of them recently. And they followed a similar storyline. In the dream, she was marrying Birdy. They were exchanging their vows when the officiant (KC) asked if anyone objected. Out of nowhere, a man in a mask appeared. He had a gun and was aiming it at Guin. A shot rang out, and the next thing Guin knew, she was screaming.

She realized she was screaming in real life and immediately turned on the light. She looked around, expecting to see a masked man in her bedroom. But there was no one there, except for Fauna, who had been disturbed by Guin's screams and was now looking at her.

"Sorry," said Guin.

She looked around, then made her way to the bathroom. When she was done, she crawled back into bed, glancing around to make sure no one was there. She was scared to close her eyes, but eventually they closed on their own. And before she knew it, she was sound asleep.

CHAPTER 22

Guin still felt on edge when she finally got up. The dream had shaken her. So much so that she texted the detective, asking if he had learned anything about the anonymous letter.

No reply. Typical. Though, to be fair, it hadn't been twenty-four hours, and it was still early.

She got out of bed and decided to go for a beach walk. Although she had work to do, it could wait.

She walked the eight minutes to the nearest beach access, then made her way down to where the water lapped against the sand. There were a half-dozen or so shell seekers out, including her friend Lenny, who was talking with their friend Bonnie, who volunteered at the Shell Museum.

"Lenny! Bonnie!" called Guin, waving at them. She quickly walked to where they were standing.

"Guin!" said Bonnie, smiling at her. "We were just discussing the Shell Show."

"Oh?" said Guin. "You entering something this year?"

"Maybe," said Bonnie smiling. "But that wasn't what we were discussing."

Guin looked from Bonnie to Lenny.

"Lenny's going to be one of the Scientific Division judges!"

"You are? I thought Gilbert Hodges and Linda Masters were the Scientific judges this year."

"Gil broke his leg skiing and had to bow out," said Bonnie. "And Lenny here agreed to step in."

"That's great!" said Guin. "Well, not great for Gil, but good for you. You excited?"

Guin knew it was a big honor to be asked to judge the Scientific Division.

"Yes, well," said Lenny, looking slightly embarrassed. Lenny wasn't one to preen or take pleasure in another's misfortune.

"So, you guys find any shells?"

Bonnie smiled again and reached into her shelling bag, pulling out an alphabet cone. It was a beauty, with dark brown markings that resembled letters.

"Nice!" said Guin.

"What about you, Len?"

"Go on, show her," said Bonnie.

Guin looked from Bonnie to Lenny. Lenny reached into his bag and pulled out a mostly whole junonia.

"You found that here?"

Lenny nodded.

"Wow. I've never found a junonia on Sanibel. Or anywhere else. May I see?"

Lenny handed her the junonia.

"It practically landed in front of him," said Bonnie.

"I wish one would land in front of me," said Guin.

"You and me both."

"Which way are you headed?"

"I'm headed home," said Bonnie. "I got out early."

Guin looked over at Lenny.

"I'm heading back, too. Got stuff to do."

"Okay," said Guin, a bit disappointed. "Well, see you around."

"If not, we'll see you at the wedding," said Bonnie.

At the mention of the wedding, Guin began to feel anxious again.

"You okay, kiddo?" asked Lenny, sensing her distress.

"I'm fine. Just got a lot on my mind. Anyway, I should start walking. Nice seeing you both."

Guin walked just past Beach Access #7, then turned around. When she got home, she made herself some coffee. Then she went to take a shower. When she got out, she saw she had a voicemail from Craig. She immediately called him back.

"Got your message," she said, as soon as he answered. "What's up?"

"Can you come over here?"

"You can't tell me over the phone?"

"I'd rather not," he replied.

That sounded a bit ominous.

"Okay," said Guin. She thought about her list of things to do. "I can be there in half an hour. Will that work?"

"Fine," said Craig.

Guin rang the doorbell and waited. A minute later Craig opened the door. Guin followed him into the living room.

"So what couldn't you tell me over the phone?"

"Would you like a glass of water?"

"I'm good," said Guin.

They sat across from each other.

"So…?"

Craig rested his hands on his knees and looked down at the slightly worn carpet, then up at Guin.

"I made some inquiries into your fiancé's friends, Boris and Natasha."

"They're not his friends."

"Good to know. Because you don't want to be mixed up with those two."

"It's a bit too late for that."

"I mean it, Guin."

Guin could tell by the look on Craig's face that he was serious. She waited for him to go on.

"Boris Sokolov is what in the old days they called an apparatchik, a loyal member of the Communist party or servant of the government."

Guin cocked her head. Where had she heard that term before? Then she remembered: Birdy had used it to describe Boris.

"Apparently Sokolov's family has ties to Putin. They vacation together on the Black Sea."

"How do you know that?"

"I have my sources."

"So, are you telling me that Boris is a spy?"

"Not exactly. More of a handler."

"Birdy said he was an administrator at Moscow State University. So that's just a cover?"

Craig nodded.

"His official bio lists him as an administrator at Moscow State University. But I have it from reliable sources that his real employer is the Russian Federal Security Service or FSB."

Guin swallowed.

"And Natasha? Wait, don't tell me." She thought about the character in Birdy's book, Natalia, who was an assassin trained by the Russian government. "She's secretly a hitman."

She was half-joking, but Craig wasn't laughing. In fact, the look on Craig's face told her she had guessed correctly.

"Are you sure?"

"Not a hundred percent, but my source is pretty reliable."

Guin leaned over and put her head in her hands.

"You okay? Sure I can't get you some water?"

Guin wanted something stronger, but she told Craig water would be great. He got up and went into the kitchen, returning a minute later with a glass. Guin took a sip.

"What else did you find out? Please don't tell me Birdy works for them."

"Them?"

"The Russians."

"Not as far as I know."

"Thank God."

"Though I could always ask my source to do some more digging. Make sure."

Guin groaned.

"What am I supposed to do, Craig?"

"That depends."

"On what?"

"How much you love him."

Guin put down the glass and stared at the carpet. She had promised Birdy she wouldn't tell people the real reason they were getting married. But she knew Craig could keep a secret. And she needed to confide in someone other than the detective.

"There's something I need to tell you," she said, looking up.

She then told Craig about Birdy's proposal and his relationship with Natasha and Boris. When she was done, Craig shook his head.

"What?" said Guin.

"You say you don't love him, but you must care an awful lot about him to put your life at risk like that."

"I didn't realize I was risking my life when I agreed."

"You can always back out."

"But if I do, I'm worried something will happen to him."

"Birdy can take care of himself. It's you I'm worried about."

"And what do I say to my mother?"

"Your mother?"

"She's flying in for the wedding. She's told everyone.

She'll be mortified if I call it off. And I'll never hear the end of it."

She hung her head again.

"Look, it's possible my source was wrong."

"Really?" Though Craig had pretty much confirmed what the detective had told her.

"Like I said, it's possible. Though I've never known her to be wrong before."

Guin felt helpless, not a feeling she liked.

"Well, thanks for your help," she said, getting up.

"You going to be okay?"

"I don't know."

She paused.

"Did your source say anything specifically about Birdy and Natasha?"

"What do you mean?"

"Birdy said they were lovers. But did they ever work together?"

"I'll see what I can find out."

"Thank you," said Guin. "I should go."

Craig walked her to the door.

"It's not too late to back out, Guin."

But Guin felt it was.

CHAPTER 23

Guin drove home along Middle Gulf Drive, lost in thought. She had just merged onto Casa Ybel Road when she heard what sounded like a gunshot. Immediately, the Mini swerved to the right. Guin's first instinct was to hit the brake, but she remembered what she had learned in her driver safety class and took her foot off the gas pedal, maneuvering the Mini onto the grass. Fortunately, there was no one immediately behind her.

The Mini came to a stop and Guin turned off the engine and got out. She went around to the passenger side and took a look at the tire. It was completely flat. She stared at it for a minute, wondering what could have caused the blowout. She hadn't noticed anything on the road. Then again, she hadn't been paying attention. She glanced around to see if there was a broken bottle or glass anywhere, but she didn't see anything.

She called AAA and was told a tow truck would be there within an hour. Not wanting to wait by the side of the road that long, she asked the operator if the tow truck driver could call or text her when he was around fifteen minutes away.

Fortunately, she wasn't far from Shelly's. She could always go over there and wait, assuming Shelly was around. She took out her phone again and called her friend. Shelly picked up after a few rings.

"You at home?" Guin asked her.

"Yup, just putting the finishing touches on a couple of pieces."

"Would it be okay if I came over?"

"When were you thinking?"

"Now, if that's all right. I had a blowout over on Casa Ybel, and AAA says it could take an hour for the tow truck to get here."

"Sure, come on over. You okay? You want me to pick you up?"

"I don't mind walking. Though if you could give me a ride back when the tow truck driver calls…"

"No problem. I'll leave the front door unlocked."

Guin again went and looked at the tire and shook her head. What could have caused it to explode like that? She grabbed her bag and locked the car. Then she headed off to Shelly's.

"And you didn't see anything on the road?"

Guin shook her head.

"There could have been a nail. I've had that happen before. But you should see the tire. It's completely flat. With a nail, it's typically a slow leak."

"Well, I'm just glad you're okay."

"Me, too," said Guin.

They were standing in Shelly's kitchen.

"You want to show me what you've been working on?"

"Sure," said Shelly.

Guin followed Shelly to her workroom, which was filled with jewelry making tools and supplies.

"Ta-da!" said Shelly, gesturing at one of the tables, which was covered with necklaces, bracelets, earrings, and rings in various stages of production. Guin took a look.

"So, are you moving away from using shells and sea glass?"

Shelly nodded.

"I've been teaching myself metalwork, creating shells and sea life out of silver and gold and semi-precious stones. It's been tough going, but I think I'm finally getting the hang of it."

Guin picked up a silver ring with a sea turtle on it.

"This is adorable."

"I'm glad you like it. It took me days to get that one right. Steve's been ready to kill me, I ordered so much silver and gold. But I reminded him that it's not his money."

"Well, I have no doubt you will sell out."

Guin picked up a pair of silver earrings in the shape of sea stars.

"How much are these?"

"For you, twenty-five."

"That's way too little. How much did it cost you to make them?"

"You don't want to know."

"I'll give you fifty."

"That's way too much."

"How about we split the difference? I'll give you thirty-seven fifty."

"Make it thirty-five and we have a deal."

Guin smiled.

"You drive a hard bargain. Deal!"

"Let me just clean them up for you."

Shelly took the earrings. As she was wiping them off, Guin's phone began vibrating. It was the tow truck driver. He'd be at her car in fifteen minutes. Guin thanked him and told him she'd meet him there.

"That was the tow truck driver," Guin informed Shelly.

"So I gathered."

"He should be at the Mini in fifteen. Could you give me a lift back over there?"

"Sure thing," said Shelly, handing Guin back the earrings,

which she had wrapped in tissue paper.

Guin thanked her and pulled out thirty-five dollars from her wallet, which Shelly pocketed.

"Shall we?" said Shelly.

Guin nodded, and they headed to Shelly's car.

The driver looked at Guin's tire and shook his head.

"You're lucky. That's a real bad blowout."

Tell me about it, thought Guin.

"Can you tow it to the Sanibel Service Center?"

"Yup," said the driver.

Guin and Shelly watched as the tow truck operator slowly loaded the Mini onto his truck. Then they followed him to the service center.

"A bullet?!" said Guin.

She had gone back over to Shelly's to await the call from the Sanibel Service Center. They had been busy when the tow truck driver unloaded the Mini, but they promised to take a look before the end of the day.

"A pretty big one, too."

Someone fired a bullet at my car? Guin's mind felt like it was about to explode. She could have been killed!

"Looks like one of them hunting rifle or sniper bullets," said the man. "You're lucky it only hit your tire."

I'll say, thought Guin.

"Can you hold onto it?"

"Sure."

"What about my tire? Can you replace it?"

"Yup, but not today."

"When?"

"Maybe tomorrow. Gotta contact our supplier."

Guin sighed.

"Okay. Please let me know as soon as you get it. I really need my car. And hold onto that bullet."

The man said he would. Then they ended the call.

"Bullet?" said Shelly, entering the living room and catching the end of the conversation.

Guin nodded.

"Apparently someone shot out my tire."

"Are you serious? You should call Detective O'Loughlin."

"And tell him what?"

"That someone shot at you!"

Guin shook her head. She knew what would happen if she called the detective.

"If you don't call him, I will."

Guin looked at her friend. She could tell by her expression that Shelly meant it.

"Fine, I'll call him."

"Now," said Shelly.

The two women stared at each other for several seconds. Then Guin took out her phone and called the Sanibel Police Department.

"Detective O'Loughlin, please."

Shelly was watching her. Guin shooed her way, but Shelly didn't budge.

Guin was surprised when the operator put her right through.

"O'Loughlin."

"It's Guin."

There was silence on the other end of the line.

"Someone shot at me over on Casa Ybel."

"Are you okay?"

"Yes, fortunately. But the Mini needs a new tire."

"Where are you and the car now?"

"I'm at Shelly's. The car's over at the Sanibel Service Center. The guy there found the bullet."

"I'm heading over there now."

"I'll meet you."

"You stay put."

Guin was about to argue with him, but he had already hung up.

Guin looked at her phone and growled. She saw Shelly looking at her.

"He hung up on me! Would you take me over to the Sanibel Service Center?"

"Let's go!" said Shelly, grabbing her bag.

They arrived at the service center a short time later. The detective pulled in right after them and scowled when he saw Guin.

"What are you doing here?" he growled.

"It's my car," Guin retorted.

The detective continued to scowl but didn't say anything when Guin followed him. (Shelly stayed by her car.)

"Detective O'Loughlin, what can we do for you?"

"I want to see the lady's car."

"Sure thing," said the mechanic.

He led the detective to an area over to the side where the Mini was parked. The detective squatted down and took a look at the deflated tire.

"Any other damage?" he asked the mechanic.

"Nope. Just the tire. She's a lucky lady. That bullet we found could've done some serious damage."

"May I see it?"

"It's in the office."

The detective followed the mechanic to the office, with Guin trailing behind. The mechanic opened the top drawer of the desk and pulled out a rag. Inside was the bullet. It was the biggest bullet Guin had ever seen. Not that she had seen many bullets.

The detective eyed the bullet, then rewrapped it and placed it in an evidence bag.

"You need anything else, detective?" asked the mechanic.

"I'm good," he replied. Then he turned and left.

"Hey!" called Guin, running after him.

The detective stopped.

"Will you tell me what you find out?"

The detective looked at her.

"I told you to stay out of this."

"I can't do that."

The two of them stood facing each other, next to the detective's car.

Then the detective got in and drove away.

"The nerve of him!" Guin said to Shelly.

Shelly shook her head.

"What is it with you two?"

"Nothing," said Guin, not wanting to discuss the detective.

"It didn't look like nothing."

"Yeah, well," said Guin.

"Come on, let's go," said Shelly. "You want to come back to my place or should I take you home?"

"Would you mind driving me back to my place?"

"No problem."

Guin took a few steps toward the Mini. It looked so forlorn, sitting there off to the side, tilting to the right.

"I'll see you soon, old friend!" she called.

The mechanic stepped outside.

"Take good care of my baby!" Guin said to him.

He gave her a thumbs-up. Then Guin turned and headed back to Shelly's car.

CHAPTER 24

Guin fixed herself an omelet for dinner. Then she turned on the TV. She needed something light and fluffy, like the omelet, to distract her.

She flipped channels, finally settling on the Food Network. As she ate, staring at the television, her phone began to vibrate. She picked it up without looking at the caller ID.

"Hello?"

"You don't call, you don't write…"

"Very funny. What's up, Lance?"

"Oh, good, you remember my name."

Guin made a face.

"I just wanted to check in, see how you were doing."

Guin thought about telling him about her car, but she didn't want to worry him.

"I'm fine."

"You know you only say that when things aren't fine."

Guin sighed. Her brother knew her too well.

"You nervous about the wedding?"

Guin hadn't actually thought about the wedding that day. "Not really."

"You sound blue. You sure you're okay?"

"Sorry. Been kind of a crazy day."

"You didn't find another dead body, did you?"

"No, thank God."

"Just checking. So, anything I can do to cheer you up?"

"No, just hearing your voice makes me feel better. Though, speaking of the wedding, any way you and Owen can come down before Tuesday? Shelly and Steve are throwing a barbecue for me and Birdy Sunday, and I'd love for you to be there."

"Sorry, no can do. I have a big client meeting Monday. And we're not really the backyard barbecue types."

Guin smiled. Her brother and Owen were snobs when it came to food. And she knew he didn't think much of the food options on Sanibel.

"Oh well. So are Mom and Philip still flying down this weekend?"

"As far as I know. Haven't you spoken to her?"

"Not recently."

Guin knew she owed her mother a call but had been putting it off.

"You should call her."

"I know."

"Well, I have to run. Owen and I have dinner plans."

"Going anywhere good?"

"Some new raw food place that opened near the gallery."

"Raw food?"

"It's all the rage. Supposed to be very healthy."

"Well, enjoy."

"Ciao. Love you."

"I love you too."

They ended the call and Guin shook her head. Guin loved her brother, but she could never lead his life.

She looked down at her phone.

"May as well get it over with."

She entered her mother's number and waited as the phone rang.

"Guinivere?"

"Hi, Mom."

"I had almost forgotten what your voice sounded like. Everything okay? It's been ages since I heard from you."

Guin rolled her eyes. Her mother was prone to hyperbole—and inducing guilt trips on her children.

"Sorry, I've been busy."

"With the wedding? I told you I'd be happy to help out."

"Thanks, but as I told you before, the wedding's being handled."

Her mother sniffed.

"So are you and Philip still flying down this weekend?"

"We are. Though we're coming Sunday now."

"Oh?"

"We're getting together with the Claydons Saturday. So we changed our flight."

"What time do you get in?"

"I'm not sure. Why?"

"Some friends of mine are throwing me and Birdy a barbecue Sunday evening. I thought you might like to come."

"It would have been nice if you had told me about it before, Guinivere."

"I just found out."

Her mother sniffed again.

"Well, we can't make it. I told Harriet we would dine with her and Alfred Sunday, assuming our flight isn't horribly delayed."

Guin sent up a silent prayer of thanks.

"No big deal. Enjoy your dinner with Harriet and Alfred."

"Besides, we'll see you Tuesday."

"Tuesday?" said Guin.

Her mother sighed.

"Really Guinivere, you should have your memory checked. I told you to keep Tuesday open."

"You did?"

"We're having a family dinner. It's all arranged."

"It is?"

"Yes, we're going to La Moraga in Naples. Alfred says the food is excellent."

Alfred was Harriet's son, who Guin's mother had tried to fix her up with, unsuccessfully.

"Um, okay. What time?"

"Seven-thirty."

"Got it. Seven-thirty. And should I bring Birdy?"

"No, it's just immediate family." Guin thought that odd but didn't say anything. "Now if you'll excuse me," said her mother. "Philip and I were watching a movie on Netflix."

Well, that was a new one.

"Of course. Have a good night."

"Same to you."

They ended the call and Guin shook her head.

The next morning, Guin went for another beach walk. She had a lot on her mind and wasn't in the mood to chat. So she was glad when she didn't run into anyone she knew. She waded into the water, searching for shells, hoping to find a junonia or a lion's paw. But despite sending a silent prayer to Poseidon, her shelling bag remained empty.

She made her way to Beach Access #1, then turned around. On her way back, she decided to poke around a shell pile and picked up a few lettered olives, a couple of mini horse conchs, and a handful of orange and purple scallops, but nothing to brag about.

As she approached Beach Access #4, where she had started, she stood and looked out at the Gulf. The water was a bit choppy, and it was chilly, so she didn't stay there long. But she wanted one last look. Then she turned and headed back down the path.

Guin had just started work on one of her Shell Festival articles when her phone began to vibrate. It was the Sanibel Service Center, letting her know the new tire should arrive just after lunch. Guin asked if that meant she would be able to get the Mini that evening, and the man said he thought so. He would give her a call later to let her know for sure. Guin thanked him, put her phone away, then went back to work. But she couldn't concentrate. She stared down at the drawer, then removed her phone and called Birdy.

"Can you come over?"

"When?"

"Now?"

"I'm in the middle of something."

"Someone shot at me yesterday," Guin blurted.

"What?!" said Birdy. "Why didn't you call me? Are you okay?"

Before Guin could reply, Birdy announced he'd be right there and ended the call.

Twenty minutes later, the doorbell rang. It was Birdy. He grabbed her by the arms as soon as she let him in and looked her over.

"You don't appear to be injured."

"It was my tire that got shot, not me, fortunately."

"Are you sure you didn't just run over a piece of glass or a nail?"

"Positive. I saw the bullet."

Birdy didn't say anything.

"Let's go outside," said Guin.

Birdy looked confused but followed her to the backyard.

"I need to ask you something, and I need you to tell me the truth."

"I've always told you the truth, Guinivere."

Guin highly doubted that but didn't say anything. She took a deep breath.

"Are you a spy?"

"Excuse me?"

"I know about Boris and Natasha."

"What is it you think you know about them?"

"I know they're both employed by the Russian government."

"Lots of people are employed by the Russian government. Doesn't mean they're all spies. Though no one actually uses that term. It's only used in movies and spy novels."

"That may be, but I have it on good authority that Boris and Natasha are spies or whatever the proper term is."

Birdy smiled.

"You have quite an active imagination."

"I'm not imagining it, Birdy. I heard it from reliable sources."

"And who are these 'reliable sources'?" he said, using air quotes, which infuriated Guin.

"Don't patronize me, Birdy."

"I am not patronizing you, Guinivere. I am just curious to know who your sources are."

"I cannot reveal them."

"Ah yes, journalistic ethics and all that. Well, your sources are wrong."

"I don't think so."

They stood there eyeing each other, neither saying anything for several seconds.

"And what about you?"

"What about me?"

"Are you a spy?"

"I think you're confusing me with the character in my books."

"I don't think so."

"What is this about, Guin?"

"Someone shot at me yesterday. I could have been killed. I think I deserve some answers."

"I thought you said it was your tire and that you were fine."

Guin crossed her arms over her chest.

"Semantics. You should have seen the tire. It was ripped to shreds. The mechanic said the bullet that did it came from a hunting or sniper rifle."

"Oh, and the mechanic is a ballistics expert?"

Guin made a face.

"My sources also informed me that Natasha is a pretty good shot."

"Your sources again," said Birdy. "Need I remind you, Natasha is in Orlando, over four hours away?"

"She could have easily driven here."

"What about her lectures?"

"I doubt she lectures twenty-four-seven."

Birdy sighed.

"What is it you want me to say, Guinivere?"

"I want you to tell me the truth. Are you a spy?"

"No, I am not a spy."

Guin didn't believe him.

"I think we should call off the wedding."

"We are not calling off the wedding."

"Give me a good reason not to."

Birdy quickly closed the distance between them.

"How's this for a reason?" he said, pulling her into an embrace, taking Guin completely off guard.

When Guin opened her mouth to protest, Birdy bit her lip and pulled her closer, slowly kissing her. As if on autopilot, Guin found herself kissing him back. Instantly, Birdy's kisses grew more passionate, and Guin heard herself softly moan.

"From the moment I first saw you, I wanted you," he whispered into her ear. "I would never let anything happen to you."

He kissed her neck, gently biting her, and Guin felt a rush of heat in her nether regions.

"Let's go inside and continue this in the bedroom," he said, his voice a low growl.

Suddenly Guin came to her senses and pushed him away.

"Leave. Now."

"But we were just getting started."

"It was a mistake."

"Don't be ridiculous. We're about to be husband and wife."

"I need you to go," Guin said, trying not to shake.

"Fine, I'll go. But admit it, Guinivere, you wanted me, just as much as I want you."

"Go!" Guin practically shouted.

"Very well. I'm going. Though what about your car?"

"I'll call Shelly. She can take me over to the service center when it's ready. Now please, leave."

He started to go then stopped.

"I'll pick you up at five-forty-five on Sunday."

Guin looked confused.

"What are you talking about?"

"The barbecue? The one your friends Shelly and Steve are throwing in our honor?"

Right. She had forgotten.

"I'll meet you there."

"Don't be ridiculous. You're on the way. And it will look odd if we don't arrive together."

Guin sighed. She was tired of arguing.

"Fine. I'll see you then."

"Are you sure you're okay?"

"No, I am not okay," she said, some of her anger returning.

Birdy took a step toward her, but Guin stopped him.

"Don't. Just go."

Birdy remained where he was, then finally turned and headed toward the driveway. Guin waited in the backyard. Only when she heard his car drive away did she go back inside. She immediately called Shelly.

"Any word on your car?"

"The tire's supposed to arrive after lunch. Could you give me a lift once it's on?"

"Sure. Just let me know when. So, any word from the detective?"

"Not yet."

Guin thought about telling Shelly about Birdy, that he had kissed her, but she realized how that would sound. After all, they were about to be married.

"Hello?"

"Oh, sorry. What did you say?"

"Never mind. Just call me when the Mini's been fixed."

"Will do. And thanks again for helping me out. I hate to impose."

"Nonsense. That's what friends are for."

CHAPTER 25

Guin called the Sanibel Police Department and asked to be put through to Detective O'Loughlin. She was told he was unavailable, so she left a message instead—then sent him a text. She paced around the kitchen, hoping the detective would call her back. Finally, she gave up and went back to work.

Around one-thirty she went into the kitchen to eat something, tucking her phone into her back pocket. She fixed herself a peanut butter and jelly sandwich and leaned against the counter as she ate it. She was staring out at the pond behind her house when she felt her backside tingling. It was her phone. She pulled it out and saw "Sanibel Service Center" on the caller ID.

"This is Guin," she said, answering.

The man at the service center informed her that they had received the tire and her car would be ready after three. Guin thanked him, then texted Shelly, asking if she could give her a lift to the service center later. Shelly wrote back, saying no problem.

Guin finished her sandwich, then returned to her office. She was in the middle of her article on the Sanibel Shell Festival when her phone started moving across her desk. It was the detective.

"Did you find out anything about the bullet or the note?" she asked him, not bothering to say hello.

"The note was clean. No fingerprints, other than yours, and no watermarks."

"What about the envelope?"

"Same. Though there were a couple of smudged prints they couldn't identify."

Guin sighed.

"What about the bullet?"

No reply.

"Come on, Bill. Give me something. I have a right to know."

Guin heard what sounded like a sigh.

"Ballistics identified it as a .338 Lapua Magnum."

Guin had no idea what that meant and said so.

"It's a long-range cartridge, developed by a Finnish firm. It was used in the Afghan and Iraq wars. But today it's used by militaries, law enforcement agencies, and guys looking to get their ya-yas out."

That may have been the most she had ever heard the detective speak.

"What about hitmen?"

There was no reply. Guin tried again.

"So, in other words, it's the kind of bullet you might use if you wanted to shoot someone's tire from far away."

Again, silence.

"What about the weapon? Was there any sign of it? Your guys search the area?"

"They did."

"And?"

"They didn't find anything."

"So whoever shot me took the weapon with them."

That meant her tire-shooter was still out there.

"Which is why you should call off the wedding," said the detective.

Guin made a face.

"You were lucky, Guin. The next time you may not be."

"Whoever it was was just trying to scare me. I'll be fine."

Or so she tried to convince herself.

"You won't be safe until you distance yourself from McMurtry."

"You're just jealous."

As soon as the words came out of her mouth, she regretted them.

There was silence again. Then the detective spoke.

"I need to go."

Before Guin could say anything, he ended the call.

Guin was tempted to call him back. But what would be the point? She sighed and looked back at her monitor. She was in no mood to write about the Shell Festival now. Instead, she searched for ".338 Lapua Magnum" and discovered the cartridge was used in something called an Orsis T-5000, a Russian sniper rifle supposedly used by Russian President Vladimir Putin's protective detail and Russian military personnel.

She immediately pictured Natasha and Boris. But how could she prove they were involved? It wouldn't be easy.

She was immersed in more research when the doorbell sounded, causing her to jump. She looked at the clock on her monitor. It was three o'clock, the time she had told Shelly to get her. She turned over her phone and saw that the message light was flashing. There were several texts from Shelly.

The doorbell rang again, and Guin got up.

"Coming!" she called.

She peered out the sidelight and saw Shelly standing there.

"I was beginning to worry!"

"Sorry," said Guin. "I was busy doing research and didn't hear my phone."

"You ready to go?"

"Let me just grab my bag."

They arrived at the Sanibel Service Center a short time

later. Guin saw the Mini parked in the same spot, but it was no longer leaning to the right. She smiled, then went into the office.

There was a woman seated at the desk, a computer in front of her. Guin went over and introduced herself. The woman called to one of the mechanics. He came over and explained that they wound up putting two new tires on the Mini, as the other front tire was a bit worn, to make sure the car was properly balanced. Guin thanked them and paid.

Shelly was waiting for her outside.

"So?"

"All good," said Guin. "You can go."

"You sure?"

Guin nodded. I'm sure. She went over to the Mini.

"Hello, old friend," she said, placing a hand lovingly on the hood. "I'm sorry about your tire. But you should be good as new." She paused. "Just to be on the safe side, though, why don't we go home via Periwinkle?"

Before Guin knew it, it was Sunday. She was getting ready for Shelly and Steve's barbecue when her mother texted her, letting her know she had arrived and reminding her about Tuesday. Guin rolled her eyes. Then she returned to getting dressed.

She knew Shelly and Steve's barbecues were informal affairs, but this one was different. This time, all eyes would be on her, and Birdy, and she heard Bettina's voice in her head, telling her not to embarrass him. So, after much second-guessing, she finally pulled on a pair of skinny jeans; a white, off-the-shoulder top; and a pair of high-heeled sandals. She stared at her face in the mirror and applied some makeup. Then she ran her fingers through her hair, scrunching it to bring out the curl. (She had washed it earlier and put in some gel, so it wouldn't frizz.)

"Not bad, if I do say so myself," she said to her reflection.

Something rubbed against her leg. She looked down and saw Fauna.

"What do you think, kitty cat?"

Fauna tilted her head, then proceeded to lick her paw.

"Okay, let's go to the kitchen and I'll give you some food before I go."

Fauna followed her and watched as Guin poured dry food into her bowl. She looked up at Guin, and Guin could swear the cat was frowning.

"Sorry, kitty cat. That's what's for supper."

Fauna continued to look at Guin, then went over to the cat bowl, sniffed, and began to eat.

"I'll be back later," she told the cat.

There was no reply.

Guin picked up her phone and saw she had a voicemail message. It was from Birdy, letting her know he would be a few minutes late. Guin frowned. She hated being late.

She called Birdy back, but he didn't answer. She gave him fifteen more minutes, then called him again. Again the call went to voicemail.

"Fine," she said, grabbing her keys. "I wanted to go on my own anyway."

She sent him a text, telling him she'd meet him at Shelly and Steve's. Then she headed to the Mini.

There were cars parked up and down Shelly and Steve's street. Had they invited the whole island? It seemed that way.

Guin went up to the door and rang the doorbell. Someone shouted, "It's open!" and Guin let herself in.

She made her way out to the lanai, which was open to the backyard. There were a couple of dozen people already there, and Guin saw several of her friends from the Shell

Club, including Lenny and Bonnie. Steve had apparently also invited several of his fishing buddies, most of whom Guin knew. Detective O'Loughlin was one of his fishing buddies, and Guin worried that the detective would be there. But she didn't see him.

"There she is!" said Shelly, spying her. She looked around. "Where's Birdy?"

"I don't know. He was supposed to pick me up, but he was a no-show."

"Did he call?"

Guin sighed.

"He left me a message saying he'd be a few minutes late. Then nothing. I finally told him I'd meet him here."

"I'm sure he'll show."

Guin glanced around again.

"So, Steve didn't invite Detective O'Loughlin, did he?"

"I don't think so," said Shelly. "Why?"

"I just saw a number of his fishing buddies here and... I didn't want things to be awkward."

"Awkward?"

"You know."

"What is going on with the two of you?"

Guin sighed.

"He wants me to call off the wedding."

"Is he jealous?"

"No. It's just..."

They were interrupted by the sound of familiar voices coming towards them. Guin froze. It couldn't be. Birdy wouldn't. Then she turned and saw her. It was Bettina all right, Birdy's drop-dead gorgeous, full-of-herself agent.

"Guinivere, so good to see you."

Guin took in Bettina, who stood nearly a foot taller than her and was dressed as though she had just stepped off a yacht. (And for all Guin knew, she had.) Suddenly, Guin regretted her clothing choice.

She looked over at Birdy, who was dressed in a button-down shirt and chinos. The two of them looked like they belonged together. And Guin again wondered how Bettina felt about Birdy marrying her.

"Sorry about earlier," Birdy quietly said to Guin. He didn't look happy.

"No worries," Guin replied, trying to act nonchalant.

"Shelly, you remember Birdy's agent, Bettina Betteridge?"

Shelly had been staring at them and quickly pulled herself together.

"Of course! Glad you could make it. Help yourselves to drinks and food."

"I could use a drink," said Birdy. "Bettina?"

Guin watched as he led Bettina away.

"Well, that was awkward," said Shelly. "Did you know he was bringing her?"

"I had no idea. But I intend to find out."

CHAPTER 26

"Birdy," said Guin, going up to him and Bettina. "Could I have a word?"

Birdy turned to his agent.

"Would you excuse me?"

"Of course," said Bettina.

She gave Guin a reptilian smile, and Guin led Birdy inside the house.

"I'm sorry about not getting back to you," said Birdy. "Bettina insisted I pick her up. Then, of course, she made me wait."

"How did she even know about the barbecue? I certainly didn't mention it. I didn't even know she was in town."

"She came down last week to see Briony."

"So they're on speaking terms?"

Briony was Bettina's sister, a photographer who had once dated Birdy and had been seeing a married man in Naples the last time Guin saw her.

"They patched things up just before the wedding."

"Wedding?"

"You didn't know?"

"Should I have? Who got married? Not Bettina."

"No, it was Briony."

"Who did she marry?"

Birdy smiled.

"Dick Grayson."

"The former CMO of Natura? He got divorced?"

Birdy nodded.

"And left Natura. Started his own company with Briony."

"Well, I'll be."

"And they have a baby."

"A baby?"

Guin was shocked. Briony hadn't struck her as the maternal type.

"Bettina's the godmother."

So that's what had brought the two sisters together.

"Well, I'm happy for them. But how did Bettina hear about the barbecue? I didn't tell her about it."

"I'm afraid that's my fault," said Birdy. "I may have mentioned it in passing."

Guin glanced back out toward the lanai and saw Bettina chatting with Paul and Cindy Astley, who owned a restaurant in Fort Myers Beach.

"Looks like she's finally found someone to talk to."

Birdy peered out. Bettina and the Astleys were exchanging cards.

"Bettina never misses a business opportunity."

"We should probably get back out there."

"Lead on," said Birdy.

Guin had been pleasantly surprised by Birdy's behavior. Instead of just talking about himself, or lecturing people about the local flora and fauna, he seemed to be engaged in actual conversations, with both the Shell Club people and Steve's fishing buddies. She even saw him laughing. And he ate two of Steve's famous bratwurst—and told him they were the best brats he ever had—which had Steve beaming.

Guin shook her head. This was an entirely different Birdy from the one she was used to. And she wondered which Birdy was the real one.

As for Bettina, her expression alternated between bored and annoyed. And she spent more time interacting with her phone than with the other guests.

"What's with her?" Shelly asked Guin.

"That's just Bettina."

Shelly shrugged, then excused herself. She went around the lanai, asking if people wanted more food or something to drink. Guin watched her, marveling at her hostess skills. Then she spied Craig. He was nursing a beer and in observation mode.

She went over to him and looked to see who he was watching.

"You interested in Bettina?"

"Is it that obvious?"

"Only to a trained observer like me," said Guin, smiling. "What were you thinking?"

"That she seems out of place. And annoyed."

Guin glanced at Bettina. She did seem rather out of place in her chic palazzo pants, black halter top, and stilettos. And she did seem annoyed, scowling down at her phone. Though that was how Bettina typically looked.

"Yeah, this isn't exactly her crowd."

Craig nodded and took a sip of his beer.

As they watched, one of Steve's fishing buddies went up to Bettina, no doubt trying to chat her up.

"How much you wanna bet she blows him off?"

"No bet," said Guin. "It's a given."

They watched as Steve's friend chatted with Bettina or tried to. Bettina smiled politely but was clearly not interested. A minute later, she excused herself and went over to Birdy and whispered something in his ear. Birdy frowned, then excused himself and followed her inside.

"I wonder what that's about," said Guin. "You think I should follow them?"

"I think you should stay here and chat with your guests."

Guin was torn.

"You're probably right." She looked around. "Where's Betty?"

"She's over there," said Craig, pointing to a cluster of women.

"Ah," said Guin. "Okay, I'll go over and say hi. You care to join me?"

"No thanks."

Guin smiled and made her way over. Halfway across the lanai, she was stopped by Jimbo Leidecker, a friend of Steve and Craig's who had become a friend of hers. (Jimbo was dating a woman named Sally who lived down the street from Guin, and she saw the two of them often on her morning walk.)

"That Birdy's a real fine fellow," said Jimbo.

"Mm," said Guin, not knowing how to reply.

"I hope you two will be very happy."

"Thanks."

She looked around. "Is Sally here? I don't think I saw her."

"No, she couldn't make it."

"Sorry to hear that."

"Not as sorry as she was."

Guin tilted her head.

"She's a huge Wren Finchley fan."

"Ah," said Guin.

"She's read both his books and couldn't believe it when she heard the two of you were engaged."

"Well, technically, I'm engaged to Birdy, not Wren."

"Tell Sally that."

"Well, I'm sure I could arrange for Birdy to sign Sally's books and chat with her."

"Really?" said Jimbo. "She'd love that."

"I'll get back to you."

"Thanks. Though try to make it sooner rather than later, so Sally doesn't pester me too much."

Guin smiled.

"I'll try. Now, if you would excuse me?"

"Of course!" said Jimbo.

Guin had been on her way over to see Betty, but Bettina and Birdy still weren't back, and her curiosity was getting the better of her.

She made her way inside, but they weren't in the living area or the kitchen. She went down the hallway to Shelly's jewelry studio. The door was closed, but she could hear voices. She leaned in but couldn't hear what the people were saying. But it was definitely a man and a woman. Suddenly the door opened, causing Guin to stumble.

Bettina glared at her.

"Eavesdropping?" she said.

Guin righted herself, trying not to look embarrassed.

"I was just wondering where Birdy had gone and then heard voices coming from Shelly's studio."

"I'd like to go back to the hotel now, Birdy," said Bettina, ignoring Guin.

"Call a cab."

Bettina looked shocked.

"You won't drive me?"

Birdy shook his head.

"I should stay. Call Island Taxi."

"You want me to take... *a taxi*?"

Guin was not-so-secretly delighting in Bettina's distress.

"You do it all the time in New York. I'm sure you can manage." He turned to Guin and placed a hand on her back. "Shall we?"

Guin nodded and allowed Birdy to steer her back to the party. When she glanced back, Bettina was gone.

"Will she be okay?" asked Guin, as they walked back out onto the lanai.

"She'll be fine. I should have never agreed to pick her up in the first place. But you know how Bettina can be."

Guin did.

"I confess, I was a bit upset when I didn't hear back from you. But I understand. She is your agent, after all."

"Thank you. But it's still no excuse for her bad behavior."

"I'm used to it."

"Oh look! There's the happy couple now!" It was Steve. "Are you two ready for dessert?"

"Sure," said Guin.

Steve and Shelly exchanged a smile.

"Be right back!" said Shelly.

A minute later, Shelly reappeared with a large fruit platter.

"That looks great!" said Guin.

Shelly smiled.

"But wait, there's more!"

She went back inside and returned bearing a large sheet cake, decorated with birds and seashells and the words *Congratulations Birdy + Guin!*

"Oh, wow," said Guin, staring at the cake.

"I had it made specially at Bailey's," said Shelly, placing it on the table next to the fruit.

"They did a good job."

"Which one of you wants to cut it? How about you do it, Birdy?"

"I'd be honored," he said, smiling at Shelly.

Shelly beamed.

He cut the first piece and placed it on a plate.

"Who wants a corner?" he called.

"Ooh, I'll take it," said Bonnie. "I know I probably shouldn't, but it looks so good!"

Birdy proceeded to cut several more pieces, placing each one on a plate, which Shelly and Guin handed out.

"Guinivere," said Birdy, handing Guin a piece.

"Thanks," she said, taking it. "Aren't you going to have one?"

He picked up a plate and then cut off a piece with his fork. Before Guin knew what he was doing, he had maneuvered the fork near her mouth.

"Here you go, darling."

Guin was embarrassed but opened her mouth. Everyone applauded as she chewed, causing her cheeks to turn red. Finally, she swallowed, then forced herself to smile.

"Now feed him a piece!" someone called.

Guin continued to smile, though she wanted to scream.

"I think Birdy's capable of feeding himself," she said to the crowd.

"Boo!" called several of Steve's fishing buddies, who had clearly had a few beers.

"Go on, Guin," said Shelly. "Give the man a piece of your cake."

Guin felt her cheeks getting redder. Birdy smiled, and Guin cut off a piece of her cake with her fork and fed it to Birdy.

"It tastes almost as sweet as you," he said, after he had swallowed.

That elicited a roar from Steve's fishing buddies.

"Yes, well," she said. "I think we can feed ourselves now."

The guests moved away, and Guin took Birdy aside.

"You didn't have to lay it on so thick," Guin admonished him.

"I meant every word," he replied, continuing to smile.

Guin rolled her eyes.

"Sorry to interrupt."

It was Lenny.

"You weren't interrupting. What's up, Lenny? I'm so glad you could make it."

"Thanks for inviting me. I haven't had a brat in years."

Guin smiled at him.

"Anyway, I just wanted to say goodbye. I'm heading out."

Guin leaned over and gave him a kiss on the cheek.

"Thanks for coming."

Lenny nodded, then looked up at Birdy.

"You take good care of my Guinny."

"I promise," said Birdy.

Lenny eyed him, then made his way to the front door.

"Nice old man," said Birdy. "He clearly cares about you."

"And I care about him. I really hate having to lie to him," she said quietly.

"It doesn't have to be a lie, you know."

"What do mean?"

"It means that I care about you, Guin. And when I promise to love, honor, and protect you, I'll mean it."

Guin studied him. He looked sincere. But she didn't feel the same way.

"I'm sorry, Birdy. But you know how I feel."

"Feelings change. I'm sure once we spend some more time together…"

Guin shook her head.

"I don't think so. As soon as Natasha and Boris go back to Russia, I'm ending this charade."

"Guin!"

Guin turned to see her friend Lorna, the assistant director of the Shell Museum, coming towards her. She plastered a smile on her face.

"I'm leaving," said Lorna. "But I didn't get a chance to congratulate the two of you."

"That's okay," said Guin. "Thanks for coming."

"Of course!" said Lorna. "I wouldn't have missed it for the world."

"How are things at the museum?"

"Busy! We're still recovering from the Under the Sea gala."

"How was it?"

"Packed!"

Guin smiled.

"I'd love to do lunch and catch up."

"Me, too," said Lorna. "Well, gotta go! Congrats again, you two."

"Speaking of leaving," said Birdy. "I should shove off too."

Guin raised her eyebrows.

"Nothing nefarious. I just have some work I need to do."

"At nine o'clock on a Sunday?"

"It's Monday in New Zealand."

"Very well. Thanks for coming."

"Don't be ridiculous. It was my pleasure. And after all, I'm the guest of honor."

He smiled, then leaned down and gave Guin a kiss on the cheek. Then he whispered in her ear.

"If you get lonely later, text me."

Before she could reply, he was gone.

"Can I help you?" Guin asked Shelly and Steve after the rest of the guests had left.

"We got this," said Steve.

"Okay. Then I guess I'll be heading out. Thanks again, for everything."

"Our pleasure!" said Steve. "You know Shelly loves a party."

He smiled at his wife, who smiled back at him.

Guin sighed to herself. Shelly and Steve had been college sweethearts. And they still looked madly in love with each other. If only her marriage had been as happy.

She saw herself out and made her way to the Mini. As she headed home, she saw a pair of headlights behind her. Not that unusual, as there weren't that many roads on

Sanibel. But it made her nervous.

The headlights continued to follow her onto West Gulf Drive, and Guin started to feel panicky.

You're being paranoid, she told herself. But she couldn't shake the feeling.

She made the turn into her cul-de-sac and was relieved to see the headlights continue down West Gulf. She released the breath she didn't realize she was holding, then pulled into her driveway. She stayed in the Mini another minute, to make sure the car hadn't turned around and followed her. But the street remained dark. Finally, she got out and quickly made her way inside.

CHAPTER 27

Guin went into her closet to change and saw the garment bag with her wedding dress. She unzipped it and took out the dress. Although it was white, it looked more like a cocktail dress than a wedding gown, which was what Guin had wanted. Though not her mother.

Her mother, even though she knew this was a second marriage, wanted Guin to wear something traditional and white. Guin had refused. As a compromise, Guin agreed to get something white, and her mother agreed to no ruffles, lace, or beading. And they had both been happy with Guin's ultimate choice, a classic-looking white cocktail dress that Shelly had found. It had a 1950s vibe, with its flared skirt, fitted waist, and off-the-shoulder sleeves. And it reminded Guin of something Audrey Hepburn might have worn.

As luck would have it, the dress fit perfectly. So she was able to take it home with her. And it had hung in the back of her closet ever since.

Guin looked at the dress and sighed. It really was lovely. And she knew the wedding would be lovely too. But it was all a sham. And her heart hurt a little at the thought. Of course, she could still call the whole thing off. But they had gone this far. And the fact that someone was trying to scare her off only made her more determined to go through with it. Besides, it wasn't as though she and Birdy would really be married.

She took one last look at the dress, then placed it back in the garment bag and zipped it up. When she returned to the bedroom, she saw the message light on her phone blinking. Her brother had texted, wanting to know how the party had gone. She called him instead of texting him back.

"So, how was it?"

"Actually, it was nice."

"Just nice?"

"In my book, nice is good."

"Never settle for nice, Guinivere."

"You sound like Mom."

"It's still good advice. So, you ready?"

"No."

Neither spoke for several seconds.

"Getting cold feet?"

"No, it's just…"

Guin was tempted to reveal the truth to her brother but held her tongue.

"Well, hang in there. Owen and I will be there in a couple of days for moral support."

"Thanks. What time is your flight Tuesday?"

"An hour no one should be up. I don't know why Owen booked us on such an early flight, but *c'est la vie.*"

"So, what are we talking about, seven?"

"Eight."

"Eight isn't that early."

"It is when you don't go to bed until two."

"Maybe go to bed earlier?"

Lance sighed.

"Well, at least you'll be here for the big dinner," said Guin.

"That's probably why Owen has us leaving at such an ungodly hour."

Guin yawned.

"Am I keeping you up?"

"Sorry," said Guin. "Long day, and I had a couple of beers at the party."

"You're such a lightweight."

"I know."

"Well, I'll let you get off to dreamland."

"Thanks, but we can chat for a few more minutes."

Guin let out another yawn.

"That's okay. I'll see you Tuesday. Goodnight, Sis."

"Goodnight, Bro. Thanks for checking in."

They ended the call, and Guin yawned for a third time. Then she grabbed her book and got into bed.

Guin was up early Monday. She had a lot to do, but it looked like a beautiful day. So she threw on a pair of capris and a t-shirt and headed to the beach.

There were waves in the Gulf, and the tide was high, so she didn't expect to find a lot of shells. But that was okay. Just being outside and breathing in the fresh sea air made her feel more at ease, less anxious. (And she had been feeling anxious a lot recently.)

She passed by a couple fishing and said hello. There were also a handful of shellers. She stopped by the sign for Beach Access #6 and looked up. Over a dozen brown pelicans were sitting or sleeping in a nearby tree. They always seemed to hang out in that one particular tree, and she always wondered why. What was it about that tree and not, say, the one next to it?

Guin continued to watch the birds. As she did so, several more pelicans joined their friends. She stayed there for another minute, then continued down the beach.

Guin made herself a large pot of coffee when she got home and spent the rest of the morning working on articles. Ginny had cut her some slack because of the wedding. But as it was the busy season, with more activities and events happening on and around Sanibel, all of the writers were expected to write more.

Guin didn't mind. She liked being busy. And the work helped keep her mind off of the wedding—and the honeymoon.

At the barbecue, several people had asked where she and Birdy were going. Birdy had said it was a surprise, and Guin had just smiled. While she loved visiting new places, she wasn't looking forward to going away with Birdy, especially as they would be traveling as husband and wife. And she wanted to know what to pack.

Guin got up to go to the bathroom. When she got back, she checked her phone. There was a message from Birdy.

"Meet me for lunch."

Guin thought about not responding, then texted him back.

"When?"

It was already noon.

"One o'clock at Jean-Luc's."

Guin thought about telling him she was busy. Then she felt her stomach rumble. And she did love the food at Jean-Luc's.

"OK. See you at Jean-Luc's at 1," she typed back.

Birdy replied with a smiley face.

Guin looked at the clock on her monitor. It was almost one. She needed to go. She thought about changing but decided not to.

She arrived at Jean-Luc's Bakery a little after one. The place was hopping. And she understood why. Everyone loved Jean-Luc's crusty baguettes, delicious French pastries, and yummy sandwiches.

She saw Jo, one of Jean-Luc's young helpers, and smiled at her. Jo smiled back but was too busy to do more. Jake was with her.

She waited off to the side for Birdy, watching as Jo and Jake did a kind of pas de deux behind the counter. They would smile at each other every time they touched, which Guin found endearing. She wondered if the two young people, who had known each other before coming to Jean-Luc's, were dating.

There was a brief lull and Guin went up to the counter.

"I see you two are working hard."

"It's been crazy!" said Jo.

Jake nodded.

"You'd think we were the only place on the island to grab a sandwich."

"Where's Jean-Luc?" Guin asked, glancing toward the back, where the kitchen was located.

"He's out," said Jake. "But he should be back soon."

"Is he running errands? Very unlike Jean-Luc to not be here during the lunch rush."

The two twenty-somethings exchanged a look.

"He's, uh, busy," said Jake.

"Sorry I'm late," came a familiar voice. "Would you believe I got pulled over for speeding? I was only going thirty-seven." Birdy looked at the display case. "Everything looks delicious. What do you like, Guinivere?"

"I like the turkey, brie, and Granny Smith on a baguette—and the crepes."

"Hmm…" said Birdy, looking at the menu. "I think I'll have the ham and cheese baguette and a sparkling water."

"And I'll have the mozzarella, tomato, and pesto baguette," said Guin. "And a sparkling water."

"Switching it up?" said Jake.

"I am."

She smiled at him, and he smiled back.

"For here or to go?"

Guin looked at Birdy.

"We'll sit outside."

"Very good," said Jake.

He made the two sandwiches, then wrapped them and placed them in a bag along with the sparkling waters.

"You sure I can't interest either of you in a pastry?"

Guin eyed the pastry case.

"I'm going to pass."

"For you, sir?" said Jake.

"Give me one of those fruit tarts. I can't resist something sweet and juicy," he said, glancing over at Guin, a smile on his face.

Guin wanted to slap that smile away.

Jake placed the fruit tart in a small box. Birdy paid. Then Jake handed him the box along with the bag.

They were a step from the door when Detective O'Loughlin walked in. Guin froze.

"Detective O'Loughlin! How fortunate to run into you," said Birdy. "Maybe you can help me? One of your associates issued me a speeding ticket earlier, which was completely absurd as I was barely going over the speed limit."

The detective scowled, and Guin wished she could vanish.

"Do you think you could have it dismissed?"

"No," replied the detective. Then he headed to the counter, not saying a word to Guin.

"I highly recommend the ham and cheese baguette," Birdy called.

"Let's go," said Guin. She opened the door and pulled Birdy after her.

"I don't know what you see in the man," said Birdy, once they were outside. "Isn't he a bit old for you?"

It was true the detective was a dozen years older than Guin, but she had never thought of him as old.

"Let's sit there," said Birdy, pointing to one of the outdoor tables.

They sat and Birdy removed the sandwiches and sparkling waters from the bag. Neither said anything as they began to eat.

"I've been meaning to ask," Guin said, when she was about a third of the way through her sandwich. "Will you have any family at the wedding?"

As far as Guin knew, Birdy's parents had died in a car crash, and he had no siblings.

"Sadly, no," said Birdy, continuing to eat his sandwich.

"So, no brothers or sisters?"

Birdy shook his head.

"I was an only child."

"Any aunts or uncles or cousins?"

Birdy put down his sandwich.

"Why do you want to know?"

"Well, we are getting married. And it seems like something a wife-to-be should know."

"My mother had an older sister, but they weren't particularly close. And I haven't seen her since the funeral."

"And your father?"

"Another only child."

"And does your aunt have any children?"

Birdy gave her an indulgent smile.

"A daughter, whom I barely know. I'm afraid my family wasn't very good at procreating or staying in touch. I'm the last of the line."

"Where were you born?"

"In Hawaii. My father was stationed there."

"Was he in the military?"

Birdy nodded.

"He was in the Navy. He and my mother were living on Oahu when I was born, and we stayed there until I was nearly seven. Then we moved around a fair bit. But it was in Hawaii that I developed my passion for birds."

"Isn't that a bit early to become a birdwatcher?"

"Not at all. My parents both worked, and I had to entertain myself. There were dozens of birds where we lived. All you had to do was look out a window or go outside. I loved the different colors and the songs they would sing to each other."

Birdy smiled at the memory.

"I would ask my parents what kind of birds they were. They didn't know, so they bought me a book. Soon I was an expert. Then, for my sixth birthday, they bought me a camera."

"That's pretty young to get a camera."

"I was precocious, and they knew I would take good care of it. I had told them I needed one to capture all the birds I saw." Again, he smiled. "Sadly, we moved soon after."

"To where?"

"First to Washington. Then to Florida, California, Japan, and Korea."

"Wow," said Guin. "That's a lot of moving around. What about school and friends?"

"I was an autodidact."

"So, you didn't go to school?"

"I did, but I learned more on my own. Eventually, they sent me to boarding school."

"And friends?"

"I had a few. But it was tough, moving around so much."

"And you continued to study birds?"

Birdy nodded.

"I did. It was the one constant in my life. Eventually, my folks settled in the D.C. area. But by then I had gone off to college."

"Where did you go?"

Birdy smiled at her.

"I'm surprised you have to ask, being a crack investigative reporter."

Guin knew he was teasing her, but his patronizing tone annoyed her.

"I know you got your Ph.D. from Cornell. I just don't remember where you went for undergrad."

"Do you need to know in order to marry me?"

"No, I just…"

Guin let it drop. Though she did have one more question.

"And have you ever been married?"

"No. Though…"

They were interrupted by a shadow looming over the table.

CHAPTER 28

"Birdy! I've been trying to reach you, but you haven't returned my calls or texts," Angelique pouted.

"I've been a bit busy, Angel."

"Still, you could have spared a few minutes for your old friend."

Guin watched the exchange and saw Jean-Luc out of the corner of her eye. Angelique followed her gaze and smiled.

"Jean-Luc!" she called. "Come over here!"

Jean-Luc reluctantly came over.

"Do you two know Jean-Luc Fournier?"

"I do indeed," said Guin, smiling at the proprietor of the bakery.

Angelique looped her arm through one of Jean-Luc's.

"And how do you know Jean-Luc?" Guin asked her.

"Oh, Jean-Luc and I go *way* back," she replied, her mouth forming a seductive smile.

"If you would please excuse me," said Jean-Luc stiffly.

"Of course!" said Angelique.

Jean-Luc gave a little nod, then extricated himself and headed toward the back of the bakery.

"*À bientôt!*" called Angelique, waving her hand.

Guin saw the way Angelique was looking at Jean-Luc. It was the same look she had given to Birdy at the party, the look of a cougar about to leap on her prey.

"So, uh, you and Jean-Luc…" said Guin.

Angelique was still looking at the bakery. She sighed.

"Isn't he wonderful?"

"What about your husband?"

"You mean my soon-to-be-ex-husband?" she scowled. "I hope he rots in hell." She replaced her scowl with a smile. "Well, I must be going." She went over to Birdy and gave him a kiss on each cheek. "*Au revoir, cheri!* And call me. There's still that matter we need to discuss."

Birdy nodded, and Guin watched as Angelique walked to her car. As soon as she was gone, Guin turned back to Birdy.

"What was that all about?"

"Just Angelique being Angelique."

"What is that supposed to mean?"

Birdy finished his sandwich, then balled up the paper it had been wrapped in and placed it in the paper bag.

"I need to go," he said, getting up.

"But you haven't eaten your fruit tart."

"You take it," he said, pushing the box towards her.

"But…"

"No buts. Take it."

"Fine," said Guin.

"Good. I'll call you later."

He sauntered off towards the parking lot. Halfway there, he pulled out his phone. Guin wondered who he was talking to. She watched him for a minute, then looked down at her sandwich. There was still a third of it left, but she was no longer hungry. And Birdy had taken the bag. Guin got up, taking the sandwich and the pastry box with her, and went inside the bakery.

"Could I get a little bag?" she asked Jake.

He handed her one, and she thanked him. She then glanced back toward the kitchen.

"Is Jean-Luc back there?"

Jake nodded.

"Okay if I go see him?"

Guin had been in the kitchen before, but she didn't want to go back there without Jean-Luc's permission.

"Let me ask."

He disappeared into the kitchen, emerging a minute later. "He says it's fine."

Guin thanked him, then went back.

"And what brings you to my kitchen?" asked Jean-Luc. "Come to sneak a look at your wedding cake?"

Guin had asked Jean-Luc if he would make the wedding cake back in December, and he told her that he would be honored to, that it would be his present to her. She had balked, knowing how much wedding cakes cost. But he had insisted. It was the least he could do for her, after all her help. And Guin had given in. Even if the wedding was just for show, she loved a good wedding cake. And she knew Jean-Luc's would be delicious.

"Don't you know it's bad luck to see your cake before the wedding?"

"I thought it was just the dress."

"*Non*," said Jean-Luc.

"Well, as much as I'd love to sneak a peek at the cake, that's not why I'm here."

"Oh?" said Jean-Luc, looking up at her.

"No, I wanted to ask you about Angelique Marchand."

"Ah. Don't tell me you are jealous?"

He said it with a twinkle in his eye.

Guin smiled at him.

"No, I'm just curious about her. How do you two know each other?"

"We met in Paris, many years ago, when she was studying there."

"Did you two date?"

Jean-Luc looked wistful.

"I was working at a *patisserie* near the school she was attending. She would stop by for a croissant and *un café*.

Soon, she was there every morning."

"And you would talk?"

"She would smile and try to engage me in conversation, but I was too shy to say more than a few words at first."

"So, what happened? What changed?"

"One day she asked me out. I said no. I thought it not right. But she was persistent. So finally, one day I said yes."

"And?"

Jean-Luc smiled.

"Those were some of the happiest days of my life."

"So, what happened?"

"She went back to Montreal when school was over, and I stayed in Paris."

"And you never saw her again?"

"We exchanged a few letters. But… Eventually, she wrote that she was getting married. And I moved on and married too."

"And now you've found each other again."

"*Oui.*"

"And you had no idea she was on Sanibel?"

"*Non.* Not until she walked in my door. You can imagine my surprise."

Angelique seemed full of surprises. And Guin could have sworn she had her sights set on Birdy. Was she using Jean-Luc to make Birdy jealous?

"Just be careful."

"*Je sais.* She is not yet divorced. But…" He shrugged. "Her husband, he is not here. And we are both adults. Now, if you will excuse me. I must get back to my pastry."

"Okay," said Guin.

She made to leave.

"And do not worry about your cake," called Jean-Luc. "It will be ready in time."

Guin turned to him and smiled. Then she had a thought.

"Will you be going with Angelique to the wedding?"

"I am meeting her there. We thought it best not to arrive together, *n'est-ce pas?*"

Guin nodded.

"*Au revoir* then. I'll see you soon."

"*À bientôt,*" said Jean-Luc. Then he went back to his pastry.

Guin picked up her mail on her way in. There was another envelope without a postmark. Just like the previous one. Even the block letters were the same. She froze, then tucked the envelope between the other pieces of mail. As soon as she was back inside she called the detective on his cell phone. It went to voicemail. She left him a message, telling him it was urgent. Then she sent him a text. He called her back two minutes later.

"What's the emergency?"

"I got another letter. At least I assume it's another letter. I haven't opened it."

"Bring it to the police department."

"When?"

"Now."

She put her phone and the pile of mail in her bag and left.

Guin watched as the detective carefully opened the envelope. She had insisted on staying and seeing what was inside. Gingerly, he removed a thin piece of paper. It looked just like the previous note, with the same computer-generated all-cap lettering.

"STAY AWAY FROM BIRDY… OR ELSE. THIS IS YOUR FINAL WARNING."

"What do you think it means?"

"It means you should call off the wedding."

"The wedding's only three days away. And if anything the letter is more reason to go through with it."

The detective scowled.

"And how do you figure that, Nancy Drew?"

Guin wrinkled her nose.

"Clearly, someone doesn't want me to marry Birdy. I want to know why." She paused. "Unless you're the one sending me the anonymous notes."

The detective continued to scowl.

"It's a federal crime to send death threats via the U.S. Postal Service."

"Though technically, the letter was hand-delivered. And it didn't explicitly say my life was in danger."

"Whatever," said the detective. "You really think I'd risk my career on something so juvenile?"

Guin felt a mix of emotions.

"So who did send the letters? And did the person hand-deliver them or have someone else do it?" Suddenly it hit her. "The security cameras! They capture everything!"

The detective was looking at her.

"My next-door neighbors, the Bregmans," she explained. "They have those security cameras on their house. I had totally forgotten about them. They record everything, and one of them is pointed right at my mailbox. Well, sort of. But the footage should show us who put the letter there. Unless it was done in the middle of the night. Though the moon was pretty bright last night."

"I'll speak with them," said the detective.

"I can do it," said Guin.

"You stay out of it."

"But…"

Guin closed her mouth, then opened it a few seconds later.

"Will you at least let me know if you find out anything?"

The detective gave her a look, the one that said, "this is

police business, and you are on a need-to-know basis."

Guin regretted mentioning the security cameras. Though the detective would no doubt have thought of them eventually. If he hadn't already. Well, if he didn't want to play nice, she would just go speak to the Bregmans herself.

"What about that bullet you found, the one that pierced my tire?"

"What about it?"

"Did you find the gun that fired it or the person?"

"Not yet."

"Did you speak with Boris and Natasha?"

Again the detective gave her the look. Guin sighed.

"Can you tell me anything?"

"Call off the wedding."

They stood there glaring at each other, like two wrestlers at the start of a match. Then the detective's phone began to ring. He went to answer it.

"O'Loughlin," he said. He nodded, then turned to Guin. "I trust you can see yourself out?"

Guin stood there for a few more seconds, then turned and left.

CHAPTER 29

Guin pounded down the steps to the parking lot. She got in the Mini and slammed the door.

"Grrr!" she growled. "That man is so infuriating!" She gripped the steering wheel. "Fine. You want to keep me out of your investigation? I'll just do some investigating on my own."

She turned the key in the ignition and backed the car out of the lot. As soon as she got home, she went over to the Bregmans. She rang the doorbell and knocked on the door.

"Coming! Coming!" called a male voice. "Hold your horses. I'll be right there."

A minute later, Sam Bregman, a diminutive man around Guin's height, opened the door.

"Guinivere, what can I do for you?"

"Do you have a minute?"

"For you, I have all the time in the world."

"Who's at the door?" called a female voice. It was Sam's wife, Sadie.

"It's Guinivere, from next door," Sam shouted back.

"Is everything okay?" she asked, still shouting.

A few seconds later, Sadie appeared.

"Guinivere. What can we do for you?"

"Is it okay if I come in?"

"Of course!" said Sadie. She hit her husband. "You didn't invite her in?"

Sam opened his mouth to protest, then quickly shut it. Guin smiled and stepped through the door.

"Now tell me," said Sadie. "Is something wrong? You haven't found any more dead bodies, have you?"

"No," said Guin. "But I do have another favor to ask you."

She felt guilty asking them again to see footage from their security cameras, but she had nowhere else to turn.

"Ask away," said Sam. "We can always say no."

"It's about your cameras. Someone put something in my mailbox earlier, a letter. But it wasn't delivered by the mailman. So I was hoping you could help me find out who left it."

"Huh," said Sam. "That detective asked me the same thing."

Guin frowned.

"And did you give him the footage?"

"I sent him a copy. I still have the original."

"May I see it?"

Sam hesitated.

"He told me that if you asked, I should tell you no."

Guin deflated.

"Well, thanks anyway. Sorry to have bothered you."

She turned to go. Sadie hit Sam.

"You going to let her leave?"

"What am I supposed to do?" said Sam. "The detective said—"

Sadie cut him off.

"Neighbors help neighbors. Show her the footage, Sam."

"But…"

Sadie gave him a look, and Sam sighed.

"I'll show you what I sent the detective."

"You sure?" asked Guin. "I don't want you getting into any trouble."

"What trouble?" said Sadie. "The detective didn't say anything to me."

Guin smiled. She liked her new neighbors.

Sam led her to his office.

"Just give me a minute," he said, sitting in front of his computer.

Guin watched as Sam futzed.

"The detective said to send him the footage between nine and noon. There!" he said. "All set. You ready?"

Guin nodded.

Sam hit play. Nothing was happening.

"Can you fast forward it a bit?"

Sam nodded. "Sure."

The videotape sped up.

"There!" said Guin, pointing. "Stop it there!" Sam paused the footage. "Now rewind it a bit."

Sam rewound the video, stopping it when a biker appeared. She was wearing a helmet and sunglasses, so you couldn't see her face. But it was clearly a woman, judging by the outline of her body. Though Guin supposed it could have been a man disguised as a woman.

"Okay, now hit play again," Guin commanded.

Sam obeyed, and the two of them watched as the biker looked around, withdrew an envelope, and placed it in Guin's mailbox. Then she looked around again and quickly peddled away.

"You want me to keep going?" asked Sam.

"No, that has to be her." But who was she? "Can you play it again, Sam?"

Sam looked up at Guin and smiled.

"I always wanted to have someone say that to me."

Guin smiled back at him. Sam rewound the tape and replayed the footage.

"Stop there!" Guin commanded, as the biker started to peddle away. Sam paused the videotape. Guin squinted. It appeared that the biker had a ponytail, a blonde ponytail if she wasn't mistaken.

Sam looked up at her.

"You want me to keep going?"

"No," said Guin, straightening up. "I think I have what I need."

Sam was looking at her.

"And you won't mention this to the detective?"

"Mum's the word," Guin told him.

Sam went to get up, but Guin told him she could see herself out. She headed down the hall and was almost at the front door when Sadie stopped her.

"This is for you," she said, holding out a small box.

Guin peered at the box.

"What is it?"

"A wedding gift."

"You didn't have to get us anything," said Guin, feeling guilty. She had invited the Bregmans to the wedding but told them no presents. In fact, she had told all of her guests that if they wanted to do something for the bride and groom, they should make a donation in their name to one of the local nonprofits.

"It's just a little something," said Sadie. "Really more of a belated housewarming gift. Please, take it. You can open it later. Or now."

Guin took the box.

"Go on," said Sadie.

Guin opened it. Inside was a beautiful amulet. It looked like an open hand with an eye in the middle, surrounded by hearts and leaves in a pretty blue-green stone.

"It's a *hamsa*," Sadie explained. "A Jewish symbol of luck and protection. I figured you could use some."

"It's beautiful," said Guin, examining the amulet.

"You should hang it somewhere where you spend a lot of time."

"I'll do that. Thank you."

Sadie beamed.

"Our pleasure."

Sadie walked Guin to the door.

"That Mr. McMurtry is so handsome. You're one lucky lady."

Sadie was smiling at her, and Guin forced herself to smile back.

As soon as she got home, she took out the amulet. She held it up against several walls, unsure where to put it. Unable to decide, she put it back in its box. She would find the perfect spot to hang it later. First, though, she needed to figure out who the mystery letter carrier was.

Guin had fixed an image of the woman in her brain. Although the video footage was grainy, Guin could tell the biker was in good shape, tall, with blonde hair long enough to tie back into a ponytail. Immediately, she thought of Natasha, Bettina, and Angelique. All three were tall, blonde, and athletic-looking. And all three loathed her. Of course, the biker could be someone else entirely. Merely a messenger. But Guin didn't think so.

Guin sat down in front of her computer and pulled up a picture of Natasha. She was supposedly in Orlando, teaching. Though she could have driven down to Sanibel. But then why bother with the bike?

Next Guin found a photo of Angelique. She was older than Natasha but looked to be in good shape. And if she was really seeing Jean-Luc, why would she care if Birdy was marrying someone else? Still, she had seen the way Angelique looked at him. And she clearly wasn't fond of Guin.

Then there was Bettina. Bettina had never liked her, and Guin had always suspected Bettina had wanted her relationship with Birdy to be more than just professional. But Birdy had told her he wasn't interested. And Guin couldn't really see Bettina printing anonymous letters, then hopping on a bike to deliver them. If Bettina wanted to scare Guin off, she'd do it to her face.

Guin sighed. Maybe she was being paranoid.

She again thought about the detective. Could he have

sent the letters, despite his denial? It would be easy enough for him to have a bike messenger deliver them. Guin sat back and frowned. Then her phone started to vibrate. She glanced down and saw her mother's number on the caller ID. Just what she needed. Not. Guin thought about letting the call go to voicemail. But then she'd have to call her mother back. So she picked up.

"Hi, Mom. Everything okay?"

"Everything's fine. I just wanted to remind you about tomorrow. Do you need me to give you the information again?"

"I got it, Mom. And don't worry, I'll be there."

"Just make sure you're not late."

Guin rolled her eyes.

"Anything else?"

"As a matter of fact, yes. Philip and I had a lovely dinner with Harriet and Alfred. Such a catch that Alfred. It's a shame you two didn't get together."

"Yes, well," said Guin. "As you recall, we were both seeing people at the time."

"And now he's engaged," sighed her mother. "To a very successful real estate agent, I might add."

"That's nice," said Guin.

"They're getting married at the Ritz in March. Philip and I were invited. I'm not sure we'll go, but…"

"Is there something else you needed, Mother? Otherwise, I should go. I have a lot to do the next couple of days."

Her mother huffed.

"Fine. I did volunteer to help, you know."

"This is work stuff, Mom."

"Very well, go do your work stuff. I'll see you tomorrow."

"I'll see you tomorrow," said Guin.

She ended the call, then put her head down on her desk. Her mother drove her crazy. Her phone began to vibrate. She groaned. It was probably her mother again, saying she forgot something. She glanced at the caller ID. It was an unfamiliar number. She thought about ignoring the call but wound up answering.

"Hello?" she said.

"Ms. Jones?"

It was a male voice, with some kind of accent.

"Speaking."

"This is Boris Vladimirovich."

"Excuse me?"

"Boris Sokolov," said the man with a sigh.

Guin sat upright. *Boris? What did he want? And how did he get her number?*

"What do you want, Mr. Sokolov?"

"Please, call me Boris."

"What do you want, Boris?"

"You Americans are so suspicious."

"I'm a little busy, Boris. Please get to the point."

Boris tutted.

"And so impatient too."

Guin waited.

"You and I should meet."

"Like I said, I'm a bit busy."

"I was thinking we could meet for dinner," he said, ignoring her.

"I'm afraid that's out of the question. I have plans tomorrow and Wednesday."

"I was thinking this evening."

"I'm afraid I won't make it to Orlando in time for dinner."

"I am not in Orlando. I am on Sanibel."

Guin stared. If Boris was on Sanibel, did that mean Natasha was too?

"Meet me at Dante's at seven."

"Uh…" said Guin.

"And come alone."

Before Guin could reply, the call ended.

CHAPTER 30

Guin had thought about not showing up. Then she realized that if Boris knew her phone number, he likely also knew where she lived. And the last thing she wanted was for him to show up at her door. So she changed her clothes, brushed her hair, put on a little makeup, and headed out to meet him, giving Fauna some food before she left.

The restaurant was crowded, and Guin wondered why Boris had wanted to meet her there. Surely he'd pick a more private spot? But the more people the better, as far as she was concerned.

She spied him immediately. He was seated at the bar, nursing a beer. Guin went over.

Boris smiled as soon as he saw her. Then he swallowed the rest of his beer and signaled to the bartender.

"Come," he said, getting up. "I had them reserve a booth for us."

As far as Guin knew, you couldn't "reserve" a booth at Dante's, but she didn't say anything.

"My date has arrived," Boris informed the young woman in charge of seating people. "Please show us to our booth."

"They're just clearing it," she told him.

The three watched as a booth near the end was cleared.

"This way," said the young woman, grabbing two menus. She waited until they had sat down, then placed the menus on the table. "Your server will be over in a moment," she informed them.

Guin watched as the hostess made her way back to the front of the restaurant. Then she turned to Boris.

"So, what was so important that I needed to drop everything and meet you for pizza?"

Boris smiled.

"I thought you Americans loved pizza."

Guin continued to eye him.

"Shall we order something to drink?" He signaled to a server, who came rushing over, and ordered a large beer.

"Guinivere?"

"I'll have a High 5."

The server nodded, then went over to the bar.

"No vodka?" Guin asked.

Boris grinned.

"When in Rome. Or Sanibel. Besides, I enjoy the local ale."

Their beers arrived a few minutes later. Boris raised his glass.

"*Budem zdorovy!*"

Guin tilted her head.

"It means 'cheers.' Now come, raise your glass!" Boris commanded.

Guin reluctantly raised her glass and Boris clinked his against it.

"So, why am I here?" she asked him, after they had some beer.

"You Americans, always in a hurry," Boris tutted. "Let us enjoy our beers and order some food."

Guin sighed. She was clearly not going to get anything out of this man until he was good and ready.

"Fine."

They picked up their menus.

"You want to share a pizza?"

"An excellent idea," said Boris.

"What would you like on it?"

"You may choose."

"I typically get a large pie with mushrooms and onions."

"Sounds delightful."

"I also recommend the chicken wings and the ribs."

"We shall order both."

"I can't eat that much."

Boris looked at her and frowned.

"You are too skinny. You should eat more."

Guin was spared having to respond by the return of their server.

"Are you ready to order?" she asked them.

"We are," Boris replied. "We would like one order of your coal-fired wings. One order of your coal-fired ribs. And one large pizza with mushrooms and onions."

"What size order for the wings and ribs? We have ten pieces or twenty for the chicken, and you can either get a half rack or a whole rack of ribs."

"We will have ten pieces of the chicken and a full rack of your ribs."

"Very good," said the server, noting everything on her pad.

"Now that that's taken care of," said Guin, "tell me why you insisted on meeting with me this evening."

Boris sighed and looked at her.

"Very well. I shall tell you. I wanted to see what kind of woman had netted our elusive bird."

Again with the bird metaphor.

"And?"

Boris was studying her.

"How much do you know about our mutual friend?" he asked her.

"I know that he's a world-famous ornithologist and wildlife photographer, as well as a bestselling author."

Boris gave her an amused smile.

"Anything else?"

"I know that his parents died in an automobile accident and that he has no siblings."

"Is that what Birdy told you, that his parents died in an automobile accident?"

Guin nodded. Though she suddenly got a bad feeling.

"Did they not die?"

"Oh no, they are most assuredly dead," said Boris. "But it was no accident."

"It wasn't?"

Boris shook his head.

"They were removed."

"Removed?" said Guin, not understanding.

Boris formed his right hand into the shape of a gun and pretended to shoot. Guin swallowed.

"They were assassinated?"

"Such a crude term," said Boris, a look of disgust on his face. He took another sip of his beer, no doubt to wash down the bad taste.

"Then why say they died in a car crash?"

"Oh, they died in a car crash. But like I said, it was no accident."

Guin shivered, remembering her recent automobile "accident." Was that what had happened to Birdy's parents, only with a far worse result?

"I don't understand. Who would want to kill Birdy's parents?"

"What did Birdy tell you about them?"

"Just that his father worked for the U.S. Navy and that they moved around quite a bit. I think his mother worked, too, but I don't remember what she did."

"They were spies."

"Spies?" said Guin, staring at him.

Boris nodded.

"Did they work for you?"

Again, Boris smiled.

"No. Though we made them a most generous offer. Sadly, they refused."

Guin flinched.

"Were you responsible for their deaths?"

Boris shook his head.

"As much as I'd like to, I cannot claim credit. That honor belongs to our dear friend Natasha."

Guin froze.

"Natasha killed Birdy's parents? Does Birdy know that?"

"Why else do you think he tracked her down?"

Guin clutched her beer.

"Was he planning to kill her?"

"That may have been his intention, but…"

He shrugged.

"But what?" said Guin, leaning forward.

"He fell in love with her."

Guin stared at him.

"Birdy fell in love with the woman who killed his parents? I don't believe it."

Again, Boris shrugged.

"Believe it or not. It is the truth."

Sure, Natasha was a very attractive woman. But she couldn't imagine Birdy being truly in love with her. Not if she murdered his parents. There was something Boris wasn't telling her.

"What about Natasha? I heard she was in love with him."

"Is that what he told you?"

"He said Natasha was obsessed with him. That she thought they would be together forever."

Boris didn't say anything.

"Was that not true?"

"Oh, Natasha believed they would be together. Until Birdy betrayed her."

"He betrayed her?"

Boris nodded.

"How?"

Boris looked at her.

"It is all in the book."

"The book? What book?"

"The one your fiancé wrote, his big bestseller."

Guin stared across the table. Birdy's—or Wren Finchley's—latest book, *Shot Through the Heart*, involved a beautiful Russian assassin named Natalia, who falls in love with an American spy, who seemingly falls in love with her, only to betray her near the end of the book. But Birdy told her the book was a work of fiction.

Boris was nodding.

Guin opened her mouth to say something, but their server had reappeared.

"Here you go!" she said, placing the chicken wings and ribs on the table. "I'll bring your pizza out in a few."

Guin looked down at all the food. She was no longer hungry. But Boris insisted she eat. So she ate. Halfway through the appetizers, the pizza came out. Guin groaned inwardly.

"I'll be back with some fresh plates!" said the server. As soon as the plates arrived, Boris served Guin a slice.

Guin glanced at it.

"Come, come," said Boris. "Eat!"

Guin cut a small piece of pizza and popped it into her mouth. But it tasted bitter.

Boris ate three slices of pizza and insisted Guin take the rest home. She reluctantly agreed.

"So," she said. "Am I free to go?"

Boris smiled.

"Would you two like anything else?" It was their server, who had magically appeared.

"I'm good," said Guin.

The server looked at Boris.

"Coffee."

Guin wanted to leave, but something held her back. Finally, Boris was done with his coffee and asked for the check.

"Well, thanks for dinner," said Guin, as Boris paid.

They left the restaurant together. At the base of the stairs, he stopped her.

"Be careful."

"Be careful?"

"Birdy has betrayed many people. He will betray you, too."

Guin got a chill. She watched as Boris made his way to a dark SUV. Then she headed to the Mini.

As she drove home, Guin replayed their conversation. What did Boris mean? Would Birdy harm her? She couldn't imagine him doing something to hurt her, but something was niggling at the back of her head.

CHAPTER 31

As soon as Guin got home, she called Birdy.

"We need to talk."

"Would you like to come over? It's a beautiful evening, and my deck has a front-row view of the stars."

Guin hesitated. While Birdy's deck was tempting, she was not in the mood to be tempted or distracted.

"Come here."

"I love it when you give me an order. Give me a minute and I'll be right over. Should I bring my toothbrush?"

Guin ground her teeth.

"No. Just bring yourself."

"I hear and obey."

He arrived half an hour later and rang the doorbell.

"I take it this was not a booty call," he said, seeing her face.

"No."

"May I come in?"

Guin led him to the living area.

"Have a seat," she commanded.

Birdy smiled as he took a seat on one of the couches.

"I like this new forceful side of you, Guinivere. You would make an excellent dominatrix."

Guin could feel her cheeks grow warm, but she ignored the sensation. Birdy patted the space next to him. But Guin chose a spot across from him.

"So, what did you want to talk about? Has Bettina been meddling again?"

"Not that I'm aware of. I just had dinner with your friend Boris."

Birdy frowned.

"And why, pray tell, were you having dinner with Boris?"

"He insisted."

"Did he give you a reason?"

"He said he wanted to get to know me, learn more about the woman who had captured your heart."

Birdy smiled.

"You find that amusing?"

"I do."

"He also told me something interesting about you."

"Oh? And what did he have to say about me?"

"He told me that Natasha killed your parents and that I shouldn't trust you."

Guin watched Birdy's face for a reaction, but his expression remained the same.

"So, what do you have to say for yourself?"

"I say you should take what Boris says with a grain of salt."

"I don't know. He was pretty convincing."

"Guin, you know me."

"Do I? Do I really?"

Birdy looked at her.

"What can I say to convince you?"

"You can tell me the truth. Did Natasha kill your parents?"

Birdy looked conflicted. Finally, he spoke.

"She did. But there were mitigating circumstances."

"Mitigating circumstances?"

"She didn't have a choice."

"Didn't have a choice? There's always a choice."

"She was following orders."

"Whose orders? And why would anyone want to kill your parents?"

"She didn't know they were my parents."

"So, what, that makes it okay? She killed two innocent people, Birdy! Why are you defending her?"

She was staring at Birdy, and again he looked conflicted.

"What aren't you telling me?"

Birdy sighed.

"The work my father did was very sensitive in nature."

"You said he was in the navy. Was that a lie?"

He shook his head.

"What about your mother?"

"She was a translator."

"Who for, the navy?"

"No, another branch."

Guin's mind was whirring.

"The work my father was doing was highly classified, but the Russians somehow found out about it. My mother was the one who discovered it." As if reading Guin's thoughts he added, "she was fluent in Russian."

"And they what, tried to recruit him, and when that failed sent Natasha to kill him?"

Birdy was looking at her.

"Seriously?"

"Natasha was recruited by the Russian Security Service while serving in the military. She was a crack shot, one of only a handful of women the FSB recruited as snipers. It was her first mission."

"I thought you said she was an ornithologist," Guin said sarcastically. "So that was a lie?"

Birdy looked pained.

"She is an ornithologist. It wasn't a lie."

"So, what? Killing people is just her side hustle?"

Birdy's lips twitched.

"So how did you find out about Natasha and your parents?"

"It took years of digging. I was told it was an accident. But I didn't believe the report."

"Did you know who she was when you met her at that birding conference?"

Birdy looked at her, and Guin felt naïve.

"So you did know. And what were you planning to do, kill her?"

"I wanted to, but…"

"But you didn't. Why not?"

"I was told not to."

"By whom?"

"I can't tell you that."

"Can't or won't?"

"Does it matter?"

"Go on."

"The plan was to use her, find out what she knew. She was a valuable asset."

Guin was starting to understand.

"So you, what, seduced her?"

Birdy gave a slight nod.

"Were you in love with her? Boris says you were."

"Boris is mistaken."

"So, what happened? Boris said you betrayed her."

"Boris has a big mouth."

"What's his connection to Natasha anyway? Is he in love with her?"

"He's her handler, though I know he has feelings for her."

"I see," said Guin. Her head was starting to hurt.

"And how did you betray her?"

"She thought I would marry her."

"And then what, she'd defect to the United States?"

"No," said Birdy. He was giving her that look again, and suddenly Guin understood.

"She thought you were going to defect to Russia?"

Birdy didn't say anything. He didn't have to. Guin knew the answer. She shook her head.

"So you seduced her, fed her false information, got her to confess government secrets, then left?"

"Something like that."

"Oh my God, you are a spy!"

"I am not a spy, Guinivere. I told you…"

"Yeah, yeah, yeah. To-may-toe, to-mah-toe."

Birdy ran a hand through his hair. He suddenly looked tired.

"It's complicated. And the less you know, the better."

"So why is Natasha really here? Is she planning on dragging you back to Russia?" She paused. "You're not going to sleep with her again, are you?"

Birdy smiled.

"Why are you smiling?"

"You're jealous."

"Jealous? Of Natasha? Please." The very thought was ludicrous.

Birdy continued to grin.

"Admit it. There's a part of you that is just a tiny bit jealous."

"I'll admit, she's stunning, and clearly intelligent, and a bit intimidating. But in order to be jealous, I'd have to actually want you."

"Ouch," said Birdy, placing his right hand to his heart. "You wound me, Guinivere."

Guin rolled her eyes.

"So why is she here? The truth, please."

"I'm not entirely sure."

"So the story you told me, about us needing to get married. Did you make it up?"

"I didn't make it up. I told Natasha that I was settling down, charting a new course."

"Let me guess: she didn't believe you."

"No, which is why I had to prove it to her."

"I see," said Guin. "And what about Boris? Why is he here?"

"Probably to make sure I don't try to seduce Natasha again and get her to defect."

"Is that a possibility?"

"No."

Various thoughts pinged through Guin's brain.

"So could Natasha be the one trying to kill me?"

Birdy shook his head.

"I don't think so. She knows if anything happened to you, I'd never forgive her."

"Maybe she doesn't care about forgiveness."

"If Natasha wanted you out of the way, you'd already be dead."

Guin didn't know whether to be comforted by that or alarmed.

Birdy got up and took a seat next to Guin. Then he gently placed his hand on her cheek and forced her to look him in the eye.

"I would never let anything happen to you," he said.

Guin swallowed. His hand felt warm, and she could feel his breath. They sat there, looking at each other for several seconds. Then Birdy lowered his hand.

"I should go," he said.

Guin stared. That was not what she was expecting him to say.

"Unless…"

"Unless?"

"Unless you want me to stay?"

Guin could hear the hope in his voice.

"No," she said. "You should go."

He looked at her for another minute, then got up.

"Actually," said Guin, as she followed him to the front door. "I do have one more question."

Birdy stopped and turned.

"Yes?"

"Where are we going on our honeymoon?"

Birdy smiled.

"Thinking about the honeymoon, are we?"

Guin felt her cheeks grow warm.

"Just tell me where we're going so I know what to pack."

"All I will say is that it could get a bit chilly, especially at night."

"Thank you."

"Though, of course, I'd be more than happy to keep you warm at night," he added suggestively.

"Get out," said Guin.

Birdy grinned and opened the door.

CHAPTER 32

That night Guin dreamed she and Birdy were being chased by Russian agents. It had been terrifying yet strangely exciting. It was like being in a Bond film or one of Birdy's thrillers, with exotic locales and derring-do. When she awoke, her heart was racing, and it took her a minute to realize where she was. She glanced around, half expecting a Russian spy to jump out and aim a gun at her. But the only jumping was done by Fauna, who was hungry and wanted her breakfast.

Guin smiled at the feline and stroked her soft black fur.

"You're not a Russian secret agent, are you, Fauna?"

Fauna tilted her head, then tapped Guin with her paw.

Guin smiled.

"All right. Let's get you some food."

She got up and headed to the kitchen, Fauna trotting ahead of her.

As Fauna ate, Guin stared out the window. The sun was just cresting over the horizon. She had slept a bit later than usual and wondered if it was too late to go to the beach. Well, maybe too late to nab the best shells. But it was never too late for a beach walk.

She went back into the bedroom and quickly changed into her beach attire. Then she pulled on a baseball cap, grabbed her sunglasses, and headed out the door.

The beach was busier than usual. In part, it was due to Guin's late start. But it had also rained the night before, which typically meant more shells—and more shell seekers. Still, it wasn't nearly as crowded as the Long Island or Cape Cod beaches Guin had frequented when she lived up north. And there was still a chance she would find something.

She headed west, laser-focused on the shoreline, ignoring the people around her. If the shelling wasn't great when she got back from wherever Birdy was taking her, she'd book a trip to the Ten Thousand Islands.

She had enjoyed her outing there with Glen the year before. They had gone on a private tour with one of the charter companies as part of the day-tripper series for the paper. Guin had hoped to find a junonia and a Scotch bonnet and a great big true tulip, but there had been several other shell seekers the day they had gone, and she had been disappointed. Although she did manage to find a pretty rose murex and a couple of small true tulips, along with a handful of gaudy nauticas (also known as colorful moon snails), lace murexes, zigzag (or flat) scallops, and alphabet and Florida cones.

Glen had been more interested in taking photographs and speaking with their captain, who turned out to be a friend of a friend. But that was fine by Guin. More shells for her.

Speaking, or thinking, or Glen, she would need to have a long talk with him when all this was over.

"Ahem."

Guin looked up to see Lenny standing in front of her.

"Lenny! I didn't see you."

"Obviously."

Guin blushed.

"I guess I was a bit preoccupied."

"With the wedding, I presume."

"Actually, I was mentally planning a trip to the Ten Thousand Islands for when I got back."

"So, no pre-wedding jitters?"

Did she have pre-wedding jitters?

"Not really. Birdy's agent, Bettina, took care of everything. All I have to do is show up."

Lenny frowned.

"It's okay."

Guin had stopped being angry about Bettina's meddling, or had been trying not to think about it.

"So, how are you?" she asked. "I'm glad you came to the barbecue."

"I never turn down free food."

Guin smiled, then looked at Lenny's shelling bag.

"You find anything good this morning?"

"A few small horse conchs and a bunch of banded tulips. Going to give them to the Shell Club. They've been asking for donations for the show."

"Right," said Guin. "I forgot about the bags of shells."

Every year the Sanibel Shell Club handed out small bags filled with local shells to everyone who paid admission to the Shell Show.

"You excited about being a judge?"

"I'm just doing my bit."

"But you must be a little excited?"

"It's not easy being a judge. You need to be impartial."

"I'm sure you'll manage. Well, I should keep walking. I'll see you at the wedding."

"I remember when I got married," said Lenny, looking out into the Gulf. Guin waited. "My feet felt like two blocks of ice. I even thought about running away."

"You did?"

Guin didn't really know anything about Lenny's late wife. All she knew was that she had died from cancer many years ago.

Lenny nodded.

"I didn't think I was good enough for Ina. Her folks

thought so too. Ina came from a wealthy family, and my family was poor, at least poor compared to hers. And I was a teacher. Teachers didn't exactly make a lot of dough back then. Still don't. But Ina didn't care. She respected me. Said she'd rather marry a teacher than a stockbroker or a lawyer."

"She sounds wonderful."

"She was. Not another like her."

"And you loved her very much."

"More than anything, which is why I didn't run. I knew she'd be devastated. Best decision I ever made."

Guin had never heard Lenny talk about his wife before.

"So, no regrets?"

"None. I only wish we had had more time together."

"And did you have any kids?" He had never mentioned any. Lenny shook his head.

"We tried. Lord knows we tried. But I guess it wasn't meant to be. We had a bunch of nieces and nephews though. Ina doted on them."

"You still see them?"

"Why all the questions?"

"Call it reporter's curiosity," she said, smiling at him.

"Most of the nieces and nephews are still up north and belong to Ina. After she died, we kind of lost touch. Though I have a niece who recently moved to Florida. Said she'd try to come to the Shell Show."

"That's nice," said Guin.

"We'll see."

They walked together down the beach, neither speaking. Then Guin said she needed to head back.

"Nice seeing you, kid," said Lenny.

"Nice seeing you, too, Lenny."

As soon as she got home, Guin made herself a pot of coffee. When she was properly caffeinated, she called over to the

San Ybel and asked to speak with Hermione. Talking about weddings with Lenny had made Guin nervous that Bettina had done more meddling.

"Hermione Potter."

"Hi, Hermione. It's Guin Jones. Just checking to make sure everything's all set. Bettina hasn't made any more requests or changes, has she?"

"Actually…" she said. Guin felt herself tensing. "I just got off the phone with her."

"What did she want?"

"Just the layout."

"The layout?"

"Where everything would be positioned."

"Ah."

"Specifically the photographers."

"Photographers plural?"

"You didn't know?"

Guin closed her eyes and took a deep breath, slowly exhaling.

"How many photographers are we talking about?"

"Three, I believe. Or was it four? That's right, one is a videographer."

"I see," said Guin, trying to remain calm. "Anything else?"

"She asked for a copy of the menu."

"She didn't change it again, did she?"

"No. Besides, it's too late now."

Guin breathed a sigh of relief.

"And remind me what time the run-through is tomorrow. Is it three?"

Guin had written it down somewhere and promptly lost the piece of paper.

"That's right," said Hermione. "Three o'clock. The area is being set up as we speak."

"Great. Okay. Then I guess I'll see you tomorrow."

"I shall see you tomorrow. And don't worry, it's going to be beautiful."

"I bet you say that to all your brides."

Hermione smiled.

"I do. But it's the truth."

They ended the call and Guin phoned Birdy.

"Guinivere!" said Birdy. "I was just thinking about you."

"Oh? And what were you thinking? Wait. Don't tell me. I don't want to know." She paused. "I have a question for you."

"Fire away."

"Who's your best man?"

Guin couldn't believe she hadn't asked. But it hadn't ever come up.

"Or will Bettina be walking you down the aisle?"

Guin fervently hoped Birdy hadn't asked Bettina to be one of his groomsmen or groomswomen.

"It's a surprise."

Guin did not like surprises.

"Not even a hint?"

"No. Besides, you'll find out tomorrow."

Guin frowned.

"Another thing: What's with all the photographers? I thought we had agreed to one."

"The magazine insisted on sending their own, as did the paper."

"Magazine? Paper?"

"I thought we went over this."

Guin gritted her teeth.

"Just make sure they stay out of the bridal suite."

"Don't you want some photos of the bridal party getting ready?"

When she married Art, the photographer and his assistant had taken dozens of before and after photos of the bride and groom. But Guin had no interest in someone snapping pictures of her getting dressed this time.

"Not really."

"Suit yourself. Anything else you wished to discuss?"

Guin thought. There was a lot she wanted to discuss, but now was not the time.

"No. That was it."

"Then I shall see you tomorrow. Unless you want me to come over later?"

"I'm having dinner with my family in Naples."

"And you didn't invite me?"

"It's just immediate family."

"Isn't a husband immediate family?"

"You're not my husband yet." Though Guin did think a bit odd her mother hadn't included Birdy. Not that she minded. "Goodbye, Birdy."

She ended the call and got to work.

CHAPTER 33

Guin was in her walk-in closet, staring at her clothes. Even though Southwest Florida wasn't Manhattan, she knew that people in Naples tended to dress for dinner. Certainly, her mother and Philip would be well-dressed.

She had heard from her brother earlier. Their plane had been delayed, but he and Owen had made it to the hotel in time. Thank goodness. Guin didn't think she could deal with her mother on her own.

She again stared at her dresses. Then she eyed her slacks and tops. Should she wear a dress or a pair of pants with a nice top? After going back and forth (she felt as though she was watching a tennis match), she decided to wear one of the dresses she had bought in Naples. She slipped it on, then went into the bathroom to do her hair and makeup.

Guin made good time and arrived at the restaurant a few minutes early. The first one there. (*Take that, Mother.*) She informed the hostess she would be at the bar, then ordered herself a margarita on the rocks, no salt. Ten minutes later, her family arrived. She waved to her brother, and he came over, followed by their mother. Owen and Philip remained by the hostess stand.

Her mother glanced at her glass, then gave Guin a disapproving look. But Guin didn't care. She needed that drink if she was to make it through dinner.

"Margarita, no salt?" asked her brother.

Guin nodded.

"I may have one of those myself."

Their mother sniffed.

"Let's go to the table."

She proceeded to the hostess stand.

"We have a reservation at seven-thirty for five. The last name is Martin."

The hostess looked down at her reservation book, then smiled up at her.

"This way, Mrs. Martin."

She plucked five menus from the side of the stand and led the group to their table.

"Guinivere, you sit across from me. Lance, to my right."

"What about me, dear?" said Philip.

"To my left."

Owen, who was used to the family dynamics, just quietly took the empty seat next to Guin. He gave her a sympathetic look and squeezed her hand. Guin squeezed his back.

The hostess deposited the menus and the wine list and told them their server would be with them shortly.

"Shall I order us a bottle of wine?" asked Lance.

"Please," said his mother.

"Red or white?"

"I should think white to start," said Philip. He glanced at his wife, who nodded.

"White it is," said Lance.

He ordered a bottle of Sauvignon Blanc, then they took up their menus.

"How about we order a few appetizers to share?" Guin suggested.

"Fine by me," said Lance.

They both looked at their mother.

"Why is everyone looking at me?"

"Are you okay sharing a few appetizers?" Lance asked her.

"It depends on the appetizers."

After some back and forth, they wound up ordering four appetizers, which they ate with the white wine.

"So, has Birdy revealed where you are going on your honeymoon?" Guin's mother asked her.

"I still don't know," Guin replied. "Though Birdy told me to pack warm clothes."

"Maybe he's taking you to Scandinavia," said Lance.

"Or Alaska," said Owen.

At the mention of Alaska, Guin thought of Russia and shivered.

"I just hope it's not dreadfully cold," said her mother.

"Though on our honeymoon, we rarely left the hotel," said Philip, looking fondly at his wife, who swatted him.

"Not in front of the children!"

Guin and Lance both rolled their eyes.

"I'll send you a postcard and let you know," said Guin.

"So, where are you two going to live?" asked Lance.

"I don't know," she replied. "We haven't really discussed it."

Guin was beginning to feel uncomfortable and realized she should have asked Birdy about their living situation as no doubt other people would be asking them about it.

"I had assumed I would stay on Sanibel and Birdy would continue to do whatever it is he does."

"You mean live separately?" said her mother, looking horrified.

"Lots of couples live apart these days, at least some of the time," said Lance. "With people working in different places and blended families, it just makes sense."

Guin shot him a grateful look. But their mother didn't seem mollified.

"As you are both writers and neither of you has children,

I would think you could just pick a place. Personally, I think you should come back to New York."

"I don't think Birdy would be happy there. He prefers to be outside, preferably in a jungle."

"Surely, once you two are married, he'll be settling down? It's not too late for you to have children, you know. They have wonderful infertility treatments for couples your age now."

Guin nearly choked on her wine and telepathically said "help me" to her brother.

"That's really Guin and Birdy's business, Mother," he replied. "I'm sure once they've decided where they're going to live, they'll let you know."

Guin nodded.

"Do you know if Birdy is writing another book? I so enjoyed his first two," said Philip.

"I don't know, but I'll be sure to ask him."

"Maybe he could add a suave MI6 agent."

Guin smiled. She knew her stepfather enjoyed espionage novels and was tickled that she was marrying a writer of thrillers.

"Maybe."

A busboy cleared away their plates and a few minutes later their main courses arrived, along with a bottle of red wine. Guin knew she probably shouldn't drink more, as she had a long drive back to Sanibel, but she allowed herself one small glass of red. She needed it.

The rest of the meal went pretty much as Guin expected. Lance and Owen talked about their respective businesses, what new restaurants they had gone to, their travels. And Guin's mother told them about their various outings in the city, the local gossip, and their upcoming trip. She also peppered Guin with questions about the wedding.

Finally, dinner was over. Guin felt she deserved a medal for keeping her temper and not yelling at her mother. Philip signaled for the check, and a few minutes later they were standing in the parking lot.

"Care to go for a walk back at the hotel?" said Lance. "There are some lovely paths, which are lit up at night."

While it would take her over an hour to get home, Guin had missed her brother and welcomed the opportunity to have some alone time with him.

"Sounds great. I'll follow you over." She glanced over at Owen. "You're welcome to join us."

Owen smiled.

"That's okay. I see Lance all the time. You two go for your walk."

"Are you coming?" called their mother. She and Philip were standing by their rental car, and she looked perturbed.

"You go ahead!" Lance called back. "Owen and I are going to drive back with Guin."

Their mother continued to look put out but got in the car.

"Thank you," said Lance, as he got in the Mini. (Owen scrunched himself into the back seat.)

"What for?" said Guin.

"She would have complained the whole ride back."

"What was there to complain about?"

"She'd find something."

Guin turned to Owen.

"You okay back there?"

He gave her a thumbs-up.

"Then off we go!"

They drove to the Ritz, which wasn't far. Guin parked and Owen bid her goodnight. Then Lance took her hand and led her through the lobby to one of the paths that led to the beach. It was a cool evening, but much warmer than in New York or Connecticut.

Neither said anything for several minutes. They just enjoyed the relative quiet and the sound of the sea in the distance.

"Did you and Owen ever think about having kids?" Guin asked him, as they watched two children run around.

"We did."

"And?"

Lance shrugged.

"Between the agency and Owen's gallery, we have full, busy lives. I'm not sure we'd have time for a child."

"You'd make the time if you wanted one."

"Maybe."

They continued to walk.

"Do you think you might change your mind?"

"It's possible but doubtful."

"Mom must be disappointed there will be no little Galahad running around anytime soon."

Lance snorted.

"I think she's come to accept it. Whereas you, dear sister…"

"Oh no," said Guin, looking over at the now shrieking children, who looked to be around eight and six. Wasn't it past their bedtime? "I'm too old to have a kid. And I tried, remember?"

"That's because you and Art were wrong for each other."

"I don't think that had anything to do with it."

"Maybe."

"And you think Birdy is Mr. Right?"

"I don't know about that, but he clearly loves you."

Guin stopped.

"What?"

"Nothing," said Guin.

"You could always try to have kids."

Guin shook her head.

"Not going to happen."

"Does Birdy want them?"

Guin paused. They had never discussed kids. Why bother? The marriage would be over before it began. Though now a part of her was curious.

"I see those wheels turning," said Lance. "Even in the dark. You're thinking about it."

"We've never actually discussed it. Besides, we're both too busy to raise a kid."

"Like your job is that demanding."

"Hey!"

"Sorry."

They continued to walk, neither saying anything.

They arrived at the beach.

"It's beautiful, isn't it? Even in the dark."

"I'll give you that," said Lance. "And you can see the stars."

Guin looked up. There were little pinpoints of light everywhere.

"I should head back."

"Must you? Why don't we grab a coffee?"

"Much as I'd like to, it's late, and I have a busy day tomorrow."

"Late," said Lance. "It's not even ten-thirty."

Guin smiled.

"That's late for me."

Lance shook his head.

"You need to come back to New York, learn to stay up late again."

"Thanks, but no thanks. I like being in bed by ten and getting up with the sun."

Lance sighed dramatically.

"I guess you really can take New York out of the girl."

Guin smiled.

"Let's go."

Lance walked her to her car and gave her a kiss on her forehead.

"Goodnight, Sis. I'll see you tomorrow."

"Goodnight, Bro. And don't be late!"

"I'll try," he said, opening the door for her.

Guin got in, then waved goodbye.

CHAPTER 34

Guin didn't know why she did it, but instead of going home, she went to Birdy's. She knew it was late, but she didn't care. They needed to talk before the rehearsal, if only to get their stories straight.

She pulled into Birdy's driveway and noticed a car parked there. She raised her eyebrows. Who would be there at (she checked the clock on the dashboard) nearly midnight? She thought about turning around and leaving, but there was a light on inside, and now she was curious to know who Birdy was entertaining after dark.

She got out of the Mini and went to the front door. She peered through the window but couldn't see anything. She hesitated for a few seconds, then rang the doorbell. No one answered. She thought about leaving, then looked back at the car in the driveway and rang the doorbell again. A minute later, Birdy appeared.

"Guin?" he said, looking down at her. "What are you doing here?"

He was dressed, though he looked a bit disheveled.

"Who is it, Ptashka?" came a female voice. The accent was unmistakable. Guin felt a bit sick to her stomach. A few seconds later, Natasha, her hair down, the collar of her shirt open, appeared behind Birdy.

Guin thought about running, but that would be foolish. Besides, did she really care if Birdy was carrying on with

Natasha? (Though a niggling part of her did.) They had never said they couldn't have relations with other people. Just that no one could know.

"I didn't realize you had company," Guin stammered. "I'll go."

"Stay," commanded Birdy. "Natasha was just leaving."

"I was n—" said Natasha, before Birdy cut her off with a look.

"Fine. I will leave. But we are not done, Ptashka."

Guin waited as Natasha collected her bag, glared at Birdy, then swept past Guin, bumping her shoulder as she passed by.

"I'm sorry about that," said Birdy, ushering Guin inside and closing the door behind them.

"You have nothing to be sorry about. I didn't mean to interrupt."

Her nose picked up the smell of perfume in the air, and she wondered what Birdy and Natasha had been doing.

"Nothing happened," said Birdy, as if reading her mind.

"Even if it did, I have no right to say anything."

"Of course you do," said Birdy. "We're to be married."

"We both know it's not a real marriage."

"To me it is," he said, coming closer.

Guin was tired and had had a bit too much to drink and was feeling sorry for herself. And Birdy was undeniable good-looking, in that Harrison Ford-Indiana Jones kind of way, and he smelled good too.

Before she knew it, he was gently lifting her chin, so she was forced to look him in the eye. She could smell the single-malt Scotch he must have drunk. It was not an unpleasant smell. And his eyes were like a stormy sea.

"You want to tell me what this is about?" he said softly.

Guin wondered if this was what deer felt like when caught in headlights.

Birdy stroked her hair, then caressed her face.

"So beautiful," he said, his voice a whisper.

Then he was kissing her. Guin closed her eyes, and before she knew it, she was kissing him back.

He continued to kiss her, his kisses becoming more passionate, and before Guin realized what he was doing, he had scooped her into his arms and was making his way to the bedroom.

It was only when she saw the unmade bed that she stopped herself.

"This is wrong," she said, still in Birdy's arms.

"Wrong?" said Birdy. "I'd say this was very right. I know you want me, Guinivere, just as much as I want you."

"Put me down, Birdy. Now."

He looked confused and hurt.

"I don't understand."

"I said, put me down."

He put her down and noticed the unmade bed.

"It's not what you think."

"I don't think you know what I think."

"I think I do. You think I was having sex with Natasha."

"I do not," said Guin, but her flaming cheeks told a different story.

"I promise you, on my mother's grave, there was absolutely nothing going on between me and Natasha."

Guin studied him. She wanted to believe him, but she didn't trust him.

"Then why was she here? Isn't midnight a bit late to be discussing bird-watching?"

Birdy ran a hand through his hair.

"She said we needed to talk."

"I bet she did. So, what did you two talk about?"

"I can't tell you."

"Why, because you'd have to kill me?"

Birdy smiled.

"Something like that. Now tell me, why is it you're here?

I thought you turned into a pumpkin if you weren't in bed by ten o'clock."

"Yes, well," said Guin, feeling uncomfortable. "I was having dinner with my family, and they were asking all kinds of questions about us, and I didn't know how to answer."

"So you drove all the way over here, at midnight?"

Guin felt foolish.

"You don't know my mother. And she's not the only one with questions. We need to get our stories straight. Like where we plan on living and children."

"Children?"

"I know. But people might ask."

"Would you like to have children?"

"I don't know," said Guin. "I used to think so. But I—we, Art and I—couldn't. And now I think I'm too old."

"I don't think you're too old. Plenty of women in their forties have children."

"Do *you* want children?"

Birdy ran his hand through his hair again.

"I never really thought about it. I guess if I had one I'd love it, but…"

"So none of the women you dated talked about having kids?"

"Oh, they talked about it, but I told them I wasn't interested. But with you…"

Guin didn't want to go there.

"And what do we tell people if they ask where we plan on living?"

"What do you want to tell them?"

"Well, I want to stay on Sanibel."

"Then tell people that."

"But what about you?"

"What about me?"

"Where do you want to live?"

"Wherever you are."

Guin scowled.

"Be serious, Birdy."

"I am being serious. I told you, I want to settle down."

Guin stared at him.

"I don't believe you."

"Believe what you want. But I started writing the Wren Finchley books so I could make a living without having to travel all over the globe and could spend my nights in a warm bed instead of in a blind or up a tree in some jungle."

"I thought you loved traipsing through jungles."

Birdy smiled.

"I did when I was younger."

"You're not even fifty."

"But I feel old."

Guin didn't believe him.

"I should get going."

Birdy pulled her into his arms and whispered into her ear.

"Stay."

Guin was momentarily tempted. She was tired, and she didn't feel like driving anymore. But she shook her head.

"I can't."

"Why not?"

"Because."

"Because why?"

Guin opened her mouth to reply but a yawn came out instead.

"You're tired. You should stay."

"I can't stay."

He reached out for her, but Guin swatted his arm away.

"I'm not sleeping with you, Birdy."

"You can stay down the hall."

Guin eyed him.

"I promise I won't go sneaking into your room at three a.m."

Guin could feel another yawn coming and was unable to

stop it. And her eyes suddenly felt heavy. It was way past her bedtime, and the alcohol in her system wasn't helping.

"Come," said Birdy, taking her hand.

He led her down the hall to the guest room.

"There's a spare toothbrush and toothpaste in the drawer. Let me know if you need anything."

He turned to go.

"Could I borrow a t-shirt?"

"I'll see what I can find."

He went down the hall and returned a minute later with a t-shirt bearing the Grateful Dead logo.

Guin raised her eyebrows.

"I wouldn't have taken you for a Deadhead."

"I'm not. I just like their music."

Guin smiled and took the t-shirt from him.

"Thank you."

"My pleasure."

He leaned over and gave her a kiss on the forehead.

"Sweet dreams. If you need anything else or get lonely, you know where to find me."

"Goodnight, Birdy," she said. Then she locked the door behind him.

Guin fell asleep as soon as her head hit the pillow. Once again, she dreamed she was being chased. But this time, she was alone and had no idea who was chasing her. It was dark, and she could barely see. Then she heard Birdy's voice and felt his hand grasp hers. "Come with me," he said in the dream. "I'll save you." But she shook him off, saying she would save herself.

She continued to run, her heart pounding, when she saw a light up ahead and ran toward it. She opened her eyes and saw sunlight streaming in through the window. For a second, she had no idea where she was. Then she remembered. She glanced around, half expecting Birdy to be there. But he wasn't. She breathed a sigh of relief and fished in her bag for her phone. As it booted, she went to the bathroom. When she came out, she looked at her phone and saw that it was after eight o'clock. She couldn't believe it. She never slept so late. Then again, she rarely stayed up past midnight.

Forgetting she was still dressed only in Birdy's t-shirt and a pair of underwear, she went down the hall to the kitchen in search of coffee. As she was about to enter the living area, she heard Birdy speaking with someone, a woman. Though it was not Natasha. Unless Natasha had lost her accent. No, she recognized that voice. And before she could turn around, she saw two pairs of eyes staring at her and heard Bettina saying, "What is *she* doing here?"

"Good morning," said Birdy, smiling at Guin. "Did you sleep okay?"

Guin nodded.

"My t-shirt looks good on you."

Guin felt her cheeks growing warm.

"I should go change."

"Please don't. I think you look charming."

Bettina made a face.

"You didn't tell me *she* was here."

"You didn't ask."

"And *why* is she here?"

"Does she need a reason? After all, we are about to be married."

Bettina snorted.

"Please, Birdy. We both know this wedding is a farce."

"Be that as it may, Guinivere is my guest, and for all intents and purposes my fiancée, and I expect you to treat her with respect, Bettina."

Bettina and Guin both stared at him.

"And what are you doing here so early?" Guin asked.

"Birdy and I needed to go over a few things."

"What kinds of things?"

"Bettina came over to discuss the rest of my tour."

"I see."

"Maybe we could discuss this later?" Birdy said, looking back at Bettina.

"You can't keep putting me off, Birdy. The sponsors are getting anxious."

"They can wait a few more hours."

Bettina glared at Guin.

"Fine. When is she leaving?"

"*She* is staying. I'll see you later, at the hotel."

Bettina scowled, then gathered up her things.

"Very well. Meet me at noon at the San Ybel."

Birdy nodded, then walked Bettina to the door. Guin hung back. When Bettina had gone, Guin turned to him.

"So, when we get married, will Bettina be living with us?"

Birdy chuckled.

"No, Bettina will not be living with us. She's a good agent. She's just not so good with boundaries."

"I'll say. So what happened to that guy she was dating?"

"Which one?"

"I believe he was a racecar driver?"

"Oh, Giancarlo. That didn't work out."

No surprise to Guin. She sniffed.

"Do I smell coffee? Any left?"

"Help yourself. Though it's probably not as good as yours."

Guin went into the kitchen and poured herself a mug.

"So, what's this about your tour? You canceling our honeymoon?"

Guin was teasing him, but Birdy frowned.

"If Bettina had her way, we would be. But I told her a while ago not to book anything until March."

"I take it she didn't listen."

"No."

"And she isn't pleased."

"To say the least."

"Well, I don't really care about the honeymoon. Go ahead and finish the tour."

"Not without you."

"I'm staying right here on Sanibel. I have a job, remember?"

"You could take a leave of absence. Come with me, Guin. We'd have a marvelous time."

"What about the honeymoon?"

"I told Bettina that was non-negotiable."

"Does she know where you're taking me?"

Birdy nodded.

"But she's under strict orders not to tell you."

Guin sulked.

"She'd probably tell me out of spite."

"Don't ask."

"Fine."

"But I meant it, Guin. Come with me on the book tour. My fans would love it."

Guin doubted that.

"Thanks, but I'm going to pass. I like my job, and I can't leave Fauna."

"I'm sure Ginny would hold your job for you. Or you could write a column about our travels."

Guin was skeptical on both counts.

"And what about my cat? Is she invited on the book tour too?"

"No. But I'm sure you could find someone to look after her."

Guin shook her head.

"Thanks, but no thanks."

She glanced at the clock in the kitchen.

"I need to go."

She put her mug down on the counter and headed to the

guest room. A short time later she reemerged, dressed in the clothes she had worn to dinner the night before.

"I must say, that dress looks quite fetching on you," said Birdy, eyeing her appreciatively.

"Thanks," said Guin. "I'll see you at the rehearsal."

She made her way to the front door. She opened it to find Angelique Marchand on the other side, about to ring the doorbell. The two women stared at each other. Then Guin turned and looked at Birdy.

"You running a harem?"

Angelique frowned.

Birdy came to the door and smiled at Angelique.

"Hi, Angel. And to what do I owe this visit?"

Angelique was still looking at Guin.

"I'm just leaving," said Guin. "Make yourself at home."

She swept past Angelique, not giving her a backward glance, and headed to the Mini.

CHAPTER 35

Guin found it hard to concentrate the rest of the day. She had too much on her mind. And she was almost relieved when it was time to head over to the resort for the rehearsal. She had asked KC what she should wear, and KC had told her to wear a dress—though not her wedding dress—and bring her wedding shoes.

Guin went into her closet and took out a pretty blue and green maxi dress that made her feel like a mermaid. Then she grabbed the box with her wedding shoes. She would wait until the rehearsal to put them on.

She put on a little makeup and combed her hair, which, as usual, refused to behave. (The perils of having curly hair in Florida.) At two-thirty her doorbell rang. No doubt it was Birdy. Guin had wanted to meet him at the resort, but he had insisted on picking her up.

"So, let's go over everything one more time," said Guin, as they drove to the resort. She wanted them to be prepared should anyone ask them how they met (long story), how Birdy proposed (it was a surprise), where they would live (Sanibel, for now), and if they planned on having children (unlikely).

"Happy?" said Birdy when Guin was finished quizzing him.

"Ecstatic," she replied. "Now I won't sound like an idiot when someone asks us for our backstory."

"We wouldn't want that," said Birdy, smiling.

"So, do you know why KC wanted to meet with us before the rehearsal?"

"No idea. I assumed it was normal to meet with the bride and groom before everyone else showed up."

"I suppose." But she couldn't help feeling there was a special reason why KC wanted to see the two of them beforehand and felt nervous.

Birdy patted her on the knee.

"It's going to be fine, Guinivere. Relax."

Guin stared out the window. Didn't Birdy know that the worst thing you could say to an anxious person was "relax"?

Birdy handed the key to his SUV to the valet, then escorted Guin inside the San Ybel.

They saw KC right away. With her mane of pale blonde hair and commanding presence, she was hard to miss. She smiled at them and waved. Birdy smiled and waved back, while Guin did her best to calm her nerves.

"Birdy!" said KC, taking his hands in hers and looking him over. "Do you never age?"

"I have a portrait in an undisclosed storage room that ages for me," he replied with a devilish grin.

KC looked as though she wasn't sure if he was joking or serious. Then she playfully swatted him on the arm.

"Same old Birdy."

She turned to Guin.

"And how are you, Guin? Any pre-wedding jitters?"

Guin looked into KC's blue eyes and had the urge to tell her everything and run. But she saw Birdy looking at her and felt him squeeze her hand reassuringly and her heart rate began to slow down.

"A bit. But I guess that's usual."

KC nodded.

"It is. But you're getting a good one here, Guin. Have to admit, I never thought I'd see old Birdy here settle down. How'd you do it?"

"Do what?"

KC smiled.

"Get Birdy to propose."

"I made him coffee."

KC laughed, but it was the truth.

"Must have been some cup of joe."

"It was," said Birdy, smiling at the two women. "I knew right then that Guin was the one for me. Though she actually turned me down the first time I asked her."

"Oho!" said KC. "The plot thickens. So why did you accept him this time?"

"He made me an offer I couldn't refuse."

KC smiled.

"I can see why you like her, Birdy. Well, shall we get on with it? Let's find us a quiet nook, so we can go over a few things before the others arrive."

KC led them to a quiet area where there were some sofas and chairs and they sat down. She then took out a tablet and went over the ceremony, asking if they understood everything or wanted to make any changes.

"Did you get what I sent you?" asked Birdy.

Guin looked at him. What had he sent KC?

"I did. Thank you for reminding me." She turned to Guin. "Did you want to write your own vows, too?"

"What?" said Guin, looking from KC to Birdy. "I thought we were keeping things simple. We agreed."

"I changed my mind," said Birdy.

KC was looking at them.

"It's okay if you just want to go with the traditional vows," she told Guin.

And have everyone looking at me, wondering why the writer didn't write her own vows? Guin thought. But she didn't say anything.

"What did you write?" she asked Birdy.

"It's a surprise."

Guin frowned. She didn't like surprises.

"Just let me know later what you want to do," KC said to her. "And don't feel pressured just because Birdy went off-script. We have lots of brides and grooms who choose to recite the traditional vows."

Guin was about to say something when she saw her mother approaching. She looked put out.

"I thought we'd never make it. The traffic was appalling."

Guin saw the rest of her family walking in their direction, and was that…? She froze.

"Birdy!"

It was Ris Hartwick, her former beau, a big smile on his face. He was accompanied by a stunning Asian woman.

"Hartwick! Glad you could make it!" replied Birdy, returning the smile.

The two men greeted each other warmly. Then Birdy turned to Ris's companion.

"Ling! So nice to see you again."

Ling smiled back at him.

Guin was trying not to stare, but she couldn't help it. It had been nearly a year since she had seen Ris, and he was as handsome as ever. And the woman he was with seemed familiar, although Guin was pretty sure they had never met.

"What are you doing here?" Guin asked him.

Ris smiled down at her.

"Didn't Birdy tell you? I'm his best man!"

Guin looked from Ris to Birdy. Birdy was still smiling. She would have a word with him later.

"So, you and Birdy," said Ris. "I have to admit, I was surprised when he told me the news. But then he explained and, well, I wish the two of you nothing but happiness."

Guin glanced over at Birdy. What exactly had he told Ris?

Then Guin's mother stepped forward.

"Dr. Hartwick," she said, eyeing him, then Ling. The two had only met once, but Guin's mother never forgot a face, especially one that had dated her daughter. "And who is your companion?"

"Oh, how rude of me. This is Ling Lee, my fiancée."

Guin's eyes went wide. *Well, that was fast.* Then again… She looked at Ling. Then she remembered. The apartment she and Ris had stayed in in Sydney had belonged to someone named Ling. And there had been several photographs of the owner. It was the same Ling.

"You have a lovely apartment," Guin blurted.

Ling smiled.

"I'm so glad you enjoyed it! Ris and I are actually looking for a bigger place for when the baby comes."

Guin tried not to stare. Ling was pregnant? She was thin as a rail. She immediately thought of Ris's two children from his first marriage, twins who were in college. What did they think of Ling—and of their father having a second family? She would ask him later if she got the chance.

"Congratulations!" said Guin, forcing herself to smile. Ris was beaming. "When is the baby due?"

"Oh, not for another six months. But we're very excited."

Guin's mother cast a glance at Guin, the one that said, "And when are you giving me a grandchild?" Guin wanted to disappear.

"Well!" said Birdy, sensing the tension, "shall we get on with it?"

"Shouldn't we wait for the Marchands and Shelly?" said Guin. It wasn't like her friend to be late.

As if on cue, Shelly came charging in.

"Sorry I'm late! Minor emergency. But I'm here now."

"Is everything okay?"

"Everything's fine. I just burned my finger soldering a new piece." She held up the injured finger, which was wrapped in a bandage.

"Are you sure?" asked Guin.

"Oh yeah. Not the first time. Won't be the last."

Suddenly she noticed Ris and Ling and frowned.

"Who's she?" she said, looking at Ling.

"This is Ling Lee," said Guin, "Ris's fiancée."

"Fiancée?!" said Shelly.

Guin was saved further awkwardness by the Marchands.

"Sorry we're late," said Pierre. "Paulette couldn't decide what to wear."

Paulette shot him a look.

"It is an important occasion. And I would not want to embarrass Birdy and Guinivere."

Pierre smiled indulgently at his wife.

"*Oui, ma chere.*"

"You both look fine," said Birdy. "I believe you two know Harrison Hartwick?"

Pierre nodded at Ris.

"We've had the pleasure."

"I've missed your lectures," said Paulette, smiling at Ris.

He smiled back at her.

"And this is my fiancée, Ling."

"Charmed," said Pierre, smiling at her.

"And this is my mother Carol, my stepfather Philip, my brother Lance, and his husband Owen," said Guin.

Again, Pierre smiled.

"Nice to meet you all."

KC cleared her throat.

"Well, if everyone is here, let us proceed with the rehearsal. I'll just let Hermione know we're ready."

She took out her phone.

"Hey, Hermione. We're all here."

She listened and nodded her head.

"Okay. See you in a few."

She put her phone away and turned to the group.

"Hermione said she'd meet us at the venue. She's just

finishing something up. You want to follow me?"

They headed outside, Guin moving to walk beside Ris.

"So, when did you get here? Are you staying at your place?"

Ris owned a charming cottage in Fort Myers Beach, though for all Guin knew he had sold it.

"Sadly, no. I rented it out. We're actually staying on Sanibel, at a friend's."

"Oh?" Guin wondered which friend. "And how long are you here for?"

"A month."

"So you'll be here for the Shell Show?"

Ris nodded.

"I told Ling all about it. She's very excited."

They had reached the venue. Everyone stopped and looked around.

A minute later, Hermione appeared.

"Hello, everyone," she said in her polished English accent. "Sorry I was delayed."

"You're British," said Philip.

"I am," said Hermione.

Philip smiled.

"But you live here?"

"I do."

"A bit hotter than Old Blighty."

"I'll say. But one gets used to it."

She smiled at Philip and he smiled back.

"All right then. Shall we get started?"

CHAPTER 36

They were standing by the adults-only pool. The area was ringed with tents and cabanas and separated from the beach by a hedge and low-lying dunes. The section of the beach where the ceremony was to take place had been cordoned off with a low white-picket fence, which surrounded a makeshift floor topped with folding chairs forming two columns on either side of the aisle. At one end was what looked like a trellis, which was where the actual ceremony would take place.

"How do you keep people from interrupting the ceremony?" asked Guin's mother, frowning at the people walking by on the beach. "Why she had to have a beach wedding is beyond me," she loudly whispered to her husband.

"We hired police to guard the area, in addition to hotel staff," explained Hermione. "So there will be no unwanted guests."

Guin's mother sniffed.

"I think it's perfect," said Lance. "You always talked about having a beach wedding."

"Thank you," Guin mouthed. Though she understood her mother's concern. She shared it, albeit for different reasons. The area was quite open.

"Of course, we still need to add the finishing touches," Hermione continued. "But I promise you, by tomorrow morning everything will be all set."

"What if it rains?"

Hermione looked over at Guin's mother.

"The forecast calls for clear skies. But if that changes, we can move the ceremony inside to where the reception will be held."

Guin glanced at her mother. She was clearly not done.

"And where will the musicians be?"

"Over there," said Hermione, pointing to the pool area. "By the hedge."

"Will Guin be able to hear them?"

Hermione smiled.

"She will." She glanced around. "Now, if there are no more questions, I will leave you in KC's more than capable hands."

"What about a bridal suite? Where is Guin to get ready?"

It was her mother again.

"We have a suite reserved for Guin and her party starting at noon tomorrow."

"Not until noon? But the wedding starts at five."

"I'm afraid the room won't be available until then. But that should give you more than enough time to get ready."

Guin's mother harrumphed.

"Don't you have another suite you could give us, one that would be available at ten?"

"I'm afraid the hotel is booked."

"It's fine, Mom," said Guin, feeling embarrassed. "It'll only take me a couple of hours to get ready."

"But what about your hair? That alone will take a couple of hours."

Guin wished the sand would swallow her.

"Right!" said KC. "Let's move onto the rehearsal, shall we?"

Guin cast her a grateful look.

"We'll take it slow the first time, then run through it a bit faster the second time. Sound good? Shouldn't take long."

She glanced around the assembled group and was met with approving nods.

"Okay! Then let's begin."

Although everyone there had no doubt been to at least one wedding, they listened patiently as KC explained how the ceremony would go. Then they began. Everything was fine until they got to the vows.

"This is where you read what you wrote, Birdy," KC said, turning to him.

Birdy opened his mouth to speak, but KC stopped him.

"You can wait until tomorrow to actually say what you wrote, unless you're hot to do it now."

Guin was shaking her head no.

"I can wait," said Birdy, smiling at his bride-to-be.

Guin released the breath she was holding.

KC finished up. Then they went through the processional and ceremony one more time.

"Excellent work, everyone!" said KC, when they were done. "See you back here tomorrow! The ceremony will begin at five sharp. So make sure you're ready half an hour before."

As they headed back to the hotel, Guin took KC aside.

"Could I speak with you for a second?"

"Sure," said KC.

Guin saw her mother watching.

"Everything's fine, Mom. I just have a quick question for KC. Go along inside. I'll be right there."

Her mother didn't move. Fortunately, Lance came to the rescue, taking their mother's arm and ushering her back into the hotel. Guin mentally thanked him.

Then it was Birdy's turn.

"Everything okay?"

"Fine," said Guin, exasperated. "I just need to ask KC something. I'll be in in a minute."

Next came Shelly.

"I'm fine, Shell," said Guin, more sharply than she had intended. "I'll be in in a minute."

"I was just coming over to tell you I have to run."

"Oh, is everything okay?"

"Everything's fine. Just have to do a call. I'll see you at the dinner. And don't worry if I'm a few minutes late."

"Okay," said Guin. She had almost forgotten about the rehearsal dinner.

Shelly took Guin's hand.

"It's going to be okay. You're marrying a great guy."

She squeezed Guin's hand and smiled at her, then headed inside.

Finally, everyone had gone, leaving only her and KC.

KC looked amused.

"They're all worried I'm going to bolt," Guin explained.

"Are you?"

Guin sighed.

"No, though, to be honest, I have thought about it."

KC didn't say anything.

"It's about the vows. I feel weird about them. I didn't know Birdy was going to write something."

KC gave her a sympathetic smile.

"As I told you before, it's up to each couple—and each individual."

"I know, but…"

KC placed a hand on Guin's arm.

"If you want to write your own vows, go for it. But it's perfectly fine to recite the standard ones. Really. No need to feel anxious or guilty. Just let me know by tomorrow morning what you want to do. Okay?"

"Okay," said Guin, nodding her head. She liked this woman and felt bad about taking her away from a real wedding. Though she knew Birdy was paying her well.

"Now, if there's nothing else," said KC, "I should get going. I'll see you tomorrow."

"See you tomorrow," said Guin. Then she headed inside.

Lance was waiting for Guin when she entered the lobby. She looked around.

"Where is everyone? Did they leave?"

"No, they're in the bar, waiting for you.

"Oh?" said Guin. "What about the dinner? Shouldn't people be heading off to get ready?"

"Pierre Marchand insisted on ordering a bottle of Champagne to toast the bride and groom."

Guin sighed.

"Come on," said Lance. "You look like you could use a drink."

He took her arm and led her to the bar.

"There she is!" said Pierre, spying her. "We were getting worried you had run off," he chuckled.

He signaled to a waiter, who immediately brought over a bottle of Champagne. He popped the cork, then poured a little into Pierre's glass. Pierre took a sip and nodded. Then the waiter poured the remaining contents into the other glasses. There wasn't enough to go around, so Pierre had him bring out a second bottle. When everyone's glass had been filled, he raised his.

"To the lovely Guinivere and my good friend Birdy, may you be as happy as Paulette and I. *A votre santé!*"

"Cheers!" said the ensemble.

Guin downed half of her Champagne in one gulp.

"Easy there," said Lance.

Guin glanced around. Her gaze fell on Ris and Ling. Ling was drinking sparkling water, and Ris was looking adoringly at her. Guin felt a pang. Was it jealousy? Maybe a bit. But she was happy for them. She just wished she felt as happy as they looked.

Ris turned and looked at her, smiling as their eyes met. His smile still had the ability to dazzle her.

Another bottle of Champagne arrived, and again the waiter poured a little into each glass. Ris raised his.

"To Guin and Birdy. Long may they love and live."

"Here, here," said the rest of the group.

The Champagne was soon gone, and Pierre and Paulette got up.

"We will see you all at the rehearsal dinner," said Pierre.

"We should get going, too," said Ris, helping Ling up.

"Philip," said Guin's mother, rising and looking at her husband. Philip rose, as did Lance and Owen. Then she went over to Guin. "We'll see you at the dinner. And do try to do something with your hair."

Guin ran a hand through her curls.

Soon, everyone had gone, and it was just her and Birdy.

"Shall we?"

She followed him out to the valet stand. Five minutes later, they were in his SUV, making their way west.

"I'll get you at seven," Birdy said, after pulling the SUV into her driveway.

"That's really not necessary. I can drive myself."

The rehearsal dinner was at a restaurant in Bonita Springs that was owned by one of Bettina's clients, who had aspirations of running a restaurant empire. Bettina had arranged everything, not bothering to consult with Guin. Guin had been annoyed, but Shelly had soothed her by pointing out it was one less thing she had to worry about. Still.

"Nonsense," said Birdy. "You're on the way. And it's better if we arrive together."

"Fine," Guin sighed. She was too worn out from the rehearsal to argue. "But shouldn't we leave earlier? Cocktails begin at seven-thirty. And Bettina will be annoyed if we're late."

Birdy gave her a conspiratorial smile.

"Oh," said Guin. She smiled back at him. "Seven it is. See you."

CHAPTER 37

Guin was feeling indecisive. She had pulled out several outfits, even called Shelly, but she still couldn't decide what to wear to the dinner, and time was ticking away. She knew Birdy would want her to look her best. Knew there would probably be well-dressed women there and Birdy's business associates. But she also needed to feel comfortable.

Then there was the matter of her hair. She didn't have time to wash it or do much of anything with it. So she had twisted it up but didn't like how it looked. She let it fall. Then she tried a different updo. She stared at her reflection and sighed. Then she felt something furry rubbing against her legs. Fauna.

"What do you think, girl? Up or down?"

Fauna looked up at her, meowed, then continued to rub against her.

Guin bent down and stroked the cat, who purred at her touch.

"All right. Decision time!" she announced, heading back into the bedroom. "Eeny meeny miny moe," she said, moving her finger over the three outfits she had placed on the bed. Her finger landed on the red dress she had picked out. She made a face and thought about choosing again, but she was out of time.

Guin took the dress off the hanger, then slipped it over

her head and smoothed it over her body. It was very form-fitting, hugging her curves, and she exchanged her bikini underwear for a thong. Then she went to her jewelry box and took out her heart pendant, diamond tennis bracelet, and the engagement ring Birdy had given her.

"Now for shoes," she said.

She grabbed a box and withdrew a pair of high-heeled sandals. She slid them onto her feet and gazed at herself in the full-length mirror.

"Not bad."

She turned from side to side.

"Okay, showtime!"

No sooner were the words out of her mouth when the doorbell rang. She headed to the door, grabbing her bag on the way, and called, "Coming!"

She opened the door to find Birdy there, holding what looked like a box of flowers.

"For me?" said Guin, looking at the box. "You didn't have to bring me flowers, Birdy."

"I didn't," he replied. "The box was on your doorstep when I arrived."

Odd. Guin hadn't heard the doorbell ring. Though she had been in the bathroom.

He held out the box, but Guin made no move to take it.

"Aren't you going to open it?"

Guin shook her head. She had a bad feeling.

"Well, if you don't want to, I will," said Birdy, going to remove the top of the box.

"Don't!" Guin shouted.

Birdy looked at her.

"It could be a bomb!"

"A bomb? Guin, it's just flowers. See, there's even a sticker from the florist."

Guin shook her head.

"Put the box down, Birdy."

"Are you all right?"

"No."

"You want to tell me what's the matter?"

Guin was still staring at the box, which Birdy had placed on the ground.

"I've been getting threats."

"Threats?"

"Death threats, from someone who doesn't want me to marry you."

"Have you told the police?"

Guin nodded.

"I gave Detective O'Loughlin the notes."

"Why didn't you tell me?"

"What would you have done?"

Birdy opened his mouth, then shut it. Then he picked up the box and moved away from the house.

"Where are you going?" Guin called.

"To open the box."

He was several yards away now, and she couldn't really see him in the dark, though her outside lights were on. She waited for the sound of an explosion, but all was silent. A minute later, she saw Birdy walking toward her, the box still in his hands.

"I take it there wasn't a bomb."

"No, just a nice bouquet of flowers. And there's a card. Would you like me to read it?"

Guin nodded.

"Sorry we can't be there with you," he read. "Love from Lavinia and the clan."

Now Guin felt silly.

"It's from my aunt in Bath."

Birdy handed Guin the box. The flowers were lovely.

"I should put these in water. Be right back."

Guin hurried into the kitchen and grabbed a tall vase. She quickly filled it with water, then placed the flowers inside, leaving the vase in the sink. Then she hurried back to the door.

"Okay," she said. "Let's go."

Both of them were quiet as they headed toward the Causeway. Finally, Guin spoke.

"Why didn't you tell me you were planning on writing your own vows?"

"I didn't think it was a big deal."

"But we agreed to keep things simple."

"Number one, I don't remember ever saying that. And two, why do you care?"

"I care because it'll look odd if you wrote your vows and I didn't."

"So, write your own vows."

Guin didn't say anything.

"What did you write?" she asked him a couple of minutes later.

"It's a surprise."

"You know I don't like surprises."

"I think you'll like this one."

Guin looked over at him.

"And you don't care if I just go with the basic 'I take thee, Bertram, to be my lawfully wedded husband, to have and to hold from this day forward'?"

"As long as you say, 'I do.'"

Guin gazed out the window.

"So, will Natasha and Boris be at the dinner?" she asked a few minutes later.

"I assume so."

Guin sighed.

"You know I had to invite them."

"I know. It's just…"

"Everything will be fine. Just act like my adoring fiancée."

"Yes, darling," said Guin.

Birdy smiled.

"See, that wasn't so hard."

Guin scowled.

"Anything else I should know?"

"No. Like I said, just be yourself."

Though Guin wasn't sure who that was anymore.

They arrived at the restaurant a little after eight. The place was packed. Clearly, it was a popular spot. Birdy went up to the host stand, and a man led them to a separate room. Guin guessed there were between thirty and forty people there. Not as many as she had feared, though still a lot of unfamiliar faces. Bettina spied them and hurried over. She looked stunning in another black and white outfit, and Guin immediately felt self-conscious.

"You're late."

"There was a lot of traffic," said Birdy.

Guin glanced at him.

"Well, you're here now," said Bettina. She took his hand. "Come with me."

Bettina led him away, ignoring Guin. But Guin didn't care. This was more Birdy's night than hers.

She scanned the room and spied Shelly and Steve talking with her family and made a beeline for them.

"Guin!" said Steve as soon as he saw her. "Look at you! Va-va-voom!"

"Thanks," said Guin, smiling at him.

"So you went with the red one," said Shelly, eyeing her.

Guin nodded.

"Good choice."

"Is that a new dress?" asked her mother. "I don't think I've seen it before."

"Actually, I've had it for a while. I just don't wear it that often."

"It suits you," said Owen.

"Thanks," said Guin.

"I agree," said her stepfather. "You look *tres chic*."

So much praise! Guin wasn't used to it.

"Would you like a drink?" asked her brother.

"Please."

"Margarita on the rocks, no salt?"

Guin smiled.

"Make it a double."

Lance returned the smile, then headed to the bar.

"Do you know all these people?" asked Owen, glancing around.

Guin followed his gaze. She spied Natasha and Boris speaking with a couple she didn't know. And she saw Bettina and Birdy chatting with a couple of men she had never seen before. Guin also noticed Bettina's hand resting on Birdy's arm and told herself she wasn't annoyed by the intimate gesture.

"Not really," she replied.

Lance returned with her drink, and Guin did her best to sip it slowly, though before she knew it, it was a third gone.

"Pace yourself," Lance whispered.

Guin was about to say something but was cut off by Bettina.

"Everyone! If I could please have your attention! Dinner is about to be served. Find a table and take a seat."

There were four tables of eight in the room. Guin and her family, along with Shelly and Steve, took one.

Guin saw Birdy heading her way. Then Bettina cut him off.

"Not there, darling," she said to him, taking his arm. "This way."

Guin watched as Bettina steered him to a table on the other side of the room.

Her mother tutted.

"How rude. Who does she think she is?"

"His agent, doing her job." Her mother frowned. "It's okay, Mom. She probably wanted him to sit with his business associates."

"His place is by your side."

"He'll be by my side tomorrow."

That mollified her mother, somewhat.

She glanced around and spied the Marchands, seated at a table with Ris and Ling and four people she didn't know. Natasha and Boris were seated at another table with another group of people Guin didn't know. And then there was Birdy and Bettina's table.

Guin made small talk with her friends and family, relieved she didn't have to spend the evening putting on an act for Birdy's business associates. Occasionally, she would glance at the other tables. Several times she caught Bettina with her hand on Birdy's arm, leaning into him. Birdy didn't seem to notice, but it annoyed Guin.

She saw Ris, sitting next to Ling, looking like a lovestruck teen, while Ling spoke with Pierre and Paulette and the two other couples. Had he looked that way at her? Guin didn't think so.

She glanced over at Natasha and Boris's table. Boris seemed to be enjoying himself, but Natasha looked bored, like a sullen teen forced to attend her parents' dinner party.

As the dinner plates were being cleared away, Birdy got up and went over to Guin.

"Sorry about that."

"No need to apologize. I know this is as much a business dinner as a rehearsal dinner. I'm just grateful all these people didn't show up for the rehearsal."

Birdy smiled.

"Shall I introduce you to everyone?"

"If you must."

Birdy pulled out her chair, and Guin plastered a smile on her face.

He first led her over to the Marchands' table. They stood there for several minutes, smiling and chatting with everyone, then Birdy excused them and went over to where he had been sitting with Bettina. As Guin had suspected, the people seated there were VIPs, including two VPs from Birdy's, or Wren Finchley's, publisher, as well as two of his sponsors.

Guin smiled politely, looked at Birdy as he spoke, and answered questions when asked. Then they went to Boris and Natasha's table.

"Boris, Natasha, so good of you to come!"

Boris grinned broadly.

"You invite, we come! Besides, I never turn down free food."

Natasha frowned.

"Is everything okay, Natasha?" Birdy asked her.

"I'm bored," she announced. "Can we go now, Boris?"

"But we haven't had dessert!" said Boris. "And I have it on good authority there is chocolate involved!"

Natasha scowled.

"You can get chocolate back at the hotel."

"What's your rush, Natasha?"

Boris looked at Guinivere.

"You are looking particularly lovely this evening, Guinivere. The color red suits you."

Guin felt Boris was undressing her with his eyes but maintained her composure.

"Thank you."

"Now, Boris," said Natasha.

Boris sighed.

"Very well. Will you excuse us, Birdy? Natasha needs her beauty sleep."

Natasha glared at him.

"Of course," said Birdy. "We'll see you tomorrow."

"Ah, yes, tomorrow," said Boris. "When you put on the

proverbial ball and chain." He smiled.

Natasha was standing and tapping her foot.

"I'm coming!" said Boris. He turned to Birdy and in a loud whisper said, "These women, so demanding. Is it not so?"

Birdy just smiled, and he and Guin watched as the two Russians made their exit.

"Well, I think that went rather well, don't you?" said Birdy, as they drove back to Sanibel.

"Hmm?" Guin mumbled. She was finding it difficult to keep her eyes open.

"I said, I thought the rehearsal dinner went well."

Guin nodded then closed her eyes again. She had had only the one margarita and then a glass of wine with dinner, but she was feeling extraordinarily sleepy.

"You okay?" asked Birdy.

"I'm fine. Just sleepy," she said.

A minute later, Birdy heard gentle snoring from the passenger seat and smiled.

"Time to get up, sleepyhead," Birdy said, laying a hand on Guin's arm after he had parked the car in her driveway.

Guin didn't move.

Birdy gave her a gentle shake.

"Guin, wake up. We're home."

Guin's eyes stayed firmly closed.

Birdy gave her a firmer shake.

"Guin, wake up!"

Guin didn't so much as flinch. Birdy frowned. He leaned over to make sure she was breathing. She was, but her lack of movement bothered him. He lifted her wrist and felt for a pulse. It was weak yet stable. He thought about turning around and taking her to the emergency room, but he wondered if he was being paranoid. For all he knew, Guin was a heavy sleeper. A very heavy sleeper.

"I'm taking you back to my place," he told her, putting the SUV back in gear. But Guin didn't reply. She was dead to the world.

CHAPTER 38

"Guin."

Guin didn't move.

"Guin!"

Someone was shaking her.

"Go away," she said.

"It's nearly ten o'clock."

Guin's eyes flew open.

"What?!" She never slept that late. Ever. Her heart was pounding, and her head hurt. She looked around. "Where am I?" she said, confused. Then she spotted Birdy. He seemed worried.

"I was about to call 911."

"How did I get here?" she said, realizing she was in Birdy's bedroom. She looked down and saw she was wearing his Grateful Dead t-shirt. "And why am I wearing your Grateful Dead shirt?"

"You passed out in the car last night. Don't you remember?"

Guin shook her head.

"I tried to wake you up when we got to your place, but you were out like a light. So I took you back here. I had to carry you to bed. What did you have to drink last night?"

"Just a margarita and then a glass of wine at dinner. But that shouldn't have made me pass out like that."

Birdy frowned.

"No, it shouldn't have."

Guin rubbed her head.

"Headache?"

Guin nodded.

"I feel like I was hit with a baseball bat."

"Let me get you some water and a couple of ibuprofen."

He returned a minute later with both and sat next to her on the bed.

"Here," he said.

"Thanks," said Guin, taking the two pills and swallowing them. "I've never had that kind of reaction to alcohol before."

Guin stared out the window. Then suddenly her eyes went wide.

"Oh my God! The wedding! I need to go!"

She made to get up, but Birdy gently laid a hand on her.

"Relax. You've got time. Let me get you something to eat, then I'll drive you home."

"I'm not hungry."

"You should eat."

Guin made a face.

"You going to turn down my world-famous grilled cheese?"

Guin did love a good grilled cheese sandwich.

"Fine. But make it quick. If I'm not at the suite at noon, my mother's going to go ballistic."

"One grilled cheese, coming right up."

As Birdy made the grilled cheese, Guin went to the bathroom and got dressed. Then she headed to the kitchen.

"Here you go," he said, placing the grilled cheese on the counter, along with a mug of black coffee.

Guin closed her eyes and breathed in. She felt better already. She took a sip of the coffee. It was strong, just the way she liked it.

"This is good," she said.

"Glad you approve. Now have a bite of the grilled cheese."

She took a bite and closed her eyes again. The cheese was hot and gooey, and the bread was crispy and buttery.

"Mmm…"

Guin saw Birdy smiling at her when she opened her eyes. "What?"

"I like a woman who enjoys her food. Go on, have some more."

Guin took a couple more bites, which she washed down with coffee. Then she wiped her face and got up.

"I should go."

"But you haven't finished your sandwich."

"I'll take it with me."

"You feeling better?" asked Birdy as he pulled into Guin's driveway. She definitely looked better.

Guin nodded.

"I still don't understand, though. I didn't have that much to drink. It almost feels like I was drugged."

Birdy frowned.

Guin turned to him.

"You don't think someone put something in my wine, do you?" she said, remembering what had happened at the Marchands' engagement party.

Birdy was silent, but she could tell by his expression he was thinking.

"If you hadn't gotten me up, I would have slept right through the wedding," Guin continued. She paused. "You don't think that was their intention, do you, to have me sleep through the wedding?"

"I don't know. If you hadn't told me about the threats, and the other stuff, I would say you were imagining things. But you were pretty passed out for someone who just had a couple of drinks."

Guin nodded.

"Well, I'm okay now." She looked down at the clock. "But if I don't get my butt in gear, my mother's going to kill me."

She grabbed her bag and got out of the SUV.

"Thanks for driving me home."

"My pleasure, Mrs. McMurtry."

Guin stopped.

"You okay?"

Guin had gone a bit pale again.

She composed herself.

"Fine. Just pre-wedding jitters. I'll see you later."

Birdy waved goodbye, and Guin watched as he drove away.

You can still back out, a little voice inside her said.

"No," Guin said aloud. "I've come this far. I need to see it through." *And find out who's trying to kill or scare me*, she said to herself.

As Guin stood in the shower, letting the water cascade over her, she wondered who could have drugged her. Natasha was the obvious candidate. But Natasha had been seated on the other side of the room. Though she could have easily arranged to have something put in her drink or done it when Guin was in the bathroom. Guin frowned. Her head hurt just thinking about it.

She got out and toweled herself off. She looked at her hair, which resembled a poodle's. Fortunately, her new hairstylist, Mick, had agreed to do her hair for the wedding. So she just gave it a quick comb-through, then got dressed.

"Okay," she said to her reflection. "Let's do this!"

She packed a small bag with a change of clothes for the reception, then grabbed the bag with her wedding dress.

She had just said goodbye to Fauna and had opened the

front door when she noticed an envelope lying on her welcome mat. Her arms were full, so she placed her bags in the Mini, then went back to pick up the envelope. She thought about calling the detective, but she was already running late. So she tucked the envelope in the side pocket of the front door, then put the car in gear and headed over to the hotel. But as she drove, she kept glancing down at the envelope.

As soon as she got inside the hotel, she found an empty spot and opened the envelope, even though she knew she might be tampering with evidence. Inside was a folded piece of paper. The envelope and paper were the same as the previous notes. She unfolded the piece of paper and read.

"THIS IS YOUR FINAL WARNING," someone had typed. "MARRY BIRDY AND DIE."

She immediately called Detective O'Loughlin on his cell phone and was surprised when he picked up.

"I got another note."

"Where are you?"

"At the San Ybel. I just got here."

"Meet me in the lobby."

"When?"

"Now."

"You're here?"

"I am. Where are you?"

"In the lobby, but I don't see you."

She turned around and saw him walking toward her.

"Give me the letter," he ordered.

She handed it to him.

"I had to open it, to see if it was like the others."

The detective grunted. First, he examined the envelope. Then he read the piece of paper and turned it over. Guin watched him.

"So? Do you think it was sent by the same person?"

The detective didn't answer. He was still examining the letter and envelope.

"Hello?"

He finally looked up at her.

"When did you receive it?"

"I found it right when I was leaving. But it wasn't there when I got home this morning."

The detective raised an eyebrow.

"What time was that?"

"A little before eleven? Then I was in the shower and getting dressed."

The detective looked thoughtful.

"So the note must have been left between eleven and eleven-forty-five," said Guin.

"And you didn't see anyone?"

"No. But you could always check the Bregmans' cameras."

The detective shot her a look.

If Guin had had the time, she would have asked Sam to review the footage, but she was already running late and didn't know if the Bregmans were even at home.

The detective took out an evidence bag and placed the envelope and letter inside.

"So…?" The detective was stone-faced. "Say something!"

"You know what I'm going to say."

"I am not canceling the wedding."

"Then I have nothing to say."

Guin glared at him.

"Fine. Well, I need to go get ready."

She turned and stalked away.

"It's your funeral," called the detective.

Guin stopped and looked back, but the detective had disappeared.

"Finally!" said her mother. "We were about to send out a search party."

Guin looked over at Shelly, who silently shook her head.

"Sorry I'm late."

"You're not that late," said Shelly. "And Mick and Donna aren't even here yet."

"Is no one on time in this godforsaken place?" asked Guin's mother.

Just then there was a knock on the door.

"I'll get it!" said Shelly.

Guin wanted to tell her to ask who it was before opening the door, but it was too late. She held her breath. Fortunately, it was just Mick, her hairstylist, and Shelly's friend Donna, who was a makeup artist.

"Hey, girl," said Shelly.

"Sorry we're late," said Donna.

"Do you two know each other?" asked Guin, looking from Mick to Donna.

"Oh, yeah," said Donna. "It's a small island."

Mick smiled at Guin.

"You ready?"

"Not really," said Guin. "Sorry about the hair." She held out a wet curl.

"Don't worry," said Mick. "I'll have it looking fabulous in no time."

Guin gazed at herself in the mirror.

"You look beautiful," said Shelly, a tear in her eye.

Guin had to admit, Mick and Donna had worked wonders, and the dress was beautiful.

"Like a movie princess," said Shelly.

"I wouldn't go that far," said Guin, smoothing her dress. But she was pleased with her appearance. She looked over at her mother, who had also had her hair and makeup done, as had Shelly. "You two ready?"

They nodded.

"Then let's go."

The men had gotten ready in a different room. Guin could only imagine what they had talked about. She couldn't picture her stepfather, brother, and brother-in-law palling around with Birdy, Ris, and Pierre Marchand. But then again, Philip, Lance, and Owen were rather good at schmoozing.

Guin had thought about inviting some of her girlfriends from up north down for the wedding. Maybe if it had been a real wedding she would have. But the fewer people she had to deceive, the better. She still felt guilty about lying to her family. Well, maybe not so much to her mother. Though her mother would be furious when Guin announced the marriage was being annulled.

There was a knock at the door. It was Hermione.

"You ready?"

"As ready as I'll ever be."

Hermione smiled, then led her and the rest of the bridal party downstairs to a private cabana near where the ceremony would take place. Guin had been there once before and shivered at the memory.[*]

The music began and Guin closed her eyes. Pierre and Ris would go first, followed by Birdy. Then Lance and Shelly would walk down the aisle, followed by Guin's stepfather and mother, who would be accompanying Guin.

Guin heard the change in the music and braced herself. Philip squeezed her hand.

As she made her way down the aisle, Guin glanced to her left and to her right. She registered Angelique sitting with Jean-Luc and thought she saw Angelique frowning, but she

---

[*] See Book 2, *Something Fishy*

ignored it. She quickly scanned the crowd for Natasha and Boris but didn't spy them.

She reached the end of the aisle, where Birdy and KC were waiting for her. They were smiling. Guin smiled back nervously.

"You look incredible," said Birdy, in a hushed voice, squeezing her hand.

Guin could feel her heart hammering against her rib cage. She knew the wedding was just for show, but it felt very real.

"Dearly beloved and honored guests," began KC, "we are gathered here today in this beautiful spot to join Bertram and Guinivere in the union of marriage. Marriage is an institution not to be entered into lightly…"

Guin's heart was beating so loudly, she could barely hear what KC was saying. She glanced out at the people gathered there. She saw her mother and Philip and Lance and Owen in the front row. And she saw the Marchands and Ris and Ling on the other side.

Over there were Jean-Luc and Angelique. And she spied Craig and Betty and Lenny and Bonnie. All of them were looking at her.

She quickly scanned the rows of seats for Natasha and Boris, but she didn't see them. She also didn't see Bettina. But she assumed she was probably giving orders to one of the photographers or at the reception, making sure everything was perfect.

A flash went off, startling Guin. Birdy squeezed her hand.

"So if anyone here can show just cause why this couple cannot lawfully be joined together in matrimony," KC intoned, "let them speak now or forever hold their peace."

Guin glanced out into the crowd. Then she felt a sharp pain in her right shoulder. Someone shouted her name. Then she fainted dead away.

CHAPTER 39

"Thank God."

Guin opened her eyes and saw Birdy looking down at her, the expression on his face a mixture of worry and relief. Her vision was a bit blurry, and her head, right shoulder, and right arm hurt. She looked down and realized she was in a hospital bed and that her right side was heavily bandaged.

"What happened?" she asked Birdy.

"You were shot."

Guin closed her eyes, trying to remember. She recalled standing at the altar. Then being hit with a sharp pain near her right shoulder blade. Then nothing.

"You're going to be okay though. The bullet missed your vital organs."

"Good to know." She opened her eyes and spied Detective O'Loughlin standing near the door. "Did you catch the gunman?" she asked him.

The detective nodded.

"And?"

"He's not talking."

Guin registered that it was he, not a she.

"Anyone I know?"

"You know any hitmen?"

"So, you think it was a professional hit?"

"Looked that way."

"Does the guy have a record?"

"We're running a background check. But we don't think he's from around here."

"Here as in the Sanibel-Fort Myers area?"

"Here as in this country."

Guin continued to look at him, wishing he'd come closer.

"What does that mean?"

"It means he's not a native."

"Where's he from?"

"Judging by his accent? I'd say Eastern Europe or Russian."

Guin turned to Birdy.

"You catch a glimpse of him?"

Birdy shook his head.

"You wouldn't happen to know any Eastern European or Russian hitmen vacationing in the area, would you, Mr. McMurtry?" the detective asked him.

Birdy's expression turned sour. He didn't respond.

"Anyone else get shot?" Guin asked Detective O'Loughlin.

"No," he replied.

"Though your mother and one of the other guests fainted," said Birdy.

"Are they okay?"

"Your mother's fine. In fact, she claimed she didn't really faint."

Guin smiled.

"And the other one?"

"Also fine."

"And no one else was shot or injured?"

"No," repeated the detective. "There was only the one shot. He knew what he was doing."

Guin frowned.

"So, when can I get out of here?"

"When the doctor says it's okay," said Birdy.

"Any idea when that might be?"

"Soon, hopefully."

Guin turned back to the detective.

"How did you catch the gunman?"

"We had men stationed around the venue. Officer Pettit saw him right after the shot was fired and tackled him."

"Very brave of him."

The detective grunted.

"He should have taken him out before he took the shot."

"What about the gun?"

"The shooter dropped it, but we found it."

"You think the shooter was the same guy who took out my tire?"

"It's possible. Ballistics is running tests on the weapon."

"And is Officer Pettit okay?"

"He'll live."

"Good," said Guin. She leaned back and closed her eyes.

"You're lucky to be alive," said the detective.

Guin didn't respond.

"I need to go."

"So go," said Guin, not opening her eyes.

The detective paused.

"I need you to promise me something."

Guin opened her eyes and looked over at him.

"I need you to promise me that you'll stay out of this."

"You know I can't do that."

The detective scowled and looked at Birdy.

"You seem to be good at persuading her. Convince her to stick to human interest stories and restaurant openings."

"I'll try, but I doubt she'll listen."

"I'm injured, not deaf, detective," Guin said, scowling back at him. "And it's my life. I deserve to know who wanted to end it."

"Fine. Be stubborn," said the detective.

He glared at her, then turned and left.

A few seconds later, there was a knock on the door. Guin wondered if it was the detective, coming back to tell her he was sorry. But, of course, it wasn't him. It was the doctor. He entered the room and went over to Guin.

"How are you feeling?"

"Great," said Guin sarcastically.

He picked up her chart and examined it. Then he went over to her right side.

"May I?" he asked.

"Be my guest."

Guin closed her eyes and grit her teeth as he examined her. The pain was excruciating.

"So, am I going to live?" she asked him when he was done.

He smiled.

"Yes. You were very lucky. The bullet just missed your subclavian and axillary arteries."

Guin had no idea what he was talking about, though it sounded like good news.

"Sorry. It means your shoulder should be fine in a few weeks."

Guin jerked, then winced.

"A few *weeks*?"

She winced again.

"Are you in a lot of pain?"

"I am, but I can handle it."

She desperately wanted something for the pain, but she was afraid of getting hooked on painkillers.

"You don't need to suffer, Ms. Jones. I can prescribe something to ease the pain."

"I don't want opioids."

The doctor smiled.

"I'll prescribe something non-addictive."

"Thank you."

He went to leave, but Guin stopped him.

"When can I get out of here?"

"We want to keep you under observation for another

twenty-four hours. To make sure there's no infection and you're healing properly."

Guin wasn't happy about staying in the hospital overnight, but she didn't protest.

"Thank you, doctor," she said politely.

"You're welcome," he replied. "I'll see you in the morning."

He left, and Guin turned to Birdy.

"You don't have to stay."

"Nonsense," he replied. "My place is here, by your side."

"You can quit with the act, Birdy. We don't have an audience."

"I wasn't acting."

Guin sighed.

"Does my family know that I'm okay?"

Birdy nodded.

"Your brother and Owen are here."

"At the hospital? Why didn't you say so? Tell them to come in."

"I'll go get them."

Birdy started to go, but Guin stopped him.

"Wait. What about the wedding? I don't remember. Did we get married?"

Birdy shook his head.

"No. You were shot before KC was able to finish the ceremony."

"Thank God," said Guin, relieved.

Birdy looked hurt. Then Guin remembered something.

"I don't recall seeing Boris and Natasha. Were they there?"

"I'm pretty sure I saw them just before the ceremony. Why?"

"No reason." Though Guin had her suspicions. "Would you please tell Lance and Owen to come in?"

CHAPTER 40

Guin could tell by the look on her brother's face that he had been worried.

"Thank God you're okay," he said, clasping her left hand. "I thought I'd lost you."

"It'll take more than a little bullet to get rid of me," said Guin.

Lance squeezed her hand and smiled.

"So, how are you feeling?"

"Like I was shot. But the doctor said the bullet missed my major organs. So I should be out of here tomorrow."

"Tomorrow? Isn't that rushing things? That bullet could have killed you, Guinivere."

"But it didn't, Lancelot."

Lance scowled, and Guin mirrored his expression.

"Behave, both of you," said Owen, who had been hanging back.

Guin glanced over at him, then turned back to her brother.

"Sorry. It's just you know how I hate hospitals."

"No one likes being in the hospital, Guinivere, but your body needs to heal. It's gone through a trauma."

Guin made a face.

"Just promise me you won't try to leave until the doctor says it's okay."

"I promise."

"Good girl." He gave her left hand another squeeze.

"So, any idea who took that shot at you?" asked Owen.

"Do you think it could have been that contractor?" said Lance.*

Guin stared at her brother. She had forgotten about Tony Del Sole.

"I don't think it was him. He's on trial, and I don't think he'd be foolish enough to hire someone to knock me off while his case was being decided."

Lance didn't look convinced.

"We're just glad you're okay," said Owen.

Guin smiled up at him.

"Thank you, Owen."

Then she turned back to her brother.

"How's Mom?"

"She seemed okay when we left. Philip was with her."

"Does she know that I'm okay?"

Lance nodded.

"Well, that's good. Philip probably took her back to Naples."

"I assume so."

"Should we call her?"

"Your call. You up for it?"

Guin thought about it, then nodded.

"You sure?"

"May as well get it over with."

Lance took out his phone and made the call.

"Hi, Mom," he began. "Yes, she's fine. They're keeping her in the hospital overnight." There was a pause. "You want to talk to her?"

He looked over at Guin, and she reached out her left hand.

"Hey, Mom."

"Thank God you are all right, Guinivere."

---

* See Book 6, *Trouble in Paradise*

"As Lance said, I'm fine."

"You are *not* fine. You were shot on your wedding day. You could have died."

Guin rolled her eyes.

"But I didn't. And with luck I should be out of here tomorrow."

"Is that what the doctor said? That's way too soon. Let me speak to him."

"He's not here."

"Do not leave that hospital until I've spoken with the doctor in charge. You hear me, Guinivere?"

"Loud and clear, Mother."

"How's Birdy? Is he there with you? The poor man was beside himself."

"He's fine. He stepped out so that Lance and Owen could visit with me."

"You should have seen his face after you collapsed, Guinivere. The man was devastated."

"He was?"

For some reason that surprised Guin.

"You should have heard him, shouting for someone to call 911 and arguing with that detective. He wouldn't leave your side and insisted on going with you in the ambulance."

Guin didn't know what to say.

"I have to confess, Guinivere, I wasn't sure about Birdy when I first met him. But after today, I'd be proud to call him my son-in-law."

Guin closed her eyes. How was her mother going to react when she told him she and Birdy would not be getting married? For she knew without a doubt she could not go through with another fake wedding.

"Hey, Mom, I'm kind of tired," she said, faking a yawn. "I'll talk to you tomorrow."

Before her mother could reply, Guin handed her brother back his phone.

"Hey, Mom. I'll fill you in when we get back to the hotel."

He ended the call and put the phone away, then looked at Guin, who yawned for real this time.

"We should let you get some rest."

He leaned over and kissed her on the forehead.

"Thanks for visiting."

"Of course!" said Lance. "Just don't give the doctors and nurses a hard time."

"What do you mean?" said Guin. "I would never…"

"You know what I mean."

"Come on. Let's let Guin get some sleep," said Owen, gently pulling Lance away.

"See you tomorrow," said Lance.

Guin yawned again, then closed her eyes.

The next morning Guin was awakened by a nurse coming to check her vitals. Guin hadn't thought she had slept, the pain in her shoulder constantly waking her up, but clearly she had.

She asked the nurse if everything was okay, and the nurse informed her that the doctor would be in later to check on her. Not the answer she was hoping for, but she didn't press, remembering what her brother had said. Instead, she thanked the nurse, who smiled at Guin as she finished up.

As soon as the nurse left, Guin picked up the remote for the television. She flipped through the channels and settled on *Good Morning America*. She had only been watching for a few minutes when there was a knock at the door.

"Come in!" she called.

It was a young man, an orderly, carrying a tray. He smiled at Guin.

"Breakfast!"

"I always wanted breakfast in bed," Guin said, smiling at the young orderly. "What's on the menu?"

"French toast with fresh fruit."

"Really?" Guin loved French toast.

The orderly removed the plastic dome covering the tray.

"See for yourself."

Guin stared. It was indeed French toast, and it didn't look half bad.

"Any chance I could get some coffee?"

"Sorry, no caffeine. Doctor's orders. But there's some fresh orange juice."

"Thanks," said Guin. Though she was craving some dark roast.

"Can I get you anything else?"

"Could you refill my pitcher of water?"

"Coming right up!" said the orderly.

He took the empty carafe and returned a minute later.

"Here you go! I filled it with ice, so it'll stay cooler longer."

"Thank you," said Guin. "Any idea when the doctor will be stopping by?"

"I saw him down the hall. He should be here soon."

"Thanks," said Guin. She picked up the fork and knife and cut herself a piece of the French toast.

"Just leave your tray wherever when you're done," said the orderly. "Someone will pick it up later."

Guin nodded, her mouth full. Then the orderly left.

She had barely gotten halfway through her breakfast when there was another knock on her door.

It's like Grand Central Station, she said to herself.

"Come in!" she called, her mouth full of French toast.

It was the doctor.

"Feeling a bit better?" he asked her.

Guin nodded, then swallowed the bite of French toast.

"If I say yes, can I go home today?"

The doctor smiled at her.

"How did you sleep?"

"Not great. But I think it's because I'm not used to sleeping in a hospital, or being shot."

The doctor didn't reply. He was busy examining her chart. When he was done, he looked over at her.

"Shall we take a look at that shoulder?"

"Be my guest."

He moved the tray table aside, then gently examined her. Guin tried not to wince.

"It's going to be sore for a while, I'm afraid."

"So, can I go home? I definitely feel better than I did yesterday."

The doctor smiled.

"That's probably the pain medication. I'd like to keep you here a bit longer. Make sure everything's okay. We should have the test results back this afternoon."

"Test results?"

"Nothing to worry about."

"But if everything's okay, I can go home later?"

"If everything checks out, and there's someone who can look after you. You're going to need help for a least a week or two."

Guin frowned.

The doctor made some notes on her chart, then looked over at her again.

"I'll check in later. In the meantime, if you need anything, press the nurse-call button."

"Will do," she replied.

The doctor left and Guin looked over at her breakfast tray. She was no longer hungry. She went to grab her phone and realized it wasn't there. She must have left it in the bridal suite. Hopefully, Shelly had it.

She was about to press the nurse-call button, to find out how she could make a call, when there was another knock at the door.

"Come in!" she called, thinking it was the orderly,

coming to remove the breakfast tray. Instead, it was Craig.

"Craig! What are you doing here?"

"Betty and I have been worried sick about you."

"You didn't have to come all the way here. I should be going home soon."

Craig frowned.

"They're discharging you already?" He shook his head. "And as for not coming here, don't be ridiculous. You know you're like family to us."

Guin felt her eyes tearing up.

"You in a lot of pain?"

"No. I'm just a bit emotional. Probably the drugs." She saw that Craig had a paper bag in his hand. "What's that?" she said.

Craig looked down at the bag.

"Betty made you a little something."

He went over to the bed and handed her the bag. Guin looked inside and smiled.

"Betty's famous bran muffins."

Craig nodded.

"She made them fresh this morning."

"Please thank her for me."

"I will."

"So, you hear anything?"

"About?"

"About who shot me."

Craig frowned again.

"Shouldn't you be taking it easy?"

"I need to know, Craig. And you know the detective isn't going to tell me anything."

Craig sighed.

He was about to say something when the door flew open and Shelly rushed in.

"Thank goodness!" she said, making a beeline for Guin. "I've been worried sick. I wanted to come straight over last night, but the detective said only family."

"It's okay, Shell. I'm fine."

"You don't look fine," she said, taking in Guin's heavily bandaged right side.

"It looks worse than it is."

Shelly's face said she didn't believe her. Then she noticed Craig.

"Oh, hi Craig. Didn't see you there."

Then she turned back to Guin.

"So, how long are they keeping you?"

"Hopefully, just until this afternoon."

"Really? That seems awfully short."

"The doctor said if the tests came back negative, I could go home."

Shelly looked again at Guin's heavily bandaged shoulder.

"You going to be able to dress or feed yourself?"

"I'll manage."

Shelly shook her head.

"You're going to stay with me and Steve."

Guin opened her mouth to speak, but Shelly cut her off.

"And I won't take no for an answer."

"You can always stay with us," said Craig. "Betty would love to have you. She was a nurse, you know, back before we had kids."

"Thanks, both of you," said Guin. "But I just want to go home. And what about Fauna?"

Shelly was about to say something when Guin noticed what looked like her handbag on Shelly's arm.

"Hey, is that my bag?"

Shelly looked down at the bag and nodded.

"It is. I took it from the bridal suite. Thought you might want it."

"Bless you," said Guin. "Is my phone in there?"

Shelly checked. It was.

"You want it?"

Guin held out her left hand.

"Please."

Shelly handed her the phone. The battery was almost empty. Guin frowned.

"What's wrong?"

"The battery's almost drained, and I don't have a charger."

"I'll get you one," said Shelly.

Craig cleared his throat.

"I should get going." He leaned over. "And I'll look into that matter you asked me about," he said in a low voice.

"That would be great. Thank you."

He turned and headed to the door.

"And please thank Betty for the muffins!"

He held up a hand in acknowledgment, then left.

"So, is there anything else you need?" asked Shelly.

Guin thought.

"I don't think so. As I said, I'm hoping to be out of here tonight."

"Are you sure that's a good idea?"

"I hate hospitals. You know that."

"But you were shot."

"But the bullet didn't do any serious damage."

Shelly looked skeptical.

"Really, Shell, I'm fine."

Shelly sighed.

"Fine. Let me see if I can find you a charger."

"Thanks."

She left, and Guin turned the television back on.

CHAPTER 41

Shelly was back a short time later with a charger. Guin had no idea how she found one so quickly, but she didn't ask. She just thanked her and plugged it in. Then Shelly said she had to dash, but Guin should call her if she needed anything, including a ride home. No sooner had Shelly gone than Lance arrived, together with Birdy. Guin wondered if they had come together, but no, they just happened to have arrived at the hospital at the same time. Guin asked Birdy to wait outside while she spoke with her brother.

Lance informed her that he would be staying a few extra days, to make sure she was okay. Guin was grateful but said he didn't have to. She knew how important his business was.

"Nothing's more important than family," he told her.

Would their mother also be extending her visit? Guin asked him. He nodded. Guin was less enthusiastic about that, but she knew she couldn't order her mother back to New York.

There was a knock on the door. It was Birdy, asking if he could come in. Lance said he had to go anyway—he had calls with clients—and excused himself.

Birdy went over to the bed. He looked like he hadn't slept or shaved in days, but Guin didn't say anything. He held her left hand and again told her how sorry he was. Guin told him it wasn't his fault, though they both knew in some sense it was. Then they made small talk until there was another knock on the door.

"I'm very popular," Guin informed Birdy, smiling as she said it.

The doctor entered, and he had good news. The test results were negative, so the hospital would be discharging her that afternoon, provided she had someone at home to take care of her. Birdy informed the doctor that he would personally be attending to Guin. And while Guin scowled, she didn't say anything, wanting to leave the hospital as soon as possible.

Birdy left shortly after the doctor did, but he said he would be back to escort her home. Guin then spent the next few hours switching between reading on her phone and watching television, waiting to be discharged.

Finally, it was time to go. A female orderly came in to help Guin get dressed, then wheeled her to the elevator (the hospital requiring all patients to be discharged in a wheelchair) and out to where Birdy's SUV would collect her.

Birdy had wanted to take Guin back to his place, but she insisted on him taking her home. She was worried about Fauna and wanted to be around her own things, sleep in her own bed. Birdy relented, but only on the condition that he stay there with her. They argued, finally arriving at a compromise: Birdy would stay at her place just until her checkup. And he would sleep in the guest room.

When they arrived at Guin's house, Birdy helped her out of the SUV and opened the door for her. Then he told her he would be back later with his things. Guin told him to take his time. Birdy smiled and said he would be back in time to make dinner.

True to his word, he returned a little before six with not only a suitcase but two bags of groceries. He then proceeded to make dinner. Guin, who was reclining on the couch, watched him. She had no idea he could cook.

When dinner was ready, he brought it over to her on a tray and sat down next to her. He had made steak and roasted vegetables, along with some brown rice.

"This is really good," said Guin, taking another bite of steak. She hadn't realized how hungry she was and ate every last bite of food on her plate. "Where did you learn to cook?"

Birdy smiled.

"I taught myself. My parents both worked, sometimes quite late. I would get hungry and grew bored eating peanut butter and jelly or cheese sandwiches. So I started to experiment. A lot of my early efforts were disasters. But eventually I got the hang of it and rather enjoyed cooking for myself and later my friends."

"Well, the steak was excellent, and so was the veg. Thank you."

"My pleasure. I was thinking I would make fish tomorrow."

"You really don't have to."

"I told you, I enjoy it."

Guin looked at him. Maybe Birdy was serious about settling down. She shook her head. She couldn't really imagine him setting up house. Travel was in his blood.

"What about your book tour?"

"It doesn't start up again for a couple of weeks."

Then Guin remembered: the honeymoon.

"I hope you were able to get a refund on the honeymoon."

Birdy smiled.

"Is that what you're worried about?"

"Where were we going anyway?"

"Do you really want to know?"

Guin hesitated.

"Maybe. No, don't tell me."

Birdy was about to say something when Guin's phone started vibrating on the coffee table. It was Shelly. She picked it up and swiped.

"Hey, Shell. What's up?"

"You okay?"

"I am."

"Is Birdy taking good care of you?"

"He is."

"Good. Just checking. Do you need anything from Bailey's? I'm happy to do a grocery run for you."

"Actually, Birdy already went shopping."

"He did?"

Guin nodded.

"And made me dinner. Turns out, he's a pretty good cook."

Birdy preened.

"Is there nothing that man can't do?" said Shelly. "Well, he may be a good cook, but nothing beats my world-famous chicken soup for curing whatever ails you."

"World-famous, eh?"

Guin smiled, then yawned.

"You tired?"

"A little," said Guin, yawning again.

"Well, I'll let you go. Get a good night's rest. I'll text you in the morning."

Guin yawned again, then said goodbye. Birdy was looking at her.

"I don't know why I'm so tired," she said.

"I do," he replied. "Let me get you into bed."

Guin gave him a look.

Birdy sighed.

"You know what I mean."

"What time is it?"

"A little after eight."

"It's too early to go to bed."

"You can always read a book."

"Fine."

She made to get off the couch and winced.

"Let me help you," said Birdy, bending down.

She pushed off him with her left hand.

"I can take it from here," she informed him, once she was vertical.

He followed her into the bedroom.

"Let me help you get undressed."

"Thanks," said Guin. "But I'm good."

Birdy glanced at her right shoulder, which was still bandaged.

"I can do it, Birdy."

He didn't move.

"Fine. You stay there. I'm going to my closet."

She turned and went to get changed. But as soon as she raised her right arm, she felt a shooting pain down her right side and howled. A second later, Birdy was there.

"Are you okay?"

Guin felt as though she was about to cry. She hated feeling helpless.

"I can't get this stupid shirt off."

Birdy went over and without saying a word helped her get undressed and put on an oversized nightshirt.

"I can take it from here," she said, heading to the bathroom.

She emerged a short time later to find Birdy still in her bedroom, though he was now dressed in a pair of drawstring pajama bottoms, his top bare. Guin stared at him.

"I told you I was fine."

"But you're clearly not."

He pulled back the quilt and sheet and patted the bed. Guin didn't move.

"Get into bed."

"Not if you're here. We had a deal."

Birdy sighed.

"I'll go down the hall to the guest room as soon as you get into bed."

Guin eyed him suspiciously.

"I promise. Now, come on, get into bed."

Guin slowly walked over to the bed and got in, propping herself up against the pillows Birdy had fluffed for her.

"See? Perfectly fine."

Birdy regarded her. He clearly didn't think so. But he wasn't going to argue with her.

"Very well. I will now go down the hall to the guest room, as promised. But if you should need me…"

"I won't," said Guin. She watched as Birdy made his way to the door. "And close the door!" she called. But he ignored her, leaving the door ajar.

That night, Guin slept fitfully. Despite being surrounded by pillows, so she wouldn't roll onto her right side, she would periodically roll over anyway and be awakened by a spear of pain. She thought about taking the sleeping pills the doctor had prescribed, but she was paranoid about becoming addicted. Finally, though, she slept. And it was six-thirty when she looked at her clock.

She gingerly got out of bed and made her way to the kitchen. There was no sign of Birdy, but the coffee maker was on the counter, and the carafe was filled.

"Birdy?" she called. There was no answer.

She reached into the cabinet with her left hand to get a mug, then poured herself some coffee. She inhaled, closing her eyes. Was there an aroma more heavenly than freshly brewed coffee? She lifted the mug and took a sip. It was strong, just how she liked it.

She stood at the counter, looking out at the backyard. She realized she had left her phone in her bedroom and went to retrieve it. As soon as she turned it on, the message light began flashing.

She checked her text messages first. Craig and Shelly had both written to her, wanting to know how she was doing.

She wrote them both back, then asked Craig if he had heard anything. A few seconds later, her phone rang. It was Craig.

"Hey there," she said.

"I'm not waking you, am I?"

"I just texted you, remember?"

"Right. Sorry. I was up late, looking into that matter we discussed."

"You find out anything?"

"I did. The shooter's from Orlando, at least according to his driver's license. Though he's originally from Eastern Europe."

Orlando, thought Guin. *And Eastern Europe*. It couldn't be a coincidence.

"Did you find out who hired him?"

"He says he doesn't know. Just that he believed it was a woman."

"Why did he think it was a woman?"

"I didn't get the details."

Guin looked thoughtful.

"Anything else?"

"No. They're still questioning him. He has an attorney."

Great, thought Guin. *Now they'll never get anything out of him.*

"I can hear those gears turning," said Craig.

"I was just thinking that it can't be a coincidence that the shooter is from Eastern Europe and lives in Orlando, where Natasha is teaching."

"You may be onto something."

"I just wish I knew who left those notes."

Then she remembered: the Bregmans' cameras.

"Hey, Craig, I need to go. Check-in with you later?"

"Fine. Just remember to take it easy."

"Yeah, yeah, yeah," said Guin. "Birdy's here looking after me."

"Good. But if you need anything, just call."

"I will. Talk to you later."

She hung up, then walked back into her bedroom. She stared at her clothes. It would be impossible to change without help. And Birdy wasn't around. She looked down at her nightshirt and sighed. It was an extra-large t-shirt that came down to just above her knees. It would have to do.

She walked to the front hall closet and put on a pair of flip-flops, then left. There were lights on in the Bregmans' house. A good sign. She rang the doorbell and waited.

"Coming! Coming!" called a female voice.

The door opened to reveal Sadie Bregman. She stared at Guin as though looking at a ghost.

"Sorry for the apparel. I need a favor."

Sadie continued to stare.

"Can I come in?"

Sadie nodded and let Guin in.

"Thank you," said Guin.

"Shouldn't you be in the hospital?"

Guin smiled.

"They let me out for good behavior."

Sadie looked suspicious.

"I'm fine. Really. The bullet missed my vital organs, and there was no internal bleeding or infection. So they let me go home."

"Still, you should be in bed. You don't look so good."

"I promise I'll go right back to bed after I've talked to Sam."

Sadie raised an eyebrow.

"Is he around?"

"He's in his office. Why?"

"I need to take a look at some footage from your security cameras."

"And it can't wait?"

"No. Please, Sadie. I promise I'll go right back to bed after I see the footage."

Sadie sighed and shook her head.

"I'll be right back."

She returned a couple of minutes later.

"Come with me."

Guin followed her down the hall to Sam's office.

"Shouldn't you be in bed?" he said to her, taking in her nightshirt.

"I know, but I really need to see this footage. I won't rest until I do."

Sam and Sadie exchanged a look.

"Okay," he said. "When exactly are we talking about?"

Guin gave him the information, and Sam got a look on his face.

"That's the same footage the detective wanted."

Of course, thought Guin.

"Just give me a minute to cue it up."

"Aren't you going to offer her a seat?" demanded Sadie.

"Sorry," he said, getting up. He pulled over a chair and indicated for Guin to sit. Then he went back to his computer. "Here you go!" he said a minute later. He pressed play, and they watched.

A few seconds into the video, a biker appeared. It was a woman. And Guin was pretty sure it was the same woman she had seen before, even though she couldn't see her face since she was wearing a helmet and large sunglasses. She disappeared from view a few seconds later.

"Can you replay it, Sam?"

He nodded his head and rewound the video. Then he hit play.

"Can you replay it one more time and slow it down?"

Sam did as he was told.

As the biker zipped by, Guin thought she saw something flash on the biker's left hand.

"Stop there!" she commanded.

He paused the video, but it was too blurry to make out anything.

"Can I get a copy of the footage?" she asked him.

"Sure," said Sam. "You have one of them thumb drives?"

"Not on me," said Guin.

"That's okay," he replied. "I probably have one you can borrow." He rooted around in his drawers. "Here you go," he said, holding up a small rectangular object maybe an inch long. "Let me just make sure there's nothing important on it."

He checked and proclaimed it good to go. Then he saved the footage to it and handed the drive to Guin.

"Thank you," said Guin. "I'll give it back when I'm done."

"No hurry," said Sam.

"Can I get you something to eat?" asked Sadie.

"Thank you, but I should get home."

"You sure?"

"Really, I'm good. But thank you."

Sadie saw her to the door and told her to take care of herself.

As soon as Guin got home, she went to her office and turned on her computer. Then she inserted the thumb drive. She watched the video several times, stopping it as soon as she saw the flash on the biker's left hand. But she was unable to see what was causing it. Could it be a ring? She wished she had video editing software, but she knew someone who did.

She sent Glen a text, asking him to call her.

A few minutes later, her phone began to vibrate. It was Glen.

"What's this I hear about you getting shot?"

Wow, Guin thought. *Word traveled fast.*

"I'm fine. The shooter had bad aim."

"Glad to hear it. So, what's up?"

"I need a favor."

"Shoot."

She could hear Glen wince.

"Sorry," he said. "Poor choice of word."

"It's okay," said Guin. "Can I send you footage of a woman riding a bicycle by my house? I got it from my next-door-neighbors' security camera. I want to find out if she's wearing a ring on her left hand, and if there's anything else that may help identify her."

"You think she had something to do with the shooting?"

"Maybe. Can you take a look this morning?"

"I'll make it a top priority."

"Great," said Guin. "Thank you."

"And Guin?"

"Yes?"

"I'm really glad you're okay."

"I am too."

They said goodbye and ended the call.

Guin was in the process of sending Glen the footage when she heard someone clearing his throat behind her. She turned to see Birdy.

"Where were you?"

"Did you miss me?"

Guin made a face.

"I was out."

"Obviously. Thanks, by the way, for the coffee."

"You're welcome. Did you have breakfast yet?"

Guin thought about lying.

"No, but I've been busy. And I could really use a shower."

She immediately regretted her words.

"I'd be happy to help," said Birdy, smiling at her.

Guin knew that look.

"That's okay," she said. "I'll manage."

"Don't be ridiculous. Let me help you."

Guin gingerly lifted her right arm, to test it out, and felt pain crashing through her. She sighed.

"On one condition."

"Yes?"

"You need to keep your eyes closed."

"Really, Guinivere."

"Swear," said Guin.

"Fine. I promise not to look."

Birdy helped Guin get undressed, then helped her get into another extra-large nightshirt when she was done, Guin having decided not to bother with real clothes for another day.

"You can go now," she informed him.

"I told the hospital and your family I'd take care of you."

"That doesn't mean hovering over me twenty-four-seven. And besides, Shelly's coming over."

"Fine. But shout if you need me."

"I'll be sure to do that."

Birdy turned to go then stopped.

"By the way, Bettina's coming over later."

"What? Why?" said Guin. Bettina was the last person she wanted to see.

"She had the food from the wedding boxed up, along with the wedding cake, and wanted to personally deliver it."

Guin had forgotten about the wedding cake. But no way could she eat the whole thing.

"She should have donated everything to F.I.S.H." F.I.S.H. was the local food pantry.

"That's what Hermione suggested."

"But Bettina ignored her?"

"No, she had Hermione donate most of it to F.I.S.H., but I suggested she save some of it to give to you—along with the cake, of course. It's quite impressive. Jean-Luc outdid himself."

"Fine. So what time will Ms. Betteridge be gracing us with her presence?"

"Around five. I'm going to meet with her beforehand. Go over some things."

"Enjoy," said Guin, turning back to her computer.

"Speaking of food…"

Right, breakfast.

"I'm busy, Birdy," she said, not looking at him.

He didn't budge.

"You need to eat, Guinivere."

She continued to type but couldn't concentrate with Birdy looming over her.

"Fine," she said. "I'll go eat something."

She got up using her left arm and made her way to the kitchen.

"I can make you some eggs and toast," offered Birdy.

"I can feed myself, thank you."

"It's no trouble."

Guin saw the look on his face and gave in.

Ten minutes later, he placed a plate in front of her.

"Voila!"

She stared at the food, then placed some egg on her fork. She took a bite, then another. The eggs were done perfectly. She had a bite of the toast. It was nice and crispy. A few minutes later, the plate was empty.

"I guess you enjoyed it," said Birdy, smiling at her.

"It was all right," said Guin, not wanting to compliment him too much. He had a big enough ego.

Guin went to wash her plate, but Birdy took it from her, saying he'd take of it. She stared at him, then shrugged. Who was she to deprive him of the joy of washing the dishes?

CHAPTER 42

Guin opened her email and saw there was a message from Glen. She clicked on the link and downloaded the file he had sent her. There were several pictures, stills from the footage she had sent him. He had managed to zoom in on the biker's left hand, as Guin had asked him to, and had made some other stills too. The images were still grainy, but they were clearer than what she had been able to see pausing the video.

She stared at the photo of the biker's left hand. She was clearly wearing a ring. Guin squinted. The image was blurry, but something about the ring felt familiar. Like she had seen it before. She stared at it for a few more seconds, then looked at the other photos.

The photos confirmed that the biker was a woman. And she looked to be in good shape. She was wearing a yoga outfit (or what looked to Guin like a yoga outfit) and had her hair pulled back in a folded ponytail, so you could barely see it. But it looked to be blonde.

You still couldn't make out the woman's face as she was in profile, and she was wearing sunglasses and a bike helmet. But the more Guin looked at the photos, the more she was certain she had seen the woman before. Then again, Guin had seen and known a lot of women who looked just like the biker—tall, fit, and blonde—when she had lived in the Northeast. Though you didn't see as many of them on Sanibel.

Guin looked again at the photo of the woman's left hand. Where had she seen a ring like that? It was driving her crazy. If only the image had been sharper, less grainy. Though she knew Glen had done his best.

She picked up her phone and sent him a text, thanking him for the photos.

"Did they help?" he wrote back.

"I'm not sure," Guin replied.

"Let me know if there's anything else I can do."

"I will."

"You need food?"

Guin smiled.

"Thanks, but I'm good. For some reason, everyone's worried about me starving to death."

"Well, if you need anything, just let me know."

"I will."

Guin paused, then began to type again.

"Everything okay with you?"

"Yup."

There was another pause. Then Glen sent her another text.

"You still getting married?"

"No," she wrote back.

She waited for Glen to text her, but there was no reply, and she had a call coming in. It was her mother. She thought about ignoring it but picked up.

"Hi, Mom. What's up?"

"We thought we'd join you for lunch."

"Why?"

"What do you mean, why? I should think it would be obvious."

Guin was about to say something snarky but held her tongue.

"You really don't have to come all the way to Sanibel, Mom."

"Nonsense, Guinivere. You are my daughter, and you are not well."

"I'm not sick, Mom. I was shot."

"You know what I meant. We're coming, and that's that."

"We?"

"Lancelot and I."

Well, at least her brother would be there.

"What would you like us to get you?"

"You don't need to get me anything. I have food here."

Guin heard someone speaking to her mother in the background.

"Your brother wants to speak with you."

"Hey, Sis," said Lance, taking the phone.

"What's up?"

"I told Mom we should stop at Too Jays as I know how you like their sandwiches and it's on the way."

"In that case, get me a turkey and pastrami on rye."

"Will do. Anything else?"

"Some coleslaw." She paused. "And maybe a piece of Banana Dream cake?"

"Done. Should we get something for Birdy too?"

Guin thought for a minute.

"I think he's meeting someone for lunch."

"Okay," said Lance.

"So what time do you think you'll be here?"

"I'm thinking a little after noon."

Good, she had some time to mentally prepare herself.

"Okay, see you soon."

The doorbell rang, and Guin heard Birdy say he would get it. She hadn't realized he was there and felt bad for not ordering him something. A minute later, she heard her mother's voice. Guin took a deep breath and slowly exhaled, then plastered a smile on her face.

"Mom," she said, emerging from her office.

"You look a bit peaked," said her mother, eyeing her. "Are you not sleeping?" She turned to Birdy. "Has she been eating?"

Birdy opened his mouth to speak, but Guin cut him off.

"I'm perfectly fine, Mom. Birdy's been making sure I eat. It turns out, he's a pretty good cook."

Birdy smiled at her.

"So what are Philip and Owen up to?"

"They went to check out some art galleries in Naples," Lance informed her. He looked down at the Too Jays bag he was holding, then at Birdy. "Sorry we didn't get you anything. Guin thought you had lunch plans."

"I do," said Birdy. "Speaking of which, I need to head out."

"Who are you having lunch with again?" asked Guin.

Birdy hesitated.

"Angelique."

Guin frowned.

"Who is Angelique?" asked her mother, looking at her daughter, then Birdy.

"An old friend."

"How old?"

Guin looked at Lance, who just shook his head. Once their mother got going, there was no stopping her.

"I should get going," said Birdy. "Good to see you, Carol." He turned to Guin. "I'll be back this afternoon."

"No hurry," said Guin.

"So, where should we eat?" asked Lance once Birdy had left.

"The dining table?"

"Sounds good. Where do you keep your plates and napkins?"

Guin showed him.

"What would you all like to drink?"

"Do you have any white wine?" asked Lance.

"I think Birdy brought over a couple of bottles."

"Just one will do," he replied, smiling.

"Ha ha. Go check the fridge." She turned to her mother. "Mom?"

"Water, no ice."

Guin got her mother a glass of water, then poured one for herself.

Lunch went surprisingly well, thought Guin. Lance kept their mother in check (for the most part), and she got to hear the latest about his business and his and Owen's upcoming trip to Italy.

"Well, we should be going," said her mother a little after two. "Philip and I are getting together with Harriet later."

"Tell her I say hi."

Her mother sighed.

"It's a shame about you and Alfred. But... Birdy will make a fine son-in-law."

Guin swallowed.

"Yes, well," she said, not wanting to tell her mother the wedding was off. "So, Lance said you might be staying a few extra days."

"We were planning on it. But with Birdy looking after you, we'll probably fly back on Sunday now."

Guin breathed a sigh of relief. Score one for Birdy.

"What about you, Lance? I'd love to get together with you and Owen before you go."

Lance smiled.

"I think we can arrange something."

They got up from the table, and Guin walked them to the door. Birdy still wasn't back from his lunch date with Angelique, and Guin was feeling a bit uneasy. There was something about Angelique that rubbed her the wrong way.

"Thanks again for coming," said Guin.

"Really, Guinivere. You don't have to thank us. Just let us know when you've rescheduled the wedding. Though I hope it won't be when we're away."

"Uh…" said Guin.

"I assume the hotel will allow you to reschedule it, at no additional cost."

"I don't know about that. I'll need to get back to you."

"Do that." Her mother turned to Lance. "Are you able to drive, Lancelot?"

"I think I can manage," he replied.

He gave his sister a kiss, then escorted their mother to their car.

Guin had nodded off. She had been reading on the couch and the next thing she knew Birdy was calling her name.

"I'm back!" he said. "And Bettina's here with food."

Guin quickly roused herself. She worried she must look a mess, but there was nothing she could do.

She saw Bettina eyeing her. Guin thought she looked like a cat cornering a bird.

"Bettina, it was so thoughtful of you to arrange to have the food boxed up and donated," Guin said, plastering a smile on her face.

"It was the least I could do," said Bettina, who once again looked like she had just stepped off a yacht, making Guin feel self-conscious.

"Here, let me take that," said Guin, reaching with her left hand for the shopping bag Bettina was holding.

Bettina held out the bag, and Guin froze. On Bettina's left ring finger was an exquisite silver or platinum ring in the shape of two birds.

"What a beautiful ring," said Guin, trying not to stare.

"Thank you," said Bettina, smiling down at the ring. "Birdy gave it to me."

Guin looked up at Birdy.

"It was a thank-you, for the Wren Finchley book deal. Bettina got me a very generous advance."

Bettina preened, and Guin continued to stare at the ring. It looked a lot like the one she had seen in the Bregmans' security footage.

"Birdy had it specially made for me," said Bettina.

"So it's one of a kind?"

Bettina nodded and Guin saw the sunglasses perched atop Bettina's head.

"I love your sunglasses. May I see them?"

"My sunglasses?" said Bettina.

"Yes, I'm in the market for a new pair, and those look very chic."

"This old pair?" said Bettina, removing them. "I've had them for ages."

"May I?" said Guin, extending her left hand.

Bettina begrudgingly handed Guin her sunglasses.

They definitely looked like the pair the biker was wearing. She looked up at Bettina. Could she have been the one who left those notes?

"If you're done with my glasses," said Bettina, putting out her hand.

"Of course," said Guin, handing them back to her. "Would you excuse me a minute? I need to go freshen up."

Birdy followed her.

"Are you okay? You look a bit pale."

"I'm fine. I just need to go to the bathroom," Guin quietly lied. "I'll be right back. Why don't you fix yourself and Bettina a drink?"

Guin then made her way to her bedroom, closing the door behind her. She removed her phone from her pocket and speed-dialed the detective's cell phone, praying he'd pick up. He did.

"Thank God," she said.

"Are you okay?" he asked her.

"No. I'm pretty sure I know who left me those notes and hired the hitman."

"You do?"

Guin nodded.

"So, you going to tell me, or am I supposed to guess?"

Guin scowled.

"It was Bettina Betteridge."

"And you know this how?"

"I had Glen make some stills from the footage from the Bregmans' security camera. I noticed the biker had something on her left hand, and I wanted to get a closer look."

"And from that you deduced that Ms. Betteridge was the one who left you those notes and hired someone to kill you."

Guin nodded.

"I know you think I'm crazy, but I recognized the ring and the sunglasses. It was Bettina."

There was another pause.

"So, are you going to arrest her?"

"Are you okay?" called Birdy.

Guin put her hand over the phone.

"I'll be out in a minute!"

She returned to the detective.

"I'll have a talk with her," he said.

"You want to come over? She's here now."

There was silence on the line.

"Bill? Are you still there?"

"I'll be right over. Just do me a favor and don't do anything stupid."

CHAPTER 43

Guin went into the bathroom and flushed the toilet. Then she caught her reflection in the mirror. She did look awfully pale, or paler than usual. And her hair was a mess. No wonder Bettina was gloating.

She decided to make herself a bit more presentable. So she combed her hair and applied a little rouge. The she eyed herself in the mirror again.

You can do this, Guin, she told her mirror image. Then she made her way back to the living room.

"You're looking better," said Birdy.

Guin noticed that he and Bettina were drinking white wine. Birdy offered her a glass, but she declined. She wanted to have her wits about her around Bettina. Speaking of Birdy's agent...

"So, how long will you be on Sanibel?" Guin asked her, trying to strike a pleasant tone.

"Not a minute more than I have to," said Bettina, her disdain for the island evident.

"Though I hear it's quite chilly in New York."

"Is it now? Well, I doubt it will be cold in Naples."

Guin wasn't sure if she meant Naples, Italy, or Naples, Florida. With Bettina, you never knew. Then she remembered.

"You're going to see your sister and the baby then?"

Bettina nodded.

"Briony practically begged me to come back. She's totally overwhelmed."

"Nice that you can help out."

"Well, I am the baby's godmother. The child simply adores me. Briony says I'm the only person who can calm little Felicity down."

Guin continued to smile, though it was starting to hurt.

"And Birdy, don't forget. You promised you would visit us."

"You did?" said Guin. Birdy hadn't mentioned anything.

"I'll drive down this weekend." He turned to Guin. "You're welcome to come with me."

"That's okay," said Guin. She had no desire to spend a day with the Betteridge sisters.

Birdy was about to say something else when they heard sirens.

"Someone go over the speed limit?" said Bettina snarkily.

Guin kept her mouth shut as the sirens grew louder. Less than a minute later, she saw the detective's car pull into the driveway, followed by a loud knock at the door. She hurried to get it.

There was Detective O'Loughlin, along with Officer Rodriguez, one of the female officers on the Sanibel Island police force.

"Ms. Jones," said the detective.

"Detective O'Loughlin," she replied. "And Officer Rodriguez. What brings you here?" Though she knew perfectly well.

"May we come in?" asked the detective.

Guin opened the door wider.

"Of course."

"What is this about?" said Birdy, as the detective approached him and Bettina.

"Mr. McMurtry, Ms. Betteridge. Ms. Betteridge, if you wouldn't mind coming with us. I have a few questions I'd like to ask you."

"I mind very much. Where are you taking me? What is this about?"

"To the Sanibel Police Department. Now if you would just come with us," said the detective taking a step toward her.

Bettina didn't move.

"If there's something you wish to ask me, Detective, ask me here. I have nothing to hide."

"What is this about?" said Birdy.

Guin and the detective exchanged a look.

"It concerns the incident involving Ms. Jones."

"You mean the shooting?"

"And the death threats she received."

Guin stole a glance at Bettina.

"Surely, you don't think Bettina was involved?" said Birdy.

"We're speaking with everyone involved with the wedding, Mr. McMurtry, as well as those who might have a grudge against Ms. Jones."

"Must be a long list," muttered Bettina.

Birdy shot her a warning look.

"Now if you would just come with us, Ms. Betteridge," said Detective O'Loughlin.

Bettina glared at him.

"This is ridiculous! I demand to speak with my attorney!"

"There's no need for an attorney, Ms. Betteridge," said the detective. "We'd just like you to answer a few questions."

He sounded calm, but Guin could sense he was becoming impatient.

"Go with Detective O'Loughlin," said Birdy, laying a hand on her arm. "As the detective said, it's just routine. I'm sure you'll be back at the hotel before the end of cocktail hour," he added, smiling.

Guin wasn't so sure about that, but she didn't say anything.

"Fine," said Bettina, rising. She looked down at the detective, who was a couple of inches shorter than her in her heels. "Shall we?" Without waiting for him, she made her way to the front door, then stopped. "You coming?"

"Ms. Jones," said the detective, giving Guin a quick nod. Then he and Officer Rodriguez followed Bettina out. When they had gone, Birdy turned to Guin. She could tell something was bothering him.

"How did Detective O'Loughlin know Bettina was here?"

Guin found it difficult to look him in the eye.

"What is it you're not telling me, Guinivere?"

Guin thought about lying but knew she couldn't.

"I called him when I went into the bedroom," she blurted. Birdy raised his eyebrows. "Bettina was the one who left me those threatening notes. I'm sure of it. I'm also pretty sure she hired the man who shot me."

"That's ridiculous," said Birdy. "Why on earth would Bettina do such a thing?"

Guin gave him a look. Did he really not know?

"She was afraid of losing you."

"What are you talking about?"

"Bettina loves you and hates me. She probably thought that if you married me, I'd convince you to fire her."

"I would never fire Bettina."

"Does she know that?"

"I would assume so."

"You know what happens when you assume," said Guin. "Also, Bettina doesn't hate you."

"You sure about that? How did she react when you told her you planned on proposing?"

Birdy smiled.

"She said you'd never say yes."

"Even though you told her about Natasha and Boris and that it was the only way to save your life?"

Birdy fidgeted and wouldn't look Guin in the eye.

Guin's eyes bored into him.

"So you made up that crazy story just to get me to marry you?"

"No!" said Birdy. "Natasha really was obsessed with me. And I thought if she knew I was truly in love and settling down, she'd move on."

Guin wasn't so sure about that. Suddenly, she pictured Natasha wielding a rifle.

"Could Natasha have been the one who shot me?"

Birdy frowned.

"The police said the shooter was a man."

"I know. But hear me out. What if the man the police caught was a decoy and Natasha was the real shooter?"

"It wasn't Natasha," stated Birdy.

"How can you be sure? She's a trained sniper, a crack shot."

"Exactly. Which is why it wasn't her."

Guin wasn't following.

"If Natasha had been the one to pull the trigger, you'd be dead."

She swallowed.

The two of them were silent for a moment.

"So, any idea where she is now?"

"Probably back in Orlando."

Guin frowned. She didn't like the idea of Natasha being just a few hours away, even if she wasn't the one who pulled the trigger... this time.

"But I promise you, she won't be bothering us."

"How can you be sure?"

Birdy gave her a look, one that said, "I'm sure."

"Then that leaves Bettina."

Birdy sighed.

"I told you, Bettina would never do something that crazy."

"What about the death threats? They were hand-delivered by a blonde on a bike."

"There must be dozens, hundreds, of blondes on Sanibel with bikes."

"Not wearing the ring you gave her."

"What do you mean?"

"The Bregmans' security cameras recorded a blonde on a bike matching Bettina's description, with Bettina's sunglasses and the bird ring you gave her, cycling to and from my house at the time those notes were left."

"It could have been a coincidence."

Guin raised her eyebrows.

"I still don't believe it was her."

Guin was tired of arguing, and her stomach was starting to growl.

"I don't know about you," she said, eyeing the bag of food Bettina had brought. "But I could use some food. Think there's anything in that bag we could have for dinner?"

Birdy glanced over.

"Only one way to find out."

EPILOGUE

Over dinner, Guin and Birdy discussed what they would tell people should they ask about the wedding. Birdy tried to persuade Guin to still marry him, insisting that she would come to love him in time and even using her mother as an excuse. But Guin was adamant. If she were to marry again, it would be for love. Finally, they agreed they would tell people that the wedding was on hold until after Birdy's book tour, which would last several months. Hopefully, by then, people would have forgotten. Though Guin wasn't so sure about that.

That settled, they dug into Jean-Luc's heavenly mocha wedding cake. No sense letting a perfectly good wedding cake go to waste just because there would be no wedding.

When they were done, Guin told Birdy he could pack up his things and go back to his place. But he insisted on staying, at least until Guin fully regained the use of her right arm and could drive. And much to her surprise, Guin agreed to let him stay. A part of her had grown used to having him around—and cooking her dinner every night. And as much as she hated to admit it, Guin realized she would miss Birdy when he was gone. But she kept that to herself.

Two people she didn't miss were Natasha and Boris, who, Birdy informed her several days later, had left Orlando rather suddenly. When she asked Birdy for details, he refused to give them, saying only that they had left the country and would not be back any time soon.

As for Bettina, she had, in fact, called her lawyer and had refused to answer any questions. Which didn't surprise Guin in the least, though it annoyed her. Also annoying was Birdy's refusal to believe Bettina was responsible for everything that had happened, even though all the evidence pointed to her.

Thinking about Bettina, Guin almost felt sorry for her. She knew what it was like to be cast aside. Though Bettina's fears were unfounded, at least according to Birdy. And even though Guin firmly believed Bettina was guilty, at least of delivering the death threats (she still had a niggling feeling Natasha had been the one who shot at her car and could have fired the shot at the wedding), she didn't want to see her jailed for life. Having to wear a bright orange jumpsuit would be punishment enough.

Finally, it was time for Birdy to resume his tour. Fortunately, Guin's shoulder, while still sore, was much better, and she could now drive.

They said goodbye, and Birdy said he would write.

As the days wore on and people began asking about the wedding, Guin began to feel guilty telling people that the wedding was on hold when she knew there would be no wedding, at least between her and Birdy. Finally, after Shelly and her mother asked her for the umpteenth time when the new date would be, she broke down and told them the truth, that there would be no wedding.

Shelly took the news particularly hard. She had had visions of Guin and Birdy leading a glamorous, jet-set life, traveling to exotic locales, and inviting her to join them on some African safari or to look for rare shells in the Philippines or Japan. (Though where Shelly got her ideas, Guin didn't know. Probably from reading Wren Finchley's books.)

Also taking the news hard was her mother. She

immediately blamed Guin, saying she must have done something to scare Birdy away. Guin was tempted to tell her the truth, that Birdy had begged her to marry him, but she had refused. However, that would have made her mother even angrier.

One person who seemed happy about the news was Glen. They had gotten together shortly after Birdy had left, and after a drink (or possibly two) Guin had felt compelled to tell him the truth. He practically beamed when Guin told him she would not be marrying Birdy.

Of course, the one person she hoped would be the most pleased was the detective. She had reached out to him right after Birdy had left, inviting him over for dinner. But he had declined, claiming to be busy. Then he had gone to Massachusetts to see his new grandson and hadn't replied to any of her text messages or calls since.

When Guin asked Shelly what she should do, Shelly told her to give the detective some time. And Guin tried to. But he was still not talking to her or replying to her texts by the time the Shell Festival rolled around at the beginning of March. And Guin was worried she had lost him for good.

It was now the middle of March, and the island was in full swing. Guin knew that if she wanted to find good shells, she would need to hit the beach early, before dawn. So she had set her alarm for six a.m. And as soon as it went off, she sprung out of bed, got dressed, and headed to the beach.

The sun was just starting to rise as Guin gazed out at the Gulf. She was lost in thought when she saw two dolphins swim by and wondered if they were mates. She watched them until they disappeared from view. Would she ever find a mate again? She chided herself for being morose. Here she was, living in paradise. What did she have to feel blue about?

A wave washed over her feet, and as the water receded

Guin thought she saw something oblong with brown spots in the water. She waded in and peered down. Could it be? No, it must be her imagination.

She threw her shelling bag onto the sand behind her and waded in farther. Then she reached down as the tide was about to reclaim her treasure and grabbed it. She held it up. It *was* a junonia! She couldn't believe it. A tiny piece was missing, but she didn't care. Nothing was perfect.

She glanced around. There was no one nearby. She squealed and did a little happy dance. Then she thanked Poseidon for her gift and took a picture of it.

"What you got there?" asked a woman, who had noticed Guin taking a picture and had come over. "Is that a junonia?"

Guin nodded, still smiling. "It is."

"Today's your lucky day," said the woman. "You should make a wish."

Guin hadn't thought of that. But as soon as the woman had left, she took the shell in both of her hands, closed her eyes, and made a wish. She opened her eyes and looked at the junonia again. Then she told herself she was being silly and put it back in her shelling bag.

She had only gone a few feet when she felt her phone vibrating in her back pocket. She took it out and saw that the detective had texted her.

"You free for dinner this Saturday?" he had written.

Guin smiled and began typing him back. Maybe today was her lucky day after all.

To be continued…

Look for Book 8 in the Sanibel Island Mystery series, *For Whom the Shell Tolls*, in late 2021.

Acknowledgments

First, I'd like to thank *you* for reading this book. If you enjoyed it, please consider reviewing or rating it on Amazon and/or Goodreads.

Next, I'd like to thank my first readers, Amanda Walter and Robin Muth, who have provided invaluable advice and suggestions over the course of the series and have caught many embarrassing typos. And speaking of typos, any you may have found are solely my responsibility and not the fault of my proofreader, Sue Lonoff de Cuevas, a former Harvard expository writing instructor and professor of English (who is also my mother).

I would also like to thank Kristin Bryant, my talented designer, for creating yet another great cover, and Polgarus Studio, for making this and all my books look as good on the inside as they do on the outside.

Lastly, thanks to my husband Kenny, who patiently listens to me grouse and keeps me fed while I write these books.

About the Sanibel Island Mystery series

To learn more about the Sanibel Island Mystery series, visit the website at http://www.SanibelIslandMysteries.com and "like" the Sanibel Island Mysteries Facebook page at https://www.facebook.com/SanibelIslandMysteries/.

Made in the USA
Columbia, SC
14 June 2021

40171066R00207